LOYALTY ABOVE ALL (THERE ARE NO EXCEPTIONS)

ALSO BY MIMA

The Fire Series

Fire

A Spark Before the Fire

The Vampire Series

The Rock Star of Vampires

Her Name is Mariah

Different Shades of the Same Color

The Hernandez Series

We're All Animals

Always be a Wolf

The Devil is Smooth Like Honey

A Devil Named Hernandez

And the Devil Will Laugh

The Devil Will Lie

The Devil and His Legacy

She Was His Angel

We're All Criminals

Psychopaths Rule the World

Learn more at **www.mimaonfire.com**

Also find Mima on Twitter, Facebook, TikTok and Instagram @mimaonfire

LOYALTY ABOVE ALL (THERE ARE NO EXCEPTIONS)

MIMA

LOYALTY ABOVE ALL (THERE ARE NO EXCEPTIONS)

iUniverse books may be ordered through booksellers or by contacting:

iUniverse
1663 Liberty Drive
Bloomington, IN 47403
www.iuniverse.com
844-349-9409

ISBN: 978-1-6632-3327-1 (sc)
ISBN: 978-1-6632-3326-4 (e)

Library of Congress Control Number: 2021924908

Print information available on the last page.

iUniverse rev. date: 12/13/2021

CHAPTER 1

When you watch the news, do you ever wonder if it is the truth? How do so many networks have such vastly different takes on the same event? Why is that? The stark, serious journalists with concern in their eyes. Do you ever wonder if they investigated the stories they tell, or are they merely reading from a monitor? Do you ever watch the commercials during the break and feel overwhelmed? (*Do* you need to talk to your doctor about this new medication?)

Back to the news and more misery; Politicians are lying, wars blazing, murder, and fear. The cycle never stops. Then the hour ends with an irrelevant yet heartwarming story about a puppy or baby, so viewers aren't completely depressed.

Have you ever turned off the news and felt good? Is there a heaviness that weighs down your soul and makes you feel hopeless? Have you been informed? You naively think so until you witness something that makes you realize how things are hyped up or watered down, and sometimes, completely ignored.

"That little house on the prairie went boom," Andrew Collin dramatically raised his hands in the air while shaking his head. The skinny, blond kid caused humored expressions all around the boardroom table. "And it didn't make the news. I wonder if it was a meth lab?"

Jorge Hernandez grinned and fixed his tie. He glanced at his wife, whose eyes were averted toward the window, as she looked over the city of Toronto, attempting to conceal her smile. Beside Andrew sat Tony Allman, giving his coworker a warning look. The two men ran Hernandez Productions for Jorge, one of the most prominent businessmen in Canada.

"I do not think it was such a prairie," Jorge corrected him, humor in his voice, his Mexican accent still quite strong despite the years he lived in Canada. "It was very rural and well, who knows what some of these people hide in the country."

"Better watch what you say," Paige spoke softly, turning toward her husband, brushing a strand of blonde hair from her face. "We own property in the country now and not far from that town."

"It was a great lot," Jorge shrugged and sat back in his chair as he exchanged looks with his wife and he remembered graphic details from a day close to the previous Christmas. "So when it went for sale, I bought it. This here, it is just good business."

Jorge Hernandez knew about good business. Since moving to Canada, he had taken over the Canadian pot industry with his chain of stores, *Our House of Pot.* Jorge then created a docuseries called *Eat the Rich Before the Rich Eat You*, which led him to start a production house. Not to mention the crematorium he purchased and, of course, the bar named after his daughter, *Princesa Maria.*

And now he was getting into the news business.

"Didn't that creepy motherfucker that owned the place you bought," Andrew continued as he grabbed a nearby piece of paper and pen."Didn't he like have a fascination with psychopaths or something?"

"Let's not get into that," Tony jumped in as he sat forward in his chair, his girth almost pushing Andrew as he did. "They found a lot of weird things at that man's house when they started to go through it. Not to mention his online history."

"Such a strange little man," Paige spoke with no emotion in her voice, she glanced at her husband and looked away. "But the news barely mentioned his murder. They fixated on something else at the time."

"That there, it will not happen with *my* news," Jorge insisted. "We are going to talk about all this stuff that happens and investigate."

"Is that always in your best interest?" Andrew boldly asked with a smirk on his face, as he looked up from the paper he was doodling on. "Do you *really* want intense investigations for all these crime scenes, especially the ones where some guy ends up dead?"

Jorge gave him a humored look while Tony appeared agitated.

A knock interrupted the meeting. Jorge looked up to see Tom Makerson, the editor for *Toronto AM,* on the other side of the glass door. He nodded for him to come in.

"Sorry I'm late," Makerson said as he rushed in. His face was flustered as he ran a hand through his strawberry blonde hair while holding an iced coffee in the other. "I got tied up at the paper, and it's so hot outside..."

"A record today, they said," Paige nodded.

"As if we should ever believe anything *they* say," Jorge quipped and glanced at Tom, who showed no reaction.

"The news channels usually get the weather right," Tom pulled out a chair beside Tony and sat down. "Although, they sometimes exaggerate..."

"This they do," Jorge nodded as Tom gave a quick nod to both Tony and Andrew, who was doodling but managed to look up.

"What's up, man?"

"Tying up some loose ends at the paper before I leave," Makerson replied and turned his attention to Jorge. "Just getting the new editor settled in, help advise him, that kind of thing."

"Hey, do not help him too much," Jorge recommended with a grin. "He is, after all, going to be your competition in the next couple of weeks when we start our news."

"Trust me," Makerson assured him, leaning forward on the table. "He's not much competition. The newspaper never will be. They will always lag unless they do investigative journalism or live streams like us, and I don't think this guy will be. He's too old-school. We're on a different playing field now."

"That paper," Jorge gestured toward the wall as if it was next door. "It is as good as dead without you."

"Let's focus on what we're doing," Paige gently suggested, placing a hand on Jorge's arm, her blue eyes briefly glancing at him. "Newspapers are dying. They're...nostalgic and maybe sometimes grab your attention with a headline, but they're no real competition."

Makerson nodded.

"So, what's the idea here?" Andrew jumped in, looking up from the image he was drawing. "One broadcast a day plus like, other random ones?"

"When something comes up," Makerson replied. "We jump online. That's why people will have the option of receiving a text or some notification whenever we're about to go live."

"It's gonna be tight," Andrew nodded. "News as it happens without the other bullshit the news channels have on…"

"Well, they have sponsors who influence the narrative," Paige commented. "This online channel won't."

"Yeah, the whole independent thing might be a stretch when you're backing us," Tony gently reminded Jorge. "It's not like we make our money completely by donations."

"No, but this here will be part of it," Jorge replied. "I give the money to start up, but donations, merchandise, these here things help too."

"Plus, if you have a paid membership," Makerson said. "You have extra access to the site, more information, you can also support your favorite journalist, that kind of thing. So, yes, we have a paycheck, but our motivation is to get more eyes on us and less on the major networks, which are bought and paid for by huge advertisers or government."

"And at the end of the day," Jorge glanced around the table. "This here, it is my main goal. It is not about money although, I will have the opportunity to advertise my other businesses on the site, which also helps. We can change the rules as we go along."

"But we can't sell out," Andrew spoke up. "That's what some of these so-called indie journalists do when they get too big."

"We won't be doing that," Makerson assured him.

"But what we will do," Jorge said. "Is shake things up. Revealing truths that many do not want exposed. We must be prepared for them to fight back."

"I'm already seeing smear stories about me," Makerson shook his head. "Saying I was kicked out of the paper, that I was paid off by Jorge. They've got me painted as a pariah, so when this starts up, people will question my character."

"That was on purpose," Jorge thought for a moment. "Maybe this means one of our first projects is to question *their* character. Who owns *them* and tells them what to say."

"The whole idea of doing this is to show we're authentic," Makerson reminded them. "So it wouldn't be such a stretch to investigate them."

"Or maybe start the rumor we will be," Tony cautiously replied. "We don't want to ruffle too many feathers from the get-go."

"Me," Jorge shrugged. "I like ruffling feathers. This here is no problem."

"Maybe we should focus on getting on our feet first," Paige suggested, giving Jorge a warning look. "I think we shouldn't be too quick to get in their crosshairs."

"No, this here is war," Jorge replied to Paige but looked around the table. "And we will treat it as such. If they shoot at us, then we must shoot back."

Andrew snickered as he continued to doodle on the paper, while Tony appeared unnerved. Makerson nodded in agreement.

"We have to do something right away," Makerson said. "If they create doubt about us from the start, it's going to be an uphill battle. We have to show that we're stronger than them and more reliable from day one."

"But we should do this with our quality of journalism," Tony attempted to explain. "Not by..."

"Well, we can attack back," Makerson cut him off. "And show our integrity at the same time. It doesn't have to be one or the other."

"Ok, let's step back for a minute," Paige said with her hand in the air. "Maybe we should show integrity while carefully exposing some of these same journalists...by showing how they got stories wrong."

"That there, it is a good idea, *mi amor,"* Jorge nodded toward his wife. "Let them squirm."

"That's the idea,' She spoke in a soft tone as their eyes met. "Why don't we leave everyone here to iron out the details? Don't forget we have to make another stop on our way home."

They exchanged looks, and Jorge nodded, looking away. It was time to deal with another matter.

CHAPTER 2

"See what I did back there?" Jorge pointed toward the building that housed Hernandez Productions as they drove away. "I walked away. I allowed them to take over the meeting, and I trust them to take care of things."

"We walked away from the meeting because I said we had something else to do," Paige reminded him with laughter in her voice. "Otherwise, you would still be there, creating a battle plan."

"Well, *mi amor,* you know that I do love a good battle plan," Jorge teased her as he reached over and touched her hand. "This here, it has been my life. I cannot remember the last time I did not have one. Back in Mexico, if I did not have a battle plan, I would have been slaughtered by another cartel."

"You don't have to worry about that now," Paige replied, and they exchanged looks causing her to add, "as much."

"This here, it is true," Jorge said as he took a deep breath and focused on the road. "But I still have to watch. If I did not, there would be a book about me out there now."

"Well, there soon *will* be a book out about you," Paige reminded him with a teasing tone. "This fall."

"Well, yes," Jorge laughed. "I *mean*, a book that tells my *real* story. The one Makerson writes, it is a bit of truth and fantasy together. There is no other way that I would tell my story."

"He found a nice way of tidying things up in your biography," Paige agreed. "But you don't have to worry. Makerson's book isn't out till the fall, and no one's going to talk."

"A message was sent," Jorge agreed as he got closer to the *Princesa Maria.* "That you do not tell stories about me. The truth, it will continue to be hidden."

"That's why I say," Paige continued. "You got to keep out of the headlines. You have to step back. Keep out of crosshairs."

"I am not sure this will happen," Jorge grinned and glanced in the side mirror. "It is not possible to keep out of people's crosshairs. Especially now that I'm in the news business."

"That's just it," Paige gently reminded him. "You won't really be. You're letting the guys take care of things. They'll hire people who want to be independent so that they can tell the truth, not the corporate version. You can focus on your children, on our other projects."

"*Mi amor,*" Jorge felt the need to bring up something that had been on his mind. "I have been thinking that there is one other thing I want to do."

"Maybe you should wait," Paige spoke with tension in her voice. "I know you talked about starting a social media company, but..."

"No, no," Jorge shook his head. "Not that there is out of the question, but later. What I mean is that I think a lot about how we....about the day we found Tala."

He referred to his son's new live-in nanny. They had discovered the young Filipino while breaking into an enemy's home the previous winter. The young woman had been held hostage by a psychopath named Gerald Myers, who had bought her from a human trafficker. She lived in barbaric conditions. When they found her, she was tied to a bed, bleeding, crying, and on the brink of insanity.

"She's come a long way," Paige quietly replied. "But I don't know if she'll ever get over how he treated her."

"I know, but *mi amor,* when we found her," Jorge thought for a moment. "It was like, when I look in her eyes, there was something there that I will never forget."

"We saved her life," Paige spoke solemnly.

"I know, and this here," Jorge replied and took another deep breath. "I want to do more of this."

"What do you mean?" Paige asked. "Save people?"

"Yes, I mean, I do not know," Jorge shook his head. "I want to do more good things. You know, if we had gone to the police with this, what would happen? This man, he would not have been punished for long, if at all. Tala, she would have suffered, been deported. I think about this a lot. I think she would not have got justice."

Jorge exchanged looks with his wife, knowing that they had the same idea about what justice entailed.

"I agree," She agreed. "So you want to help people in…precarious situations."

"I do not know," Jorge shrugged. "I cannot explain. I want to help people the right way. I wish to do good but *my* way. People who deserve *real* justice."

"I like that," She gently spoke as they drove into the parking lot behind the bar. "I like that a lot."

"I know that I am hardly a superhero," Jorge stopped the SUV and turned it off. "But I feel that what I did that day, I would like to do more."

"You did a lot for Tala," Paige smiled at him. "She's just a kid."

"We both did a lot for Tala," Jorge reminded her. "She is good with Miguel."

"I know," Paige spoke in a small voice. "But I miss Juliana."

Jorge didn't reply but looked away. Their former live-in nanny was a sensitive topic.

Jorge and Paige got out of the SUV and headed to the club's entrance. It only took a single knock for the door to swing open. A tall, indigenous man answered. His dark eyes softened when he saw the couple.

"We're working on it," Chase Jacobs muttered as he moved aside to let the couple into the empty bar, quickly closing the door behind them. They walked toward the VIP room, where an older man sat, tied to a chair in the middle of the floor. Plastic was beneath him. "He ain't talking. At least, not to us."

Jorge glanced across the room to see the newest member of the group, Ricardo Rubio standing back. An angry Diego Silva appeared confrontational as he stood to face the hostage.

"We found him in the hole he was hiding in," Diego twisted his lips and turned toward Jorge, giving him a nod, a sign that said it all. The

Colombian had worked with Jorge for years, both back in Mexico and now in Canada. The two men needed few words to communicate. "He had his chance to talk."

Diego walked away as Jorge approached the man in the chair.

"Let me," Paige said before he even had a chance to speak. "I want to take care of this guy."

"But," Jorge started. "I think since he was the one who…."

"I know," Paige nodded as she calmly sat down her designer bag and rolled up her sleeves, showing no concern. "But this affects my family. And *no one* messes with my family."

The older man sitting on the chair appeared intrigued by the slender blonde that picked up her bag and walked in his direction, her shoes clicking on the floor, eventually muffled by the plastic beneath them. She wore a soft pink blouse and fitted jeans, appropriate attire for a mom, but probably not what most would expect from a trained assassin, which she was.

"So, it's time we have a conversation," Paige spoke in her usual gentle voice. The room was still, allowing music to seep through the walls. The main bar was closed for a few more hours. "My understanding is that you revealed some very incriminating information about my husband to a man who planned to write a book called *Psychopaths Rule the World.*"

"I don't know what this is about, lady," The middle-aged white man attempted to sound calm despite the beads of sweat forming on his forehead as he glanced in Jorge's direction. "I'm a reporter. If there were a story to tell, I would've done it myself."

"Would you?" Paige pushed as she watched him with interest. "You got a nice big cheque for your information."

"I don't know what you're talking about."

"Don't bother lying," Paige replied. "We have a superior hacker. He knows everything about you."

The man paled.

"We can tell you what you had for fucking breakfast," Jorge spoke in his usual abrupt manner from across the room. "Or the last time you talked to that man Gerald Myers about me and what you told him. That is, before his sudden death. We found the notes, the recordings, everything."

"If," He suddenly stopped, looking away from Jorge and back to Paige, his eyes moving down her body. "If that were the case, the cops would've been at my door when his body was found. They would've wanted to know…"

"The cops," Jorge started to laugh. "Do you think the cops know this information? We are smarter and more efficient than the police. We found everything we had to know. And then, we only had to find *you*."

"And here we are," Paige spoke in a soft voice as she reached in her purse and pulled out a hunting knife with the same ease as a tube of lipstick. She sat her bag aside and focused on the man in the chair. "So, it's time you explain where you got this information and why you told it."

"I," he watched the knife and grew nervous. "I…I didn't..."

"You didn't what?" Paige asked and tilted her head. "I would like to know."

"I didn't tell him that this information was...was for sure true," he stuttered along as he pulled his head backward. "I mean, I didn't know…"

"You didn't know this would be in a book?" Paige asked as she stepped forward while the men in the room watched her closely. "Really?"

"Well, he said," the man started. "I didn't know for sure he would…"

"That he was writing the book?" Paige asked as she removed the knife from the leather sheath that held it. "Is that what you mean?"

"Yes," He replied and nodded as she moved closer to him. "I thought he…"

"Paige," Jorge said as he walked closer to his wife. The song *Southern Nights* drifted in from the next room. "He say a lot for a man who knows nothing. I mean, we did hear him talking about what a criminal I was in Mexico. Some facts, you know, they were true. Some, they were not. So many things were wrong."

"Can you imagine if that information had gotten out?" Paige shifted her attention to her husband, which momentarily drew the man's attention to Jorge Hernandez. In one swift move, Paige swung around and drove the knife into the man's throat. His eyes were frozen in fear as blood poured down his chest. He briefly struggled, but not for long.

Paige stepped back just as the man slumped forward in the chair.

"It is nice to tie up loose ends, *mi amor,"* Jorge showed no reaction to the man's death. "This here, it makes me slightly more relaxed."

"I'll get the clean-up crew in," Chase said behind him. "And is Andrew free for the crematorium?"

"He is," Jorge replied as he looked into his wife's eyes, his primal urges suddenly taking over. "We got to go. There are other things we must attend to now."

CHAPTER 3

"They won't be back for a while," Paige reminded Jorge as they entered the safe room, a hidden location in their basement that was available to the family if danger ever struck. Of course, it was also there if the *mood* struck as a way to have some alone time. Fortunately, the house was big enough that they could disappear for some time before anyone would notice.

"*Mi Amor,*" Jorge was quick to lock the door behind them. "It is better to be safe than...interrupted."

The words were barely out of his mouth, and already, he was starting to unbutton her blouse, his breath growing heavier, as he moved in to kiss Paige. What began gentle and warm quickly grew into a fierce expression of lust as the couple rushed to remove their clothes, leaving a pile on the floor as they made their way to the nearby couch. A soft, grey blanket lay over it. Naked, Paige laid down and Jorge quickly moved on top of her.

Things moved fast. Watching his wife murder the man who had caused trouble for the couple the previous winter was enough to set his urges ablaze. He had always insisted that murder brought out his other natural and primal instincts. There was nothing sexier than a powerful woman, who could later show her vulnerable side when he needed it the most.

"Oh God," Paige moaned as he slid inside her, moving slowly at first but quickly picking up the pace as his wife wrapped her legs around him.

She gently coaxed him to move faster until they were both panting and moaning. Paige arched her back, and Jorge grabbed her ass with both his hands and pulled her closer. As he tightened his grip on her body, Jorge thought he was going to lose his mind. He let out a loud noise as his wife lost control beneath him.

Moments later, as they lay in silence, Jorge felt his heart furiously pounding as he began to relax.

"*Mi Amor,* I did not realize how much I needed that," Jorge confessed as he slowly moved away from her. "Lately, Miguel, he is so..."

"I know," Paige said as she sat up, her face still flustered. "It must be a stage he's going through. He wants to pop up in our bed at the most inconvenient times."

"But we buy him his own bed," Jorge shook his head. "I do not understand. Maria, she was never like that."

"All kids are different," Paige reminded him as she gently touched his arm. "It's a phase."

"It is putting a damper on our...alone time," Jorge leaned in and kissed her.

"We just got to keep taking him back to bed," Paige shrugged. "I don't know what else to do."

"Should we," Jorge shook his head as he slowly sat up, "get him a pet or something?"

"I don't think that will resolve anything," Paige admitted as she rose from the couch and made her way across the room. Finding her clothes, she held the pile against her body as she glanced toward the nearby bathroom. "I did some research, and it sounds like it's just a phase."

"Maria, she was so different," Jorge repeated as he ran a hand through his black hair, simultaneously shaking his head. "Are we doing something wrong with Miguel?"

"You weren't around a lot when she was his age," Paige reminded him. "And your ex..."

"This is true," Jorge nodded as he stood up. "Plus, Maria was always independent. Not that her mother was comforting, so I can see why she'd not want to go to her room at night."

"Like I said, kids are different," Paige shrugged. "Miguel has so much energy. He never wants to sleep. All of a sudden, he's in our room, giggling. Then he passes out in our bed, and you take him back to his room."

"I guess," Jorge said as he grabbed his clothes while his wife headed toward the bathroom. "*Mi Amor*, you know, what I say earlier about wanting to help people?"

"Yes," She stopped and turned in his direction. "You know, I was thinking about that. Helping Tala had a powerful effect on you. There's a connection between a victim and the person they view as their savior."

"I like it," Jorge confessed. "I feel like I am doing good."

"You like it," Paige corrected him as a grin crossed her lips. "Because it makes you feel God-like, which I don't have to remind you, is what you live for."

"Oh yes, that there does make sense," Jorge considered. "I had never thought."

"I know *you,*" Paige reminded him with laughter in her voice. "I'm not saying it's a bad thing. There's a lot of people who never get real justice, so if you can somehow help them, then that's a good thing."

"I would like to do this, *si,*" Jorge nodded as he stood awkwardly with his clothes in hand. "I think that the situations, they will come to me. I do not think I will have to look. But I hope they do."

"They always have," Paige reminded him. "You've helped a lot of people over the years, even within our group. And now, you're helping Juliana back in Mexico."

Her last comment caused him to look away as sorrow filled his heart.

"And I know," Paige continued. "There's not much we can do for her now, except make her comfortable for her last...."

"I know," Jorge spoke sadly. "It is very sad that she is so sick. I regret I cannot help her, but she is with her family, and that is all that matters."

"I think the most heartbreaking moment of my life was watching Miguel's reaction when she left that day," Paige confirmed with sadness in her eyes. "I never saw him cry so much."

"Yes," Jorge said as he recalled the emotional moment when the family's nanny was leaving for the airport. "Miguel, he cried so much. I think it was the most upsetting thing for poor Juliana. She was so heartbroken."

"We all were," Paige confirmed as Jorge took a deep breath. "But cancer..."

"I know, *mi Amor,* I know," Jorge nodded. "Even I cannot help this time."

With that, Paige burst out in laughter, startling him.

"What?"

"Jorge, that's what I was talking about," Paige reminded him as she entered the bathroom and stopped in the doorway. "You think you're God-like. *Even I* can't help her. Really?"

With that, Jorge merely shrugged and winked at his wife. She shook her head and smiled before closing the bathroom door. After both freshened up, the couple made their way upstairs.

In the living room, they found Tala playing with Miguel on the floor. He was giggling, not a care in the world. Much happier than the little boy who said goodbye to Juliana weeks earlier. If only he could save his children from pain, but it was out of his control. Soon they would receive the call that Juliana had taken her last breath. How would he tell the kids?

"Miguel," Jorge attempted to grab his son's attention, but his focus was on the game he was playing with Tala. "I guess if it is not the middle of the night when I am sleeping, he has no interest in seeing me now."

"Oh, no, Mr," Tala looked up with big, brown eyes. "He just....a little boy, he is easily distracted."

"I can see that," Jorge said as he looked at the plastic animals on the floor. "He seems...very busy."

"Oh, I get this new game for him," Tala's face brightened up. "I saw it today at the store..."

"Thank you, Tala," Paige called out from the kitchen. "But I will give you the money. You don't have to do that."

"I do not mind," Tala shook her head. "You are so kind to me."

"It is, you, who are kind to our son," Jorge smiled at her before heading to the kitchen. "That is all that matters, Tala."

"God-like," Paige muttered when he got closer to her. "That's what I mean."

"Well, Paige, I cannot help if I am the chosen one," Jorge shrugged with fake modesty. "You know, the almighty..."

Paige sighed and gave him a look.

"My ego, it is always strong," He winked at his wife as he grabbed a cup of coffee. "Is Maria home yet?"

"She has her judo lesson," Paige said as he headed out of the room.

"Great," Jorge said as he walked toward his office."Paige, if you need me?"

"I'm fine," She called out.

Once behind closed doors, he collapsed in the chair behind his desk. Taking a drink of coffee, he sat it down and felt as if he were about to drift off when his secure line rang. That could only be one person.

"Athas," Jorge answered the phone, showing little interest in talking to the Canadian prime minister. "What you want?"

"Hello to you too," Alec Athas spoke curtly from the other end of the line as Jorge reached for his coffee. "I thought you'd be happy to know that I'm rushing Tala's immigration papers through. She should be a citizen by the end of the year."

"That's the fastest you can do this for me?" Jorge attempted to instigate Athas, but it didn't work.

"You know the drill," Athas was curt. "It's a slow, long process, and this is the quickest it could be done."

"Very good," Jorge nodded. "This here is good news."

"I heard about your independent news channel," Athas changed topics.

"Yes, it is starting soon," Jorge replied. "So, if there is anything you need reported, you know where to go."

"I might have a few things," Athas confirmed.

"The election rumors for the fall," Jorge reminded him. "I would think you'd have a lot."

"I don't know if I should run again," Athas spoke honestly. "I feel like I'm surrounded by more criminals here in Ottawa than you are there."

With that, Jorge threw his head back in laughter.

"*Amigo,*" Jorge finally contained himself. "That is a sad state you are in if it is the case."

"The government isn't what people think," Athas admitted. "The more I dig up, the less I want to look. They're savages and psychopaths. Some of our former prime ministers should've been in fucking prison for things they've done in secret."

"Well, this here does not surprise me," Jorge confirmed. "But Athas, you are powerful, and when you get in a second time, make plans for what you want to accomplish and fuck everyone else."

"*If* I get in a second time," Athas reminded him. "My numbers have been down and…."

"You *will* get back in," Jorge assured him. "This here, I promise you."

Alec Athas didn't argue. He knew all about Jorge Hernandez.

CHAPTER 4

"I can't stop the world from fighting," Jorge attempted to sound humble as he looked away from everyone at the table, casually leaning back in his chair. "But you know, I would like to make it a better place in some, small way."

"Is this here a joke?" Diego Silva leaned toward Jorge, his eyes full of suspicion. "Are you on medication or something?"

Further down the table, Marco Rodel Cruz let out a laugh. The Filipino hacker immediately put his head down as if studying something on his laptop. When Jorge glanced around the table, he noted that everyone else, other than Paige, had an expression of disbelief.

"Like…what do you mean?" Chase Jacobs asked with a confused look on his face. "What are you doing?"

"Sir, some," Marco quickly attempted to redeem himself. "They start charitable organizations. You could do something like that."

"Oh no," Jorge shook his head and put his hand in the air, glancing at Ricardo Rubio, the newest member of the group, who remained stoic. He started 6 months earlier and quickly proved himself to move up the ranks. "This here, it does not interest me. I mean, I would like to do things to directly help people."

"Like…work at a soup kitchen?" Diego's eyes bulged out as he twisted his lips and glanced at Jorge's wife, who let out a laugh. "I can't see you…."

"No, no," Jorge shook his head. "You do not understand this here. What I mean is that I would like to help people get the justice that they deserve. I help in certain situations where the police are useless."

"Like most situations, sir?" Marco joked, and everyone around him laughed.

"This here, it is true," Jorge grinned before continuing. "It is like when we help Tala last year. It felt good to be there for someone who needed it, who appreciated it."

"Well, in fairness," Diego shook his head. "You were going to kill the man who was holding her hostage anyway, so it wasn't such a stretch."

"Was Clara in today?" Paige cut in, referring to the woman who checked their workplaces and homes for listening and other devices.

"Yes," Chase replied and glanced around the VIP room. "No one else gets in here after she's checked things."

"So," Diego picked up where he left off. "What I mean is that you were gonna do that anyway."

"But Diego, we did more than that," Jorge shook his head. "We helped her start a new life. The authorities had no idea she was in this country. Now, I am pushing her immigration through."

"In fairness," Diego shook his head, appearing unconvinced. "She's your live-in nanny too, so…"

"Ok, Diego, this here is not the point," Jorge cut off the Colombian. "What I mean is that this is an example. I want to help people like Tala, who feel powerless, who need help and justice. *Real* justice, not the bullshit kind the police and government pretend to do."

"Ok," Diego seemed to accept his answer and sat back in his chair. "You have an interesting version of what *doing good* in the world means."

To this, Jorge merely shrugged.

"How are you going to find out about these people?" Chase asked with interest. "I like this idea too."

"I feel that the situations," Jorge shrugged. "They will come to me. If I am meant to help, I will learn about them. It could be something someone hears, then tells me, or it could be something I see in the news."

"Speaking of news," Paige jumped in. "We're supposed to talk about the indie news channel…what is it called again?"

"HPC news, *mi amor,*" Jorge gently reminded her. "Hernandez Productions Company news but of course, we have to keep it simple. Most people, they will not even speculate what HPC means, and this here, it is fine."

"This is good," Ricardo spoke up with some hesitation. "I like this news channel, Mr. Hernandez."

"It will shake the fuck out of this city," Jorge spoke with pride. "And this country, for that matter. I want people to see the real news, not the agreed-upon narrative."

"They do not like that, sir," Marco shook his head. "Most media in this country, they are part of that group I told you about the other day. This group decides the narrative and everyone is to comply with their decision."

"What?" Chase seemed surprised. "What does that mean? Do you mean like how all the US media are owned by like six millionaires or something? Is it the same here?"

"No," Marco shook his head and turned toward Chase. "I mean, that *is* true, but it is not what I am referring to…what I mean is that there is a larger group, internationally, that creates the narrative, and all the news outlets follow it. In turn, this means that there is more power in their words since they're saying the same thing."

"So, for example," Paige jumped in. "If Jorge ran for prime minister and this organization didn't want him in, they'd make sure all these outlets would report how terrible he supposedly is because they'd be on the same page. It would seem more valid. And if they wanted him in, they'd do the opposite. It's very manipulative when you think about it."

"Oh, so if all the channels say the same things, you'll more likely believe it," Diego attempted to understand. "Because they wouldn't all say it if it wasn't true?"

"More or less," Paige nodded. "We're essentially being told what to think."

"What about Makerson when he was at the paper?" Chase asked with interest. "He didn't go with the narrative."

"Nah, they were not part of this here group Marco is talking about," Jorge replied.

"The point is," Paige continued. "This organization has a lot of power. HPC will be going against it, so we'll automatically be making an enemy."

"Like I give a fuck," Jorge shrugged. "I do not care how powerful they think they are. I am more powerful. We are here for those who don't want to be sheep."

"Good luck finding those people," Diego quipped. "Most people are sheep."

"Not always a bad thing for us," Paige reminded him. "We can work with that."

"Sir, I have the promos for HPC," Marco jumped in, glancing momentarily at Paige than Jorge. "I think you will like them."

"Fire it up, Marco," Jorge said and pointed toward the laptop. "I am anxious to see them."

"I have to change a few settings," Marco said as he tapped on the keyboard while the others waited. The group was cautious when dealing with technology, turning off their phones and laptops while meeting, even though Marco had an extra layer of security to prevent potential eavesdroppers. The IT expert knew how to reassure their privacy would be protected. "Ok, here it is."

Turning the laptop around, he pulled it back to ensure everyone could see it. A frozen image of Andrew was on the page. Marco hit a key, and suddenly the young man's voice filled the room.

"Are you seriously still watching corporate media?" Andrew was pointing toward an older-style television that showcased one of the leading Canadian news channels. "You know these guys are bought and paid for by big advertisers who dictate how *you* think, and it gets worse. Do you know that *your* tax money is paying for this shit? Are you getting your money's worth?"

Andrew grabbed a baseball bat and smashed the television screen, causing the glass to shatter as strange dust filled the room.

"Is that safe?" Paige muttered.

Jorge laughed and clapped his hands together. The group continued to watch.

"There's a reason why *my* generation doesn't trust the media," Andrew went on as shots of older news stories, which later proved to have purposely misled the public, started to flash on the screen. They moved faster and faster as he talked. "There's a reason why we don't bother with cable television. There's a reason why we don't trust politicians. There's a reason why we don't care what the establishment says. Are we even hearing the truth? Are we hearing the whole story? Are they biased?"

Andrew's face was back on screen.

"The reason why you don't trust mainstream media is because you *shouldn't."*

His face disappeared. Huge, shaky letters announcing the date that HPC News was premiering appeared on the screen, along with loud, rock music that set the tone. The ad showed the website and social media details, encouraging people to sign up for notifications.

"I like this," Jorge pointed toward the laptop. "This here, it is perfect."

"It ended like an ad for *MuchMusic* back in the day," Chase said and glanced at Paige. "You probably know what I mean. I'm not technical, but it has that whole, young, cool vibe to it."

"Yes, our target market is younger people," Paige nodded. "Tony said he's not sure if he can captivate older viewers right off the bat, but they want to start with a focus on people under forty. Hopefully, others will come around too."

"I am sure of this," Jorge shook his head. "People, they are tired of being lied to, and this channel, it will show the truth and burn them all."

"You are not going to make any friends, sir," Marco reminded him as he pulled his laptop back and closed it. "Although, when I did some research, these companies do not seem to think you will go anywhere with this channel. They are confident that no one will take it seriously."

"They are making the grave mistake of underestimating me," Jorge grinned. "But this here, it could work to my advantage. It will be easier to sneak up and cut their heads off without them suspecting."

"It's about time," Chase spoke quietly. "When Leland died, the media tried to turn it around like it was my mother's fault that he got out of the house. Rather than focus on that piece of shit, Luke Prince, who shot him, they blamed my mother."

Everyone fell silent. Each showed signs of compassion as the group shared a rare silence. It had been a heart-wrenching day a few years earlier when Chase's son wandered into a wooded area and was shot by a hunter who mistook the child for an animal. Even though he had been drinking and wildly irresponsible, Luke Prince had his lawyer create doubt in the media about the woman who was caring for Leland Jacobs at the time.

"Yeah, well, Prince is burning in hell for what he did," Jorge's face tensed up, his voice growing angry. "Leland, he was a little boy. I know, Miguel, he has also got out of the house, and you know, we were lucky because he didn't leave the yard. The news, they were wrong to say this, but the people who agreed with them are no better."

"Sheep," Diego shook his head. "They're fucking sheep."

"Yes, they are Diego," Jorge nodded. "But these people, it will not be our audience. Our audience will be people who want to know the truth. We are going to shake up the news world with our show. I guarantee it."

He turned to Paige, who gave a tense smile. Ignoring her hesitation, Jorge leaned in and kissed her on the cheek.

CHAPTER 5

"Are we ready to do this?" Jorge asked as he entered the Hernandez Productions boardroom a few days later. Both Makerson and Marco were seated at the table. Marco looked up from his computer with a wary expression on his face, while Makerson nodded, exchanging looks with the IT specialist. Jorge noted the heaviness in the room as he closed the door behind him. "Am I missing something here? We did have a meeting?"

"Yes, sir, that is true," Marco nodded. "But there is something else we must discuss."

"Ok," Jorge said as he sat across from the two men. "Will Tony be joining us?"

"No, sir," Marco shook his head. "He is busy with another project but is aware of the situation."

"What is wrong?" Jorge grew nervous but hid it. "Do not tell me there is a glitch when we are so close to launching."

"No, it is not that, sir," Marco shook his head and exchanged another look with Makerson, who put his head down. "It is more on a personal note."

"What?" Jorge asked, his defenses lowering slightly.

"Sir, do you remember when…Juliana, when we learned she was ill?" Marco asked as he leaned forward on the table. "I remember at the time, you said something about how it was surprising because she was relatively young, had no prior health conditions, and only took one medication. You said it was prescribed by her doctor, for stomach issues?"

"Yes," Jorge nodded and thought back. "It was a long name. I think it started with N, but it was because she suffered from heartburn."

"Well, that pill," Makerson jumped in and gently added. "It may have caused her cancer."

Jorge said nothing. He glanced between the two men while his thoughts ran out of control. Juliana had stomach cancer. When she announced the diagnosis, Jorge had been surprised that a woman who had lived a healthy lifestyle would develop this condition, especially without warning. Looking down, he felt saddened, but a charge of anger quickly followed.

"Do you mean to tell me," Jorge looked back up at the two men, "That this here medicine that her doctor recommended may kill her? Because if this is so, I am going to find him and…"

"He probably didn't know," Makerson cut him off, shaking his head. "He would only be going by what Big Pharma told him. They said it is safe, but the documents that we uncovered say otherwise."

"Sir, when you talk about this months ago," Marco jumped in, shaking his head. "I did not feel we got the full story. I did not want to tell you at the time, but I was highly suspicious because I have read of many medications allowed in this country, later taken off the shelves for causing harm. I recently decided to hack into this company's system and do some snooping, and this is what I learned."

"I am proposing this be our first breaking story for the channel," Makerson suggested and took a deep breath. "We'll make a big enemy from the start, but this is what you want, right?"

"What I want is to burn those motherfuckers to the ground," Jorge corrected him but calmed as he fell into thought. "But this, I do like that you have discovered this Marco, and yes, of course, Makerson, you are right. We need this to be our first, big story."

"We'll say that someone in the company released the documents in secret," Makerson went on to explain. "And show where they have been essentially killing people with this so-called harmless drug. Marco did more research into health records, and there is a strong link to a rise in stomach cancer among the patients who used the medication. Of course, we have to be savvy about how we report that part, but we can find a way to track down people who have lost a family member or currently have cancer."

"Would we be able to interview Juliana?" Makerson asked cautiously. "Or..."

Jorge didn't say anything but solemnly shook his head.

"We will bring it to light," Makerson went on. "But only if you want us to."

"*Si,*" Jorge nodded vigorously. "This here, the world must know."

"Also," Makerson cleared his throat. "It will set a tone and hopefully encourage people to bring stories to us."

"Yes, I do like this," Jorge nodded. "And I do appreciate this work. This was very good."

"It's unfortunate, the circumstances," Makerson spoke honestly. "But at the same time, we can use it to lead the way. This isn't an isolated incident. These pharmaceutical companies have no shame. They will set their mother on fire to make a buck. The list of lawsuits and lies, it's unreal to me that so many people blindly trust them."

"People, they do not want to hear the truth," Jorge reminded him. "They want to have a magic pill that solves their problems because it is easy. People want everything to be easy. It is human nature. Did you know that the doctor, he want to put Miguel on pills for being hyper? I said, over my fucking dead body."

Both Marco and Makerson laughed.

"*Your* dead body, sir?" Marco teased him, causing Jorge's head to fall back in laughter.

"Yes, you are expected to conform, or there is something wrong with *you*," Makerson spoke sarcastically.

"Yes, my son, he will never conform," Jorge shook his head. "So, are we still doing the interview about the channel today? Should we hint about the big story?"

"Sure, if you still want to" Makerson nodded. "I can post on social media we're going live soon."

After discussing a few other details, the men prepared for the interview to take place minutes later. They already knew what they would talk about and how to present it. This would be Jorge's opportunity to let the public know that he was behind the channel while sending a chilling vibe to those who might be in his line of fire.

The interview started casual, with Makerson asking Jorge mundane questions, but the two quickly got to the topic at hand.

"What made you decide to add an online news channel to your many projects?" Makerson casually asked. "You already have a lot of docuseries with your production house that exposes hidden truths so, why not just continue with that? Why the news?"

"Well, Tom, I find it very disturbing how much our corporate media misses," Jorge humbly spoke as he looked toward the camera. "You know, I have seen it in my own life, as a man in the public eye, but also, as you said, I do own a production house that exposes many things. This has opened my eyes to how much is not reported, and this is concerning to me."

"Is this why you refuse to take advertiser money for the project?" Makerson asked. "I know you are fronting the money to start, but after that, the channel will be run by donations, mainly, paid subscriptions."

"This here, it is the way of our future," Jorge replied and paused for a moment before continuing. "Unfortunately, when you have advertisers involved, they influence what is reported."

"So, no government money either?" Makerson asked with a grin on his face.

To this, Jorge's head fell back in laughter. He calmed and shook his head as he glanced across the room at Marco giggling, pulling his fedora down as if attempting to hide his face.

"No, *señor,* we will not beg for government funding for this channel," Jorge insisted. "This here, it does not interest me. Unlike *some* Canadian channels, we will not run to *papi gobierno* for money. The government is not *our* sugar daddy, and we will not be obligated to do any favors in return. We will take money from the people who feel we are valuable and wish to *donate.* The problem with our Canadian media is that much of the money is given to them by our government. It is *our* tax-paying money. So, if you pay taxes, you are giving money to the Canadian media even if you do not watch or care for it. It does not seem like a good deal to me."

"But some people would argue," Makerson jumped in with no expression on his face. "That by supporting these news channels that we're in turn, supporting Canadian television."

"Hey," Jorge shrugged casually. "They are entitled to feel however they wish. If they believe it to be true, then it is the truth to them. But I am here to tell you that if the government and advertisers are the backers of a news channel, they have a hell of a lot to say about the narrative. It only makes sense. But this here, it is a matter of opinion."

"And for full disclosure," Makerson turned his attention toward the camera. "I will be heading this news program, and it is important for me to be objective and see all sides. People deserve the truth, and I'm not suggesting they never get it from other channels however, I do share Jorge's concern regarding the money provided to run the networks. It seems like a huge conflict of interest."

"And you have worked in the news some years now," Jorge said with a shrug. "So you are aware of many things. I picked you for this new project because I knew you would be fair, concise, that you would tell the truth."

"People don't trust the news anymore," Makerson admitted with a concerned expression on his face. "And what I strive to do is to regain that trust, to listen to the people. I'm not here to tell you what to believe but to give you the facts."

"This is also my goal," Jorge nodded in agreement. Glancing across the room, Marco nodded and gave a thumbs up to them both as he viewed comments under the live stream.

"So, to wrap this up," Makerson got back on track. "The launch is coming up in a few days, any final thoughts you would like to leave with our potential viewers?"

"*Si,*" Jorge nodded. "I would like to say that we have one major story that is quite disturbing. It is a heartbreaking reality that many corporations put money above people. And this story will, unfortunately, reveal a disappointing and disturbing example of this, which is going on in Canada. I will not reveal more, but it hits very close to home for my family."

Makerson nodded solemnly.

"But this is what this independent news channel is about," Jorge said with a sinister look in his eyes as he glanced at the nearby camera. "It will expose those who should be exposed. It will tell the truth. It will address stories you want to hear. We are listening to our audience, and we are listening to the people. Our goal is to be number one here in Toronto and eventually nationally. We want Canadians to become aware and more involved in their communities. And I believe they will be once they learn the facts. We want to make Canada stronger by exposing those who try to make us weak."

Across the room, Marco nodded vigorously as he watched comments from the live stream.

The battle was about to begin.

CHAPTER 6

"So what's this about something affecting our family?" Maria boldly asked her father as soon as Jorge walked in the door. Paige stood nearby with concern on her face. "Like, did you say that to be dramatic or something?"

Jorge closed the door behind him and took a deep breath. Despite the sarcasm in his daughter's voice, there was a sense of fear behind it. Paige looked away as if she had already figured it out and he wondered how to break the news.

"Please," Jorge looked between his wife and daughter. "Is Miguel at home?"

"No," Paige gently replied. "But him and Tala should be back soon."

"Then we must go to my office," Jorge said as he began to walk in that direction. "This here, I do not wish to talk about in front of Miguel. I know he is young, but still, it is better that I do not."

"Does it have to do with Juliana?" Maria asked, this time her voice sounding more like the vulnerable little girl she used to be, causing Jorge's heart to drop. He turned and looked into her big, brown eyes and nodded as he reached out to gently touch her long black hair as the three of them headed toward his office. No one spoke until they were behind the closed door.

"What is it?" Maria quietly asked. "Did she..."

"No," Jorge shook his head and pointed toward the chairs in front of his desk. "Please, let us sit down."

His wife and daughter did as he asked while Jorge went behind the desk. He was about to speak when his secure line rang. It was the prime minister.

"For Christ sakes," Jorge complained as he sat down. "Does this man have a camera in my fucking office?"

"Just get it," Paige shook her head. "I'm sure it won't take long."

"Do we have to leave?" Maria made a face.

"No," Jorge said before picking up the phone. "Athas, what can I do for you?"

"Hello," Alec Athas said. "I saw your interview."

"So?" Jorge was sharp. "This here, it better be important, Athas. I have to discuss something with my family."

"I want to point out that your interview today was misleading," Athas automatically began to speak. "Yes, the government does fund a public broadcaster, but not completely, and as for the others…"

"Whatever, Athas, is that all you want?" Jorge cut him off. "I do not care about the details."

"I want to assure you that funding them is of no benefit to me," He continued. "Do you know how much they butcher me in their news?"

"Then cut their funds."

"But then they'll say…"

"Then *you* say," Jorge cut him off. "That the budget does not permit as much money for their fucking networks. I do not understand what is so hard about this. You are the prime minister. I would like to think you have some power."

"Sometimes, I wonder."

"That makes two of us."

To this, Athas merely sighed, and Jorge rolled his eyes.

"Look, I can't be butchered from you too, on top of the others."

"You do not have to worry," Jorge assured him. "You will come out smelling like roses, but if you have any stories to reveal, this could be helpful to both of us. If we give a favorable report about you and you are not funding us, then this looks more legit. Wouldn't you agree?"

"I would."

"Of course, if you have a family member or say, like a hundred of them, that would like to *donate* to the channel or get a paid subscription," Jorge added. "This here, it would help too. I am sure you can find some personal money in the government budget."

There was silence on the other end of the line.

"So I have to pay you off?"

"Nonsense," Jorge replied. "But I cannot report favorably on you unless I have money to run my channel. That is all I am saying."

"Ok, well, I can take money from…"

"The other news channel," Jorge finished his sentence. "That is what you do. Budget cuts, but instead, you are putting some of that money toward….I don't know. Call it something creative and find a way to funnel it through. This here, it will work for us both. You're down in the polls. That there is about to change. We will have our own polls with this channel. And it looks like you will do very well on them."

"Ok," Athas finally replied. "That sounds… reasonable."

"I am a reasonable man," Jorge replied with a grin as he glanced at his family, winking at his wife while his daughter seemed to smother a giggle.

"Thank you," Athas replied. "This might work well for me."

"It will," Jorge assured him. "As they say, it's better to work with the devil you know."

"That is also true," Athas replied.

The men ended their call, and Jorge looked back at his family. They were solemn despite his attempt to make them laugh during his conversation with Athas.

"I like how you did that," Maria said as she sat up straighter. "It was very…smooth."

"Maria, I have so many lessons for you," Jorge replied with pride in his voice. "If you one day lead this family, there is a lot you have to know, but probably most important is how to get what you want. You have to make people see what they are getting in order for them to cooperate."

"How to manipulate," Maria smiled, and Jorge was struck by her maturity, despite not yet being 15 years old. "Is that what you mean, *Papá?*"

"Maria," Jorge shook his head. "You make me sound so sinister. The point is that you have to reason with people to get what you want. Athas wants good publicity. He officially pays these clowns at the other channel with our tax dollars, and they make him look bad. He can donate to my channel and get better publicity. This will encourage him to give us some money."

"I don't mean to change the subject," Paige spoke up. "But what were you talking about in the interview today? You spoke about something affecting our family?"

"Yeah, what was that about?" Maria asked.

"I found out today," Jorge said, pausing for a moment. "That there may be a reason Juliana got stomach cancer. The doctor, he tried to say she just, what? Had the 'bad luck' of the draw? Well, it may not be that simple."

"It never is," Paige muttered, and her step-daughter gave her a sympathetic smile.

"Marco," Jorge continued. "He is amazing at his job. That is why I do so much for him. He does so much research, even when not asked."

Maria nodded in understanding.

"He tell me today," Jorge continued. "When Juliana got sick, I commented that she was a healthy woman, and she did not even take any medication except for…"

"That pill for heartburn," Paige finished his sentence and tensed up as the two shared a look.

"Wait, what?" Maria said. "Was the pill making it worse?"

"The pill, Maria, may have caused her cancer," Jorge replied and watched his daughter's face drop. "This here, unfortunately, is often the case with some prescription drugs. They help one thing while causing other issues."

"There can be other factors," Paige spoke evenly.

"Yes, this is true," Jorge continued. "But that is why we do not take many pills in this family. As I say, they may help one thing while hurting another. And there are some like Juliana's that they say they are safe then we later learn are not. Marco, he found this out, and now we are going to divulge it on our new channel."

"What?" Maria's eyes filled with tears as if just getting up to speed. "Do you mean…that Juliana never would've got sick if she had not taken these pills?"

Jorge shrugged as he watched his daughter wipe a tear away. Paige touched her arm to comfort her.

"It is…it is terrible," Jorge nodded. "They are currently trying to hide this information, but we will expose them."

"Now she's going to die," Maria said with a shaky voice. "It's not fair. She didn't do anything wrong. She never smoked or drank alcohol or…. did anything to hurt her body, but her stupid doctor gave her poison pills?"

"Her doctor," Jorge shook his head. "He may not know. He knew what the pharmaceutical rep told him."

"They rush these products on the market," Paige added. "And don't always check things carefully."

"Or cover them up," Jorge corrected her. "That is more likely."

"And it's too late for Juliana," Maria said as tears continued to fall down her face. "She's going to die. Can we do anything?"

"Maria," Jorge leaned forward in his chair. "You know that if there was anything I could do, I *would* do it. I have offered her family anything she needs. I would go to the moon to get her the cure if I could, but even my specialists cannot help her. We tried, but it has been a discouraging battle."

"She sort of gave up as soon as she found out," Paige gently added as she leaned toward Maria and put her arm around her. "We tried, Maria."

"I know," She sniffed as Jorge passed her some tissues. "I know, I just wish…before Christmas, everything was fine then suddenly, she was leaving and…"

"I know, Maria," Jorge watched his daughter with a heavy heart. "I know. We cannot do more, but we can expose this company. And Maria, you know, this here will happen. I do not let anyone hurt our family."

Jorge and his wife shared a look. She nodded but didn't say a thing.

CHAPTER 7

"You asked to see me, sir?" Ricardo seemed hesitant as he stood just inside the VIP room of the *Princesa Maria.*

"*Si,*" Jorge looked up from his phone then turned it off. "Please have a seat. We must discuss something."

Ricardo didn't reply but closed the door behind him. The young man appeared nervous. Being the newest member of the group, he always held back a bit. This reminded him of Chase Jacobs only a few years earlier. However, this lifestyle had a way of changing a person. Then again, so did life.

"Now, Ricardo, you must not worry," Jorge was quick to assure the Mexican as he sat across from him. "This here, it is not because something is wrong. I ask you here to thank you for all you have done."

"I…I appreciate all you have done for me too," Ricardo was quick to reply as he moved his chair closer to the table. "I had nothing when I come here to Canada, and as a student, it had been a struggle."

"I know this," Jorge nodded. "What Jolene did to you…"

Ricardo didn't reply. He shook his head and looked away.

"Anyway, this here is history," Jorge moved quickly past the topic of Jolene Silva. Diego's sister had proven untrustworthy again and again. Ricardo had been one of her many victims. "We do not need to speak of it, but I will say, you have proven very loyal to this here family in the past few months."

"Thank you, sir."

"And it is because of this loyalty that I would like to offer you a rather…unique opportunity," Jorge continued as he sat back and thought for a moment. "I do not know if you are aware, but the production house that I own. They are doing a television series about the Mexican cartel."

Ricardo said nothing but raised an eyebrow.

"It is, you know, a topic that interests many people," Jorge continued, casually shrugging as if it was something that didn't relate to his past in any way. "So, I suggest that maybe we do a program on it."

"Sir," Ricardo paused as if unsure what to say. "Is this…does this have anything to do with things…when you live in Mexico? I know there is also a book coming out…"

"No, the book," Jorge was quick to jump in with his rehearsed answer. "It is my life story. It tells of my meager, boring life in Mexico. I grew up and worked for my father's coffee business. You know, the people, they think it would be interesting. So I say yes, of course, if you wish. Tom wrote that book about my many businesses successes, and it is out this fall."

Ricardo showed no expression but nodded.

"No, this here," Jorge continued, observing his reaction. "The show, it will be fiction. I do not know of such things as cartels. I only hear stories."

Ricardo didn't respond. He looked anxious, as if he wanted to speak but couldn't get the words out. To this, Jorge burst out in laughter, his head falling back. He clapped his hands together, causing Ricardo to jump. Jorge enjoyed the rare glimpse of naïveté in this business.

"Ricardo," Jorge finally saw the young man relax, even if just slightly. "You know that I am teasing you. I think you know all about *me*."

"*Si,* sir," Ricardo spoke bashfully. "I did not want to disrespect you. Even before the…recent incidents, of course, I hear of you while growing up in Mexico."

"At any rate," Jorge decided to get back on track. "I need a young, handsome star to play…ah, the protagonist. And I am wondering if that might be you."

"Me, sir?" Ricardo laughed. "My English, it is not so good, and I have no acting experience"

"But that is not a problem," Jorge shook his head. "The protagonist, his English is not so good either."

There was a moment of silence before the two men broke out in laughter.

"Ok, sir, I understand," Ricardo blushed and continued to laugh. "But I have no acting experience."

"That is fine," Jorge shook his head. "Tony, he is overseeing the show, and he will work with you."

"Wouldn't he prefer a more...experienced actor?" Ricardo wondered.

"It was Tony who suggested you to me," Jorge informed him, causing Ricardo's eyes to light up. "He said he saw something in you and requested that you do an audition. And you know, maybe it will not work, or maybe you won't like, but it does not hurt to try."

"This is very nice, sir," Ricardo said and thought for a moment. "I am off school until this fall."

"It will tape in the summer," Jorge assured him. "It will go into the fall as well, but Ricardo, we can worry about school details later. If you do this and like it, it may give you another career path, and as you know, you always have work with me."

"Thank you, sir," Ricardo nodded.

"As long as you continue to be loyal."

"I know, sir. Loyalty above all."

Jorge nodded with pride on his face. The student was learning.

"Do you wish me to go to the production house?" Ricardo asked with uncertainty in his voice. "Do I need an agent?"

"I will give you Tony's number," Jorge replied. "And you can call him. He will set up an audition and take care of any details you need. You may have to join an actor's group or something. I do not know. This here, it is not my area of expertise."

"But sir, you have so many."

To this, Jorge laughed and shook his head.

"Not this one here, I'm afraid."

The meeting ended on a positive note, and Jorge was left alone in the VIP room. This was a good move. Ricardo had handled a sticky situation with Jolene for him, and now, he would be rewarded. If he succeeded as an actor, he could play other roles in Jorge's production house. Not to mention, get all the women and money he desired. It seemed like an ideal opportunity for a young man.

A knock at the door interrupted his thoughts.

"*Si?*" Jorge called out and watched the door open. Chase entered the room.

"Did you tell him?"

"Yes," Jorge nodded. "He seemed to like the idea."

"Who wouldn't?" Chase replied as he closed the door behind him. "I mean, at that age especially."

"Would you also like…"

"Nah," Chase grinned as he walked toward the table. "I think I'll pass on that one."

"Well, not everyone wants to be a star," Jorge replied. "In fairness, sometimes it is the people working behind the scenes that matter the most."

"That's true," Chase sat down. "So, he'll be playing the lead role in this new show?"

"Yes, and I think it will be popular," Jorge predicted.

"All these shows are now."

"Not just that," Jorge shook his head. "It is about an anti-hero. I think people, like the anti-hero, and even though they do not like to admit it, they may relate to it more than the regular hero."

"Do people even believe in heroes anymore?" Chase raised an eyebrow. "I mean, really?"

"This here, it is a good question," Jorge nodded. "Many of the so-called *good guys* have given us reason to not trust them."

"Look at what happened to Juliana when she trusted her doctor."

"It is a terrible thing," Jorge reached for his phone and turned it on. "My Maria, she cried her heart out when she heard about the medication. She is getting tougher, but in many ways, she is very vulnerable. Juliana was part of the family. She looked after my children like they were her own. It breaks my heart."

"Have you heard anything?" Chase quietly asked.

"It is not good," Jorge replied as his phone came to life. "It is not going to be much longer, I am afraid."

Chase shook his head and looked away.

"Ah, I see Marco has something for me to see," Jorge said as he tapped on a link. "Oh, it is a Twitter post by Andrew."

Turning his phone around, Chase read it and raised his eyebrows, nodding.

"That's a hell of a lot of likes and retweets," Chase commented.

"Well, he is talking to people his age. They do not trust the mainstream news anymore," Jorge pointed out. "And he gives a specific example from a recent story. He did not have to look far to prove his point."

"There are lots of reasons not to trust them."

"Many, they still do."

"Not his age."

"You are practically the same age," Jorge teased. "But yes, I know what you mean.

Jorge turned the phone back to see another link. This one was a video from a major Canadian news outlet, one he had taken swats at in his interview with Makerson.

"...and Jorge Hernandez has started a new project," A female entertainment reporter spoke in a bubbly, high-pitch voice. *"One that will soon take over the internet. Not only does he own a media company, producing the popular docuseries Eat the Rich Before the Rich Eat You, but now he's getting into the news."*

"Yes, Peta, he's backing an independent news channel called HPC news that he says will tell the truth and only the truth," A polished middle-aged man spoke sarcastically. Both reporters had fake smiles on their faces. *"So, basically, we're trusting the same man who sells us weed to tell us the news."*

"Well, that sounds fun, Nick."

The two continued to mock Jorge's news program.

"These two," Jorge said after the clip was over. "They are, as you say, filling in space with fluff."

"There is a lot of that these days," Chase commented. "I can't stand that show."

"Because they are fake," Jorge shook his head, staring at the still screen which continued to feature their images. "Fake smile. Fake laugh. Fake tits. It's all fake here."

"I don't know, the tits too?" Chase laughed. "They don't look like she got her money's worth."

"She works for a shitty network," Jorge grinned. "That's all she can afford."

Chase continued to laugh.

"At any rate," Jorge said as he closed the video. "It is me who will have the last laugh."

CHAPTER 8

"It's kind of like a sweet 16 party, except it's a sweet *15* party instead," Maria explained to Jorge as they sat by the pool. His attempt to enjoy a quiet morning outside wasn't going as he had planned. "I have these kids from school I want to ask and…"

"Maria, I do not want a bunch of strangers wandering around my house," Jorge cut her off, shaking his head. "You know why we cannot have this here. We talked about it before. Besides, you did not want a *quinceañera,* but you want this?"

"It's not the same," Maria insisted, which caused Jorge to be suspicious. Other than his daughter's friend, Cameron, he never saw her with any other kids. "I don't want anything fancy, just a few people."

"Who exactly?" Jorge grew suspicious. "Give me names."

"No one you'd know."

"Maria, can we talk about this when it gets closer to August," Jorge suggested. "It is the end of June. I cannot think that far ahead."

"Promise you'll at least think about it," Maria encouraged as she glanced at her phone, then back at Jorge. "I just have a few friends I want to have over…not a lot."

"I will think about it."

"And I promise not to let them out of my sight," She stood up, smoothing out her outfit. "Like, your office will be locked, and I won't let them upstairs and…"

"And if you think that we are leaving the house while you have this party, think again," Jorge suddenly caught on to what his daughter had in mind. "This here, it is not happening. We are not uprooting the family so you can have your party."

"It would only be a couple of hours," Maria whined. "I can't have my family here and baby running around while we're trying to dance and stuff."

"Maria, it is the '*and stuff*' part that worries me," Jorge gave her a dark look.

"No one will be having sex or taking drugs," Maria assured him.

"You're goddam right no one will be," Jorge shot back and noted Maria's discouraged expression as she started to walk away. "We will be talking more about this later. I would like to enjoy my morning off in the sun."

"I thought you said you never had a day off," Maria sang out as she reached the patio door. Paige was on the other side.

"Yes, well, today anyone who wants to see me," Jorge loudly replied. "Will see me *here*."

Shrugging, Maria met Paige in the doorway and went back into the house while Jorge's wife came out.

"How *is* your day off so far?" Paige asked as she glanced toward his empty coffee cup. "Need a refill?"

"Yes, and put a shot in the next one," Jorge grumbled as Paige sat down. "She wants a sweet *15* party."

"Is that a thing?"

"It won't be in this fucking house," Jorge muttered back. "I put her off. She seems to think we are going to allow a bunch of strangers to roam around and have sex in our bed while we vacate the premise."

"She said that?" Paige appeared humored.

"No, come on, Paige, I am not stupid," Jorge shook his head, quickly pulling up his sunglasses to look into her eyes. "I was 15 once too."

"I somehow doubt her lifestyle is quite the same as yours was at 15," Paige quietly spoke.

"Somedays," Jorge loudly sighed as he lowered the sunglasses again. "I do not know, Paige. She has done a lot, but overall, yes, it is different. I worry too. Does she want us out because she has something planned? She over-emphasized that they would not be going upstairs. This made me certain that they *are* planning to go upstairs. Does she have a boyfriend?"

"Did you ask her?" Paige asked.

"No," Jorge shook his head. "She would not tell me anyway. I do not even know how these things work with kids these days. Everything seems pretty goosey loosey with teens now. I do not understand."

"Let's wait and see," Paige suggested. "By August, maybe she'll have other ideas."

"I do not want a bunch of horny teenagers in my house," Jorge complained.

"Are you going to yell at kids for being on your lawn, too?" Paige quietly asked.

Jorge took a minute to catch on that she was teasing him but merely grinned.

"So," Paige pointed toward his phone. "No business today?"

"Only if people want to come to see me here."

"That's fair," Paige nodded. "It's a beautiful day."

"The perfect day," Jorge corrected her. "Not too hot, nice breeze, our neighbors are quiet…" he pointed toward Diego's house, next door. "I am content."

After Paige left, Jorge leaned back in his chair and closed his eyes. The warmth of the sun beat down on his face, causing him to relax. He needed to do this more often. With the money he spent on his backyard and pool, it seemed ridiculous he never enjoyed it. Plus, it made Paige happy when he slowed down, although Jorge secretly worried it would kill him if he slowed down too much.

A whisk of air over his face caused him to open his eyes. Expecting to see Paige or Maria returning, Jorge opened his eyes to see a large, black crow on the other end of the patio table. Unconcerned with Jorge watching him, the crow ripped a portion of a half-eaten bagel from his plate. He momentarily stopped and jerked his head sideways to look at Jorge before continuing to eat. He finally tore of another portion of the bagel and flew off.

Intrigued, Jorge wondered if he'd come back for the remainder that sat on the plate. He had barely touched his food this morning. His stomach was upset. He had received news that Juliana had slipped in a coma that morning. It wouldn't be much longer.

The patio door slid open, and Diego walked outside. For once, he was wearing shorts and a t-shirt. It was rare to see his long-time associate not dressed in a designer suit.

"I see you have also taken the day off," Jorge remarked as the Colombian approached him. Diego suddenly halted and leaned back, staring at the table with a look of horror on his face, causing Jorge to follow his eyes.

The crow had returned and was boldly pecking at the final piece of bagel. The bird continued to seem unconcerned with Jorge sitting nearby. He finally got the remainder situated in his beak and flew off.

"What the fuck?" Diego dramatically exclaimed as he walked over. "Is that your new pet or what?"

"We just met earlier today," Jorge grinned. "He come to visit me."

"Don't they say crows come to take your soul?" Diego appeared unsure whether or not to sit at the table. Nervously, he glanced around as if expecting the bird to return.

"Don't be ridiculous, Diego," Jorge laughed. "I do not have a soul."

"It's pretty hard to argue that point," Diego admitted, as he continued to look around nervously as he sat down.

"Do not worry," Jorge replied, humored. "He will not come back. There is no food left on my plate."

"Birds scare the shit out of me," Diego complained as he lifted his sunglasses to inspect the area once more. "I had one attack me once."

"What can I say, Diego," Jorge teased. "The birds, they also work for me."

Diego made a face.

"What is new in Diego's world this morning?" Jorge asked with interest. "I have not seen you much lately."

"Same old," Diego swung his arms in the air. "Bad boyfriends, work stress, same bullshit."

"Well, Diego, you must make an effort to change this here," Jorge recommended. "Life, it is short."

"Getting shorter by the day," Diego complained. "Don't get me wrong, I love being the CEO of *Our House Of Pot*, but a lot is going on. I feel like I'm tied to that place."

"Remember, you run the place," Jorge lectured him. "Other people, pay them to do the work."

"I think I need a home office," Diego wondered. "Like I could work from *my* patio on days like this."

"Do it," Jorge shrugged. "Diego, you can. You know this…"

"As long as your creepy crow stays the hell over here," Diego pointed next door to his place. "I don't want him eating off my goddam plate."

To this, Jorge laughed.

An awkward silence followed.

"We got to talk about Jolene sometime," Diego finally said. "We haven't since…"

"I know."

"Everything was left up in the air."

"It was not a good time for a lot of reasons," Jorge admitted. "but Diego, not today. I want to enjoy my morning."

Diego nodded and didn't reply, yet there was a solidarity between them that relaxed the atmosphere. Neither of them wanted to visit the topic.

"I heard you got Ricardo a new job," Diego commented.

"Yeah, he's young and handsome," Jorge quipped. "He suits the protagonist of the cartel show well."

To this, Diego laughed.

"Do not say it, my friend…"

"Hey, didn't say a thing."

"I am happy he is willing to do it," Jorge continued. "And I am also happy that Tony, he is satisfied that he will play the role well. I was not sure since he is young, inexperienced."

"Tony got him an acting coach," Diego replied. "It will be good."

"This is true."

The two men sat in silence, enjoying the sunshine until Jorge's phone beeped. Glancing at it, he lifted his sunglasses.

"Marco, he has something for me," Jorge announced. "I will tell him to come over here to have a beer…"

"A beer does sound good," Diego replied.

"He is on his way," Jorge confirmed. "He has to stop by to see Tony first."

"That means he got something."

Jorge turned off his phone, and Diego did the same.

"I hope this here means he knows who gave the final word on this drug that was supposed to be safe, that gave Juliana cancer," Jorge said as he ran a hand over his face, briefly removing his sunglasses. "Plus enough proof to expose this company for the premiere of our news show."

"It's Marco," Diego reminded him. "You know he does."

He would soon find out it was much worse than he thought.

CHAPTER 9

"Sir, it is very disturbing," Marco commented as the three men sat in Jorge's office. The dark, dreary atmosphere was counter to the warmth and light that his morning had provided. He considered how this was probably appropriate, given the topic. "It does seem that it is not *one* person that knew it was probably not a safe drug but *several,* and they still allowed it to pass."

Jorge remained silent but exchanged looks with Diego, who shook his head and looked away.

"The company," Marco pointed toward some documents he had printed off. "They purposely removed the damaging information, only focusing on the short-term effects of the drugs, which sir, were minimal."

Jorge nodded and remained quiet.

"However, everyone seemed to give a blind eye to the *potential long-term effects,"* Marco went on, pointing toward specific sections of the large document. "There is even communication between them all where they openly discuss it! They knew it might damage people later on but let it go!"

"Fucking bastards," Diego made a face. "Because they don't care."

"Because, sir," Marco shook his head. "They knew by the time the truth came out, any lawsuits would be minimal compared to the amount of money they projected making on the product. You see, that is how they weigh their options. How do they lose more money and the option that loses the least, it wins."

Jorge frowned and felt anger seething through his body.

"Look out," Diego pointed at him. "Jorge's head is about to explode. That gotta be a messy situation."

"Diego, you have no idea," Jorge said as he pulled open a desk drawer and grabbed a bottle of tequila. Then he reached behind him for three shot glasses. "My head, it *is* about to explode for so many reasons."

Marco appeared concerned as he carefully watched him, while Diego looked equally frustrated.

"You know," Jorge said as he poured the tequila. "When I lived in Mexico, I was the devil to most because I sell drugs. This made me a terrible person but, people, they *voluntarily* took my drugs. They were fully aware of what could go wrong and potential…you know, consequences. I did not lie about this. I was honest. But yet, *I* was the villain."

The two men nodded in agreement while Jorge gave them each a shot before he continued.

"But Big Pharma," He continued. "They make drugs they *know* will hurt people, and there are no consequences. If I had been caught selling drugs, I would go to jail. They *legally* sell drugs that are *proven* to hurt people, and at worse, they get some bad publicity and lawsuit. They do not go to jail. There are no consequences, and the people, they continue to take their drugs. This world, it does not make sense, and it infuriates me."

"It's true," Diego reached for his shot. Beside him, Marco was hesitant but finally did the same. "Those fuckers can get away with anything and people, they trust them! If I sell you shit that makes you sick, you would never buy something from me again. But *they* do, and it is, what? No big deal? An *honest* mistake."

"Sir, it was neither honest *nor* a mistake," Marco shook his head. "They knew what they were doing and did it anyway. They look at profit, and that is all. It is very scary. I even started to investigate some of the medications that my children have had to take in the past. No, I will not allow it again. I discussed it with my wife that we go to a naturopath or someone not corrupted by all of this here."

"Well, you see," Jorge attempted to explain but stopped to take his shot. The others did the same. He made a face and went on. "You see, the people, they see Big Pharma as a religion. It is their church, their savior, or so they think. But when we put anyone, anything, on a pedestal, it is almost guaranteed to be corrupt. When you make a God out of a mere person, a corporation, any institution, *they* believe it, and that is when the problems start."

The two men said nothing but continued to watch him.

"At any rate," Jorge turned to Marco. "I do appreciate this here information. Even though it makes me furious."

"I am sorry to have to report it."

"So, where we start?" Diego got right to the point. "Who we kill first?"

"Well, let us first put the fire under them on the HPC news," Jorge suggested. "We will watch them squirm, and then, I will decide who lives and who dies."

"My guess is the lives list is pretty short," Diego muttered.

"Well, Diego, you know me," Jorge said as he raised an eyebrow. "I do enjoy a good purge from time to time."

"Sir, you have already exposed Big Pharma in your series," Marco reminded him. "And here we are again. It is just the same…."

"I know, Marco, it is frustrating," Jorge shook his head. "And the people, they never learn."

"Then why bother to report it?" Diego bluntly asked. "Does it even matter?"

"Well, this here is the thing," Jorge replied as he leaned back in his chair in thought. "*Some* people, they will open their eyes. Those who want to keep their eyes closed will forever, no matter what proof you show them. That is just their way. They do not want to know. Meanwhile, Big Pharma, their stock will take a dip. They will get shaken up. I will make them very uncomfortable, and although that is no real justice, it does bring me some satisfaction. And we will see what happens at this point. Once things calm, maybe someone's head will be on a platter."

"These people are like fucking cockroaches," Diego complained. "They never die."

"It's Big Pharma," Jorge reminded him. "You cannot bury them. They crawl out from another rock."

"These people, they are crazy," Marco said as he shook his head.

"Yes, they are Marco," Jorge confirmed. "But not crazier than me!"

After the two men left, Jorge sat alone and read the documents Marco had brought to him. He had also dropped off copies to Tony and

Makerson, who would work furiously to throw a story together for the first episode when their news channel premiered that Monday. Although they had other staff working on the show, only the men he trusted the most would be allowed to work on something that was so highly confidential. Big Pharma couldn't learn what was coming around the corner. He wanted it to be a surprise.

"A penny for your thoughts," Paige's voice alerted him. She was standing in the doorway. "Diego and Marco let me know what was happening on their way out. I'd like to say I'm surprised, but I'm not."

She entered the room, closing the door behind her. Heading toward her usual seat, Paige carefully watched her husband as she did.

"Well, *mi Amor,* if this here news was just to attack Big Pharma," Jorge commented as he pointed toward the document on his desk. "I would say, this here is fine. Let us burn them in public. But the more Marco, he speak to me about this, the more I thought about Juliana."

Paige nodded with compassion in her eyes.

"She had worked for me a many years," Jorge reminded his wife. "Long before she was Maria's nanny. When my ex, she was on drugs, it was Juliana who brought up my little girl. She was with me for a long time and has been here since Miguel was born. She is family, and I do not like it when someone hurts my family. This here, it does not matter if it is direct or indirect. Either way, people are going to pay."

Paige nodded in understanding.

"And Paige," Jorge sat ahead in his seat. "I do not have to tell you that it will not be pretty. These people, they are more concerned about profit than they are about people's lives. We are nothing to them. Just profit. And they say *I* am evil."

"Unfortunately, that's a lot of corporations," Paige reminded him. "Not just Big Pharma, it's capitalism."

"I also made money this way," Jorge reminded her. "But you know, it always seems like these people, they wanted to do anything to keep me from doing so, from being legit. I got a lot of pushback when I start here in Canada. I was not allowed to join their club. But I have bad news for them because I'm going to tear their clubhouse down and burn it."

"I think it's justified," Paige nodded. "But wait to see the fireworks on Monday."

"There will be lots," Jorge confirmed. "And I will enjoy it."

"I've been getting notifications all day," Paige said as she reached in her pocket and pulled out her phone. "Andrew is going wild with his posts on social media."

"He is....quite aggressive in his presentation," Jorge grinned. "I like this here."

"That's an understatement," Paige confirmed as her phone came to life and she hit a few buttons. Turning it around, she showed him a still video of Andrew's face. "You gotta watch this one."

"Do it," Jorge said with a grin as he leaned across his desk as Paige moved the phone closer to him. She hit the play button, and Andrew came to life on the screen.

"Why are you still watching corporate news?"

Jorge was expecting a long rant to follow, but instead, there were quick flashes of the many stories that news agencies got wrong. This included reporters contradicting themselves, the segment making a mockery of some of Canada's most well-known journalists and reporters.

Andrew's face reappeared on the screen. He was in downtown Toronto, reaching for the door of a popular coffee shop.

"Have you ever noticed there's a narrative?"

Common and frequently used phrases began to be displayed, one after the other, with reporters from all major news channels saying them. They used the same language and same wording until everything collided together. Hip hop music started to play, causing the words to create a mock rap song, mimicking those who appeared serious, stoic on the screen.

Andrew appeared, sitting at a table, drinking a coffee.

"Who writes this stuff? And even more, why do you trust it?"

The video ended with powerful letters on the screen, showing the premier date of HPC news.

Jorge's head fell back in laughter.

"You like it?" Paige asked.

"Paige, this here," Jorge nodded as he pointed toward her phone. "This here, it will burn them all; the media, Big Pharma, I am taking those fuckers down in one fucking swoop and exposing them for the lying bastards they are. I am gonna eat the rich, and those fuckers won't have a chance."

CHAPTER 10

"But *Papá*," She started in a whiny voice that irritated Jorge. "You know it's not fair! You barely know this Ricardo guy, and you give him a role in your new show. You've known *me* my entire life, and you won't let me..."

"Maria!" Jorge snapped as he brought his hand down on the desk. "Enough! I do not like this tone you are taking with me. You act as if you have no privilege at all, but you do! You go to a private school. You have lessons in many things including, martial arts by an expert, so many things. You say you want to move up in the family, so that has been my focus. Now, you want to throw it away to be a television star? We are back to where we started!"

"No," Maria continued to whine. "I can do both. I can be on television *and* later, I can lead this family. I mean, it's almost better because no one will ever suspect a thing if I'm on television. They'll think I'm just another dumb actress."

"Maria," Jorge shook his head. "This here is an interesting argument, but you know that the best thing is to keep under the radar. You cannot do this if you are on a television screen every week."

"It doesn't have to be every week," She replied in a flat voice.

"Maria, this here, it is enough, ok?" Jorge shook his head as his frustration continued to grow, causing him to stumble on his English. "First of all, there are no roles for teenage girls on this show and, I want your focus to be on the family…unless, of course, you no longer think this is important. I have to say, Maria, it concerns me how you flip-flop around. I thought you had outgrown this acting nonsense, but it does not seem so. You are a young lady now, soon to have your number 15 birthday! You cannot continue to invest in a silly idea. You have not even acted in a long time."

"I can start again on my free days," Maria continued to insist. "*Papá,* I'm just trying to *live* my *life!*"

"Maria, there are only so many hours in a day," Jorge ignored her dramatic appeal. "You cannot do everything."

"You do!" She accused.

"I do not act, Maria."

"No, but you have a chain of pot shops, almost got into politics, own a crematorium, a film production house…"

"Yes, I own," Jorge agreed. "But I do not work at each of these places every day. I have other people run them, and from time to time. I consult with them on what I would like to see then I walk away. I do not try to do everything."

"I thought…"

"Maria," Jorge cut her off. "Normally, I would say, try everything that appeals to you, but if you want to one day lead this family, which you did approach me last year to say, then you must make it your focus. I told you that then, and I tell you that again now. You cannot go back and forth. There is too much for you to learn and too much responsibility."

Maria's face turned red, and she nodded.

"Now, I would say that you have a decision to make," Jorge said as he calmed down. "It is fine, either way, with me. But Maria, remember that my production house, it only has a few shows. You would have to compete with many for those jobs. Actors work hard to get a single role and have many auditions before they get a job. Even us, we have a lineup for each audition. Many are very talented, but only one person will get the job. Think about it, Maria. And think, what it is you want and why acting appeals to you. Being famous, it is not everything."

She nodded, her face falling.

"And if it is acting you like," Jorge continued. "Do this here at school and see, but for now, Maria, you are not getting special favors because I own the production house. This is not happening."

"I didn't mean..."

"Yes, Maria, you did," Jorge cut her off again. "You asked me for a role. You did not ask to *audition* for a role."

"But you gave Ricardo one!"

"He auditioned," Jorge replied and watched his daughter's expression drop. "We did not know for sure, but it was difficult to find the right person. Tony and I talked about him, and he suggested he give it a shot. They felt he would work with a few lessons. That is why he has the staring role in a show. He did not ask me, and actually, I had not thought of this at all. It was Tony. The starring role is very important, and we must have the best person for the job."

"I suppose," Maria said, her defenses dropped. "That's true."

"So, Maria, for now," Jorge said as he shook his head. "Please focus on the family and learning what you need to know to one day head it. This here, it is more important than a stupid acting job."

"I know."

"Please, it is a beautiful dayl," Jorge continued to calm down. "Go and enjoy yourself and not worry about these things here."

She left shortly after, and even though Jorge hated to see her look defeated, she needed to learn the truth. He would not sugarcoat anything for his children. This was not the Hernandez way.

"Are you ready?" Paige was standing in the doorway. "It's almost time."

"Yes," Jorge jumped up from his seat. "Let's go."

The couple headed to the SUV in the garage and silently got in. Jorge was nervous. His news channel was premiering at noon. The group was to meet for lunch at the *Princesa Maria* and to watch it together. Everything needed to go off flawlessly.

"I spoke to Tala earlier," Paige broke the silence as they backed out of the driveway and turned onto the street. "She's up for it."

"This here, it is good," Jorge nodded as he focused on the road. "I hope she does not just say this."

"No," Paige shook her head. "After being kidnapped last year, she has a lot of concerns for her safety, and of course, she wants to protect the children, if ever needed."

"Hopefully not," Jorge replied. "But it is always a possibility."

"I'm going to start teaching her later this week," Paige replied as she looked out the window. "I think it will be empowering to learn to shoot."

"I think it will," Jorge insisted. "She worries me, you know. She is still so nervous. Are you sure teaching her to shoot is a good idea?"

"I think that her nervousness will start to go away as she learns," Paige insisted. "Remember, I was in a similar spot as her once, and it did for me. That and learning self-defense, which we talked about too."

Jorge nodded. His wife had dealt with a traumatic event in her youth. She was the victim of an armed robbery as a young woman, her coworker murdered in front of her eyes. The experience had left her gutted. Paige eventually learned that either she focused on growing in her power, or she would fall apart.

"I think this here makes sense," Jorge nodded. "I would like this for Tala. I do not want her to be afraid."

"She'll be ok," Paige predicted as they got closer to the bar.

"This is good," Jorge nodded and changed the subject. "Maria, she come to me, wanting to be in one of my shows."

"I'm not surprised," Paige traded looks with him, and he raised an eyebrow.

"Well, I tell her, she has to choose," Jorge shook his head. "In reality, I do not want her on television, but I said, she cannot learn to run a family, plus school, plus acting. This here is too much."

"I wonder where she got the idea to take on too much," Paige teased and to that, Jorge grinned and winked at his wife.

"This was brought up," He replied as they arrived at the bar. "I had to think fast, but I feel I persuaded her."

After Jorge parked the vehicle, the couple got out of the SUV and headed for the side door that let them directly into the VIP room, which had become their preferred place for meetings.

Diego answered the door with a big grin. The delicious smell of pizza caused Jorge's stomach to growl.

"You got here just in time," He pointed behind him as the group sat around to watch a large screen television on the wall. "It's about to start."

"That's new," Jorge pointed at the screen. "I like it."

"It was a special occasion," Chase replied, in his usual seat with a slice of pizza in front of him. "And I thought, we're always watching stuff or looking at documents on the computer. This is perfect to have a better look."

"Good idea!" Jorge commented as he reached into one of the pizza boxes and pulled out a slice, placing it on a paper plate.

"Oh, he's starting," Marco spoke up, pointing toward the screen.

Jorge took his usual seat while Paige grabbed a slice and did the same. "Where's Ricardo?"

"At the studio," Diego replied as he pulled his box of gluten-free pizza closer. "He had to help Tony with auditions for another part. They thought he would have better input, you know, being Mexican and all."

Jorge nodded, his eyes returning to the screen. He watched a professional Makerson appear, welcoming viewers. Marco, meanwhile, turned his laptop around to show the number of viewers watching on the various platforms. The viewers rose as Makerson continued to talk, hinting of a shocking story to come later. He started by going through the top stories in the same way as a traditional news program. He presented things in a manner that was easy to understand, relatable, and to the point. About 15 minutes in, he switched to their breaking story promised at the beginning of the show.

"We recently received a tip that turned out to be a very alarming story about Big Pharma," Makerson solemnly spoke and paused for a moment. "I have to warn you that some of the content that you are about to hear will be disturbing, and you might want to check your medications after you watch."

"Beautiful!" Jorge joyfully clapped his hands together. "This here, it is *perfecto!*"

"Last week, we were presented with some shocking information, coming from an insider in the pharmaceutical industry..."

As Jorge gleefully rejoiced in his triumph over Big Pharma, his phone rang. As soon as he saw the number, his joy quickly sank to the ground.

He knew who this number belonged to and what it meant.

CHAPTER 11

"It is bittersweet," Jorge admitted to Paige as the two mournfully sat over breakfast. "I guess this here is the nature of the universe. It is the balance. We must take the good with the bad."

Paige quietly looked into her coffee.

"I wish I could have done more for Juliana," Jorge continued as he glanced over his shoulder as if expecting Maria to come downstairs. Breaking the news to her the previous night had been difficult enough. "But unfortunately, even I only have so much power."

Paige reached out and touched his arm with kindness in her eyes and nodded.

"You did all you could."

"I did more than most, I suppose," Jorge admitted. "But did it matter in the end?"

"You made her comfortable in her last days," Paige reminded him. "That's all you can do when someone is dying."

"I will pay for the funeral," Jorge lowered his voice and glanced toward the stairs. "Of course, anything they need."

"Are you going?"

"No," Jorge shook his head. "Her family, my reputation…it is better I do not. It was discouraged."

"They told you no?" Paige appeared annoyed. "But you…"

"Paige, no, this is fine," Jorge shook his head. "I do understand. My reputation in Mexico, it is not good. So it is better that, out of respect, I do not go to the funeral. And this is fine. The family was more than kind to me when I call last night, but I do not want to bring any shame. Most know she worked for a family in Canada, that is all."

Paige nodded.

"And well, they were pleased for the help," Jorge confirmed. "They did thank me with their whole heart, her family, so I am ok with this here."

"I can't believe she's gone."

"I know, it seems like yesterday," Jorge pointed toward the door that led to the basement apartment, where Juliana stayed. It was now Tala's home. "But, we can only move forward."

"So, what's on the agenda for today?"

"I go talk numbers from yesterday with Tony and Makerson," Jorge confirmed. "Then I go speak with Marco, see what he is learning on his end."

"Are we going to get sued for that story?"

"No, it is, how you say," Jorge thought for a moment. "The truth, but they must find a way to lie about how we got the information. It anonymously arrived at the production house. Makerson did some deep research and what it says was true."

"I can't help but wonder," Paige shook her head. "Do you think that if Juliana hadn't…"

Her sentence drifted off as her eyes watered.

"Paige, I do not know," He attempted to comfort her. "Maybe? But then again, maybe not. We cannot know. But, from what I learn, this pill definitely increased her chances of getting sick."

"It is maddening."

"It is."

As it turns out, many others felt the same way as Paige. When Jorge arrived at Hernandez Productions later that morning, Makerson and Tony were going through the comments on their social media, not to mention the many emails they received since the story broke.

"It's viral," Makerson pointed toward the laptop, while on the other side of the table, Tony nodded. "Like the whole fucking country, all over the world, everyone is talking about this story. It's trending on Twitter, which forced mainstream news to talk about it."

"Some are going to great lengths to bury it, though," Tony reminded him as he twisted uncomfortably in his chair. "Trying to downplay it as if cancer was a *rare* side effect of the drug."

"Not to mention the things we brought up about other pills," Makerson shook his head. "Although none as dangerous as that one, it still alarmed people."

"One other network is jumping on the bandwagon," Tony mentioned. "Doing a story called 'Are the drugs you take safe'?"

"This here, it is easy," Jorge shook his head, "no, they are not."

"Pretty much," Makerson confirmed.

Just then, the door opened, and in walked Andrew Collin, holding a box of donuts.

"What the fuck, you guys have a meeting without me?" He asked as he set the box down, and everyone dove to grab one. "And who said those donuts were for you? Maybe I like to eat a lot."

"It's a meeting," Jorge commented after shoving half a chocolate donut in his mouth. "You share."

"Things were a bit impromptu," Makerson confessed. "I probably forgot to text you. Did you see the response to the story online? It's crazy."

"Oh yeah, read the trolls too," Andrew confirmed as he plunked down in a chair and reached in the box of donuts. "Probably brought to you by the assholes in Big Pharma."

"Troll away," Jorge said. "This here, it does not bother me. Most people, they are alarmed by this news, as they should be."

"And Juliana..." Makerson started, as if suddenly remembering the terrible news from the previous day. Before he could give his condolences, he was cut off.

"Exactly," Jorge nodded as the others listened. "She took this pill and thought it was safe, and she got stomach cancer. And here we are."

"Fucking savages," Andrew shook his head. "They should all burn."

"Well, the day is not over yet," Jorge sharply commented.

"So, how should we follow this up?" Tony asked the others. "We're getting too much response to not do something bigger now."

"I was thinking about that this morning," Makerson said as he reached into the box of donuts. "I think by keeping it simple. Address the fact that this story from last night brought a lot of attention, maybe bring on someone who was directly affected by it, have an emotional interview."

"Hey, you lost your nanny, bodyguard lady," Andrew looked at Jorge.

"I am not going on there, crying," Jorge shot him a look.

"Like, no, I mean your daughter," Andrew shook his head. "A young girl, crying, Just a thought."

Jorge wanted to dismiss the idea but wondered if it might quench Maria's thirst for stardom, even if it was short-lived. Perhaps this would be a good move, but he'd have to talk to Paige.

"I will see," Jorge spoke evenly. "I am not sure."

"I think I know someone else," Makerson suggested as he shoved the last piece of donut in his mouth, pointing toward the laptop. "But maybe she could have a few minutes at the end or something."

"But if they find out it's Jorge's daughter," Tony made a face. "They may attack that or *her*. Also, she was a nanny. People may not have as much compassion for rich people with nannies, no offense."

Jorge shrugged with no concern.

"We wouldn't do it that way," Makerson shook his head. "She was an immigrant who was given an opportunity in a new country. Jorge helped her. She was a part of your family. It's something to consider."

"I will," Jorge confirmed as he glanced at the clock. "I gotta go. I have a meeting with Marco at the club."

"Let us know if he finds anything," Makerson suggested.

"I will send him to you later," Jorge said as he rose from the chair. "This here, it is great work. Now that we have shaken their tree, I cannot wait to see what falls out."

"Let's hope it's not lawyers," Tony said as he made a face.

"We got the info legit," Makerson shrugged. "They can't prove otherwise."

Jorge considered any potential problems as he left the production house and headed for his SUV. Turning on his phone, he noted that all seemed quiet for a change. But was it the quiet before the storm?

Traffic was starting to pick up, but he managed to reach the club just as Marco rolled up on his bike. He met Jorge at the door.

"Oh sir, we have so much to talk about," Marco seemed out of breath, his face red.

"Let us go inside," Jorge instructed as they walked into the empty club. "Would you like something to drink, Marco? You look exhausted."

"Just water, sir," Marco said as he leaned his bike against the wall and headed toward the bar, where Jorge was pulling out a bottle of water from the cooler. He handed it to him and gestured toward the VIP room.

After unlocking the door, the two men went inside.

"Sir, there is a lot of talk of lawyers," Marco said quickly. "But fortunately, I do not think they will pursue anything."

"I do not think they are in the position to…"

"That is what they say too," Marco said as he opened the bottle of water and took a long drink. "They said that their lawyers did not feel there was a case. However, they are now trying to figure out which person on their staff leaked the information."

"Makes sense," Jorge sat down, and Marco did the same. "So, no lawyers?"

"No, not unless they can prove we hacked them," Marco shook his head. "And sir, they cannot deny that it is true. The proof we presented on the news, it said it all."

"And it was a document a lot of people in the company had access to?" Jorge asked.

"Yes, sir," Marco nodded. "So, we are good that way. We will not have lawyers at our door."

"If we did," Jorge shook his head. "They would not be here for long."

"Well, the only issue that I see," Marco said as he leaned forward. "Is that they feel this is a personal vendetta from you and worry what more you will dig for, so they want to stop you but aren't sure how."

"There is no way."

"Sir, I would be cautious," Marco warned. "They are talking about how their shares have dropped, all the bad press, and they want revenge."

"Bring it on," Jorge spoke with no fear. "I can take them."

CHAPTER 12

"I have Health Canada and the public waiting for answers," Athas continued to complain through the secure line. Not that he had any sympathy from Jorge Hernandez, who merely rolled his eyes on the other end of the phone. "The drug was pulled from the shelves. Not that they had a choice, but how did it get on there in the first place? How did it pass?"

"I think you and I know how it passed," Jorge reminded him. "But you investigating all this, it will satisfy the people, but does it not take forever?"

"Pretty much," Athas admitted and let out a loud sigh. "There's already hints that my decision in this matter might affect whether or not I get re-elected."

"Of course," Jorge nodded. "You are not playing their game. a*migo.* They do not like this here."

"I don't like the fact that Canadians are taking pills that are killing them," Athas confirmed with frustration in his voice. "It's like I keep saying. The longer I do this job, the more I see how corrupt the system is."

"Of course it is," Jorge agreed. "This here, it is not news. It always surprises me how Canadians, they think they live in such a pristine and honest country. When in fact, this country, it is as corrupt as the rest of them. You just put a better face on it."

"If you say so," Athas said after some hesitation. "I'm not even sure I want to run..."

"You will run again," Jorge cut him off. "After all, if you want to fix this here mess, then you must roll up your sleeves and do so, not slink away like a coward."

"I think this is bigger than me," Athas admitted.

"Yes, but is it bigger than me?" Jorge asked him. "You tell me what you need, and I will take care of it."

"I might need some things shaken up at Health Canada."

"Just tell me what you need," Jorge repeated.

After ending the call with the prime minister, Jorge sat contemplating the last few days. It was interesting how the world worked and how the truth often shocked people. Were they so naive to trust large corporations? He assumed it came from the same side of human nature that also believed in fairy tales. But this situation was no fairy tale.

Rather than jumping in with both feet, Jorge had decided to take Paige's advice and stand back and take it in. He would allow his associates to put out the fire or start a new one. Either way, he was to watch from the sidelines. It was a fascinating view.

Turning on his phone, he went to the HPC news website to check out the videos. The first was the original story, with thousands of comments below it. Two other videos featured people who were learning of the dangerous side effects of the drug that Juliana had been taking. One man had stomach cancer, while another recently lost a family member who took the same medication. These emotional accounts angered the community, many people demanding the CEO of one of the largest pharmaceutical companies in Canada to step down.

Makerson was planning to discuss what Athas mentioned in his call for that day's episode. How did this happen? How did dangerous drugs get passed with such ease? What other drugs that seemed safe were causing other, serious health effects?

Closing the site, Jorge sat back and sighed. He glanced at a new picture on his desk of Juliana with the children. It was from a happier time when she was well. How quickly things can happen. Was that not what Paige had warned him about many times? He finally saw that she was right.

His phone rang, causing him to pause his dark thoughts and glance at the number.

"*Hola,*" Jorge answered with some hesitation.

"Hey, some geezer in a suit here looking for you," Andrew spoke bluntly. "I'm at the production house."

"Who is it?"

"I dunno," He muttered. "Something about the company we just burned."

"Is he hassling you?"

"Nah," Andrew sounded bored. "Makerson is out on an interview, and Tony is working on location for the cartel show. Just me here, and I don't give a fuck, but he insists on talking to you."

"I will be there shortly," Jorge said as he stood up from the desk and loosened his tie. "Keep an eye on him till then."

"Will do," Andrew said with laughter in his voice.

Moments later, Jorge was in his SUV and on the way to the production house. Andrew's vague details didn't tell him much about who awaited him, but it sounded like something he should deal with personally. He wondered how this person got past security, but he'd have to make sure it didn't happen again.

However, when he arrived, Jorge quickly saw why Andrew hadn't viewed the visitor as a concern. The man hadn't seen his youth in many years. He wore a suit that probably was purchased a few decades earlier, but Jorge had to admire his efforts to present himself professionally. Still, he wasn't about to drop his defenses as he approached the reception area.

"I am told you want to see me?" Jorge said as he stepped up to the man. "What can I do for you?"

"Yes, Mr. Hernandez," The elderly man stood up and reached out to shake Jorge's hand, which he did with some hesitation. "I need your help and..."

"What?" Andrew yelped and jumped up from his chair on the other side of the room, rushing over. "I thought you were a suit from Big Pharma?"

"Did you think this here old man was working at Big Pharma?" Jorge grinned at Andrew. "He probably retired forty years ago."

"Thirty," The old man corrected him, clearly not offended.

"Whatever," Jorge shook his head. "What are you here for?"

"I need your help," The old man spoke bravely, despite the fear in his eyes. "And someone told me you could be...the person who might be able to do something for me."

Jorge made a face, then pointed toward the hallway.

"Andrew, is the conference room empty?"

"Yuppers."

"We will be using it."

Jorge gestured for the man to follow him while Andrew skeptically watched. As Jorge walked by, he raised an eyebrow.

"Should I....heat the oven?" He referred to the crematorium, causing Jorge to grin and shake his head no.

Once he was in the room alone with the elderly man, Jorge sat down and watched him do the same.

"So, who are you, first of all?" Jorge asked.

"My name is Clarence," He hesitated. "Maybe it's better if I don't say my last name."

To this, Jorge shrugged.

"I talked to a young man," Clarence started. "He said that you might be able to help me."

"Is this so?" Jorge asked. "Why is that?"

"Because my only great-granddaughter, she took that pill you had the computer the other night," Clarence spoke with emotion in his voice. "And she died of stomach cancer 3 months ago. At the time, I kept telling the doctors that she never had such severe problems until *after* taking these pills, but they wouldn't listen to me. They brushed it off. They said there was no connection."

"I see."

"And she died," Clarence said and cleared his throat. "She was only 21. Never was sick before in her life. She only took those goddam pills because she would get nervous, you know, with her schooling, and I guess life in general. But they tried to say that it was cancer that caused her stomach to be upset, not the other way around."

Jorge nodded and listened. The old man seemed to be shrinking in size as he spoke, the suit he wore almost too big for him. But he was telling the truth. There was no doubt.

"I watched her die," Clarence continued and hesitated before continuing. "It should have been me. I'm an old man. And I knew it was that pill. But no one would listen."

"Well, Clarence," Jorge attempted to assure him, feeling sorry for the old man. "I am listening. I do understand. My ah....my kid's nanny, she also take this here pill. And she also got cancer."

"Was she healthy before?"

"Yes, she was," Jorge nodded. "I mean, she had stomach issues, but who does not from time to time? The doctor, I believe, told her it would be better to take this pill all the time, so she did not experience any flare-ups. I think it…ah, as my wife explained, would keep her stomach consistent."

The old man's eyes widened as Jorge spoke, and they shared a look of understanding.

"That's what the doctor told her," Clarence confirmed. "The same lie."

"This here, it may not be the doctor," Jorge attempted to explain. "You know, they are told a drug is safe, so they assume it is."

"I don't believe that, do you?" Clarence challenged. "I was suspicious when she died, so I hired a private detective, and that high and mighty doctor had a lot of money for a young man. A big house. He spent a lot of time with another young man who worked at the pharmaceutical company that sold these pills."

Jorge sat back in his seat. Clarence had his attention.

"So, you tell me…"

"Mr. Hernandez, I think they worked together," Clarence suggested.

"So, how did you hear about me again?" Jorge was suddenly curious.

"I took this information to a young detective after I saw the news," Clarence continued. "Mark Hail. He lives next to me. I went to his house. He said nothing would come out of it. The laws protect them because Health Canada passed the drug."

"So, you wanted these men arrested?" Jorge nodded in understanding, knowing the detective he was referring to; they had helped each other out in the past. "To pay for what they did? You think they conspired to make money?"

"Yes, and Mark said it would never happen," Clarence shook his head. "They are protected."

"So, Mark suggested you come here to tell your story on the news?"

"Yes, I suppose I could do that," Clarence nodded and studied Jorge for a moment before continuing. "But what I *really* want is for both of these men to die."

Jorge didn't reply but slowly nodded.

CHAPTER 13

"Calm down," Mark Hail put his hand up in the air, as he nervously attempted to assure Jorge Hernandez. "I didn't say you would kill *anyone.* I just said that if he wanted *real* justice, he would go talk to you."

"You do not think that this here is implied?" Jorge asked the young black man as he sat across from him. "Come on now."

"Clarence?" Mark asked and started to laugh. "He's like pushing 100! He's harmless."

"Oh, is this so?" Jorge countered. "He just asked me to kill these here men."

Mark Hail looked genuinely shocked. His eyes widened as he glanced around the room.

"Yeah, we did *not* talk about that," The young cop shook his head. "I thought he would want to be on your news show or something. I thought if he went and asked to speak to you, it might show the guys at the production house to take him seriously."

"This is true," Jorge continued. "He said he was next door to you, so since I want to talk to you about this, I offered to drive him home. He talked all the way here about wanting to see these men die for what they do to his great granddaughter."

Mark Hail looked stunned.

"You did not see this here coming?"

"Are you serious?" Mark shook his head. "As I said, the man is fucking old! After the story broke, he came to me and said he'd recently hired a detective and what they told him. He said it made sense now that the truth about those pills came out. I said I'd look at his report and agreed, it was shady as shit, but I also pointed out, there wasn't anything I could charge them for because they were protected. I suggested he look into a class-action lawsuit. I thought going to you and giving an interview might bring him closure."

"He wants this here closed all right," Jorge replied.

"So, what did you tell him?" Mark pushed. "I mean when he asked you to kill these men?"

"I say, you know, I will look into it," Jorge shrugged. "That is all I can do."

"Honestly," Mark replied as he stood up and headed for the next room. "The report that he brought me would've sent me over the edge too if it was about someone in my family."

"He left it with you?" Jorge called out.

"I got a copy," Mark replied as he returned to the room with a large envelope in hand. "I mean, Clarence's not wrong. The problem is that these men are both protected because Health Canada passed it, and Big Pharma was sneaky. I'm sure people would be horrified if they knew how often this kind of thing happens. I mean, remember the baby powder story a couple of years back?"

Jorge grimaced as he reached for the envelope.

"These companies don't care," Mark shook his head as he sat down. "I told Clarence that too. I wish I could do more for him, but really, there isn't much. If there's a class-action suit, it's going to drag on for years. He don't got years."

Jorge glanced over the sheets and didn't say anything. Everything Clarence had told him was true.

"The two men he spoke of were good friends since university," Mark began to explain. "When the Big Pharma guy has a new drug, he needs genuine pigs to test it. He gets the doctor to enroll his patients to try it out, and in turn, they both get kickbacks. It's completely legal, but ethically? That's another story. This specific doctor had a hell of a lot of his patients taking these drugs. And he's getting paid well to do so. I'm actually impressed by Clarence's instincts in the matter."

Jorge nodded and sat the papers down.

"Juliana, she looked after my kids for years," Jorge finally spoke. "She died from this here drug. That is how we started to look into it in the first place. I wonder if she shared the doctor. Paige would know."

"If not," Mark shook his head. "He isn't the only one. More doctors are doing the same thing."

Jorge thought for a moment and stood up.

"Can I have a copy of this?" He pointed toward the sheets.

"Sure," Mark jumped up. "Wait, what are…"

"I am not sure yet," Jorge confirmed. "I would like to get more information before I do anything."

"Maybe get your researcher on it?"

"That is my thought."

"Do I want to know if I'm going to be investigating a murder scene at some rich pharmaceutical asshole's place soon?"

Jorge gave him a dark look and grinned.

On the drive home, he turned his phone back on and called his wife.

"Where are you?" She immediately asked. "You flew out of here earlier, and I wasn't able to reach you."

"I got a thing I had to deal with at the production house," Jorge replied as he watched traffic ahead. "*Mi Amor,* can you do me a favor and find out the name of Juliana's doctor. The one who prescribed the meds she took?"

"Yeah, I have the information upstairs," She replied. "Are you….doing something on the news?"

"Something like that," Jorge replied. "I will see you soon."

He ended the call and took a deep breath. He had another stop to make.

He called Marco.

"Hey, where are you?"

"The club," Marco replied. "I was doing some work in the VIP room. Do you need to see me?"

"I got something for you," Jorge replied. "I will be there shortly."

"Very good," Marco replied. "See you soon."

When he arrived at the club, Jorge was surprised to see Diego sitting at the bar.

"Short day at work, *amigo?"* Jorge teased.

"Nah, I decided to take your advice and work in different places to get away from the office."

"So, today, you choose a bar?" Jorge carefully studied him.

"Well, technically, I'm working in the VIP room," Diego shrugged and turned around before finishing his drink. "But you know, Marco is there…."

Chase walked out of his office behind the bar and gave Jorge a look.

"Diego," Jorge cut him off. "Are you drunk?"

"Well, I had a few drinks."

"Diego, you cannot start coming here and getting loaded during the workday," Jorge warned him. "This here, it is not ok."

"I was…."

Jorge shook his head and cut him off, turning his attention to Chase. "Can we use your office to speak?"

"Yes, of course," Chase replied. "I'm just doing an order."

"Great, can you first take this to Marco?" Jorge passed him the envelope. "He will know what it is. I will be in to talk to him shortly."

"Will do," Chase replied as he took the envelope. "Is this something to do with that news story on Big Pharma?"

"Yes, it certainly does."

"Anything else you want to tell him?"

"Just to research it further."

Diego watched with interest.

"And you," Jorge pointed at his longtime friend. "You and I, we must talk."

Diego appeared nervous as he got off the barstool and started toward Chase's office.

"I know how this looks…"

"This here," Jorge cut him off. "It is not the first time this has happened."

The two men went into Chase's office and closed the door. Jorge sat behind the desk with Diego on the other side.

"Now," Jorge spoke up, and he leaned forward. "What is going on? You did not start drinking because Marco had the spot where you planned to work. I thought you were going to work from home? You know, in your backyard, in the sunshine? What happened there?"

"I got a lot on my mind."

"Why is it that when you have a lot on your mind," Jorge pointed toward him. "You decide to drink your problems away."

"This isn't exactly something I just do *now,*" Diego pointed out.

"I know," Jorge nodded. "That is my point. This is a pattern over the years."

"It's not like I'm the only person..."

"No, but you are the only person who is running my company that does this," Jorge sharply cut him off. "If it is too much to be CEO, please tell me so I can replace you."

"No," Diego automatically shook his head. "That's not...that's got nothing to do with this."

Jorge didn't have to ask. He knew what was wrong.

"Jolene."

Diego nodded.

"It had to be done."

"I know."

"But you are having issues with it," Jorge guessed. "So, what do you want me to do? Your sister, she causes a lot of problems. I could not have her in this family any longer."

"It's....she is always calling me," Diego spoke emotionally. "She's crying."

"She is manipulative," Jorge reminded him. "This is not new."

"I know," Diego agreed. "I know, and I know why you don't trust her. I get that, but there must be a way."

"Diego, I have given her many chances," Jorge reminded him. "I give her a chance after she talk to people who want to kill me, years ago. I give her a chance when she teach my teenaged daughter to shoot a gun against my wishes. I give her a chance after..."

"I know," Diego cut him off and took a deep breath. "Jorge, she has nothing without us. You ostracized her from the group. This is her family.

She calls me, begging to come back. She says her life means nothing if she can't be a part of us. She is willing to do anything to come back."

"Diego, she causes so much misery," Jorge reminded him. "And not just to me, but she has to Ricardo, to Chase…she always argue with Tony at the production house. I did not know to trust her. She does what she wants and does not listen."

"I know," Diego spoke solemnly. "Believe me, I know. But our parents aren't well, and Jolene is my only blood relative left. And she calls me and for a long time, I didn't answer, but her messages became so desperate, and I was scared she would do something…"

Jorge took a deep breath and thought for a moment.

"Diego, I will reconsider," Jorge finally replied, seeing the surprise in his longtime associate's face. "But *only* because of you, and there will be severe consequences if I take her back and she does anything again. I will take it under consideration."

"That is all I ask," Diego's face lit up. "That's all I want."

CHAPTER 14

"Sir, this is interesting," Marco pointed toward the envelope on the table as Jorge entered the room. He waited until the door was closed before swiftly changing the topic. Pointing toward the door, Marco seemed to be carefully picking out his words. "Is he..."

"Honestly, I am not sure," Jorge replied, sighing loudly. He collapsed in the chair at the end of the table. "This here is not the first time I have found him this way."

"Sir, I do not think it's a rare thing," Marco spoke in a low voice. "I mean, it is not my place to say, but..."

"No, I am wondering the same, Marco," Jorge nodded. "This concerns me. He talked a great deal about Jolene and her anxieties, but me, I think this is what you call...you know when you say something about another person, but you mean yourself?"

"Projection, sir," Marco nodded. "And I think you are right. He hasn't been quite the same since Jolene left town."

"I am not sure about before," Jorge replied. "I suggest that he go see her for a few days, take some time off. I think this would be good for him."

"I think you are right, sir," Marco nodded. "I thought...I didn't think that she was allowed to speak to anyone in the group since..."

"Well, that is, for the most part, the case," Jorge nodded. "But since they are blood relatives, I could not say no. But at the same time, I have to wonder if this was the right decision. She has manipulated him, and now he worries for her. I am not saying her depression is not normal, but at the same time, she was lucky to even have a life with everything she has done over the years. The trust has not been there for a long time. I have tolerated her because of Diego, but that is all."

"I understand, sir," Marco nodded. "I can monitor her again if you wish. I stopped after she was gone for about a month."

"Maybe, this here is a good idea," Jorge nodded. "I still do not trust her. I said to Diego that I may allow her back, but she will be on a short leash this time. I do not know what I will do, but I will see. Diego is going to visit her. Let's see how that goes first."

Marco nodded.

"That is a problem for another day," Jorge continued and glanced at the envelope on the table. "So, that is some interesting information."

"Yes, where did you get this, sir?"

"Long story," Jorge suddenly felt exhausted. "The point is that we were not the only people suspicious. This old man was too. He come to see me today, and well, this report says it all."

"Sir, I have been researching the men in the report," Marco pointed toward the envelope. "The problem is that what they are doing is not illegal. So, there are no repercussions for their actions."

"Well, that remains to be seen." Jorge insisted and raised his eyebrows.

"Did you share this with Makerson?"

"Not yet," Jorge confirmed. "I am not sure if we will get names involved if I do."

"You do not want to get sued."

"I may be paying these men a visit myself," Jorge confirmed. "I am going to check with Paige when I get home. If this man mentioned in the report was also Juliana's doctor, then I plan to have a conversation with him."

Marco nodded, his expression full of sadness.

"This is a terrible thing," Marco spoke honestly. "It concerns me."

"Athas is looking into it now to see what can be changed," Jorge informed him. "But he is going against the giant of giants. They have a way of always winning even when they shouldn't."

Jorge left shortly after, feeling drained and defeated; he headed home.

At one time, this entire situation would've invigorated him. Killing both men wouldn't have been a second thought. But these days, he was left feeling defeated. These people were like rats; you might catch one in a trap, but there was generally two more behind, ready to replace them.

Walking into his house, he felt some regeneration upon seeing his son in the kitchen with Paige. The little boy was eating a cut-up apple at the table.

"Snack time?" Jorge asked as his eyes met with his wife's, her expression remaining blank.

"*Papi,* here," Miguel picked up a piece of apple and pointed it toward him. "Eat this."

Jorge shook his head.

"No, Miguel, that is for you," Jorge said as he sat down beside his son, gently touching his arm. "But *gracias!*"

The little boy looked at him with fascination and proceeded to eat the piece of apple, saying nothing.

"So, did you find out anything?" Jorge asked Paige.

"I did," Paige nodded. "But Jorge, maybe we should…"

"I had an old man come to see me today," Jorge cut her off as he rubbed his forehead. "His great-granddaughter, she was also prescribed the same pill as Juliana for her stomach issues. The doctor said she had to take it all the time to make sure it did not flare up again. She died. A very young woman and she died of stomach cancer."

Paige bit her lower lip and looked away.

"So, you see, this here is hard to let go," Jorge continued. "She was their test subject. That did not work out so well for her."

"Dr. Hamilton," Paige replied. "That was the name."

"It is different from what I saw today," Jorge replied. "However, Marco, he is looking up the doctors that were testing this drug for a specific Big Pharma rep. I suspect he was on the same list."

"So, he…"

"Might be a different kind of test subject," Jorge finished her sentence, and she nodded in understanding. "They did not care."

"Even Makerson's report," Paige shook her head. "There was a lot of people, especially in Toronto, that took that medication regularly."

"It is scary," Jorge confirmed. "Now, do you see why I do not trust doctors? Pills? This here is why. I do not wish to be part of an experiment."

"Have you talked to Alec?"

"Yes, I talk to Athas earlier," Jorge confirmed. "But what can he do? These companies are powerful. They will fight him every step of the way."

Paige didn't reply.

"Then Diego was drunk at the bar."

"What?" Paige spoke sharply, alarming Miguel, who watched her with intrigue. "What the hell is that about?"

"Jolene," Jorge replied. "She is working on him."

Paige shook her head.

"I tell him to take a few days off, go see her," Jorge said with a shrug. "That I would reconsider allowing her back in the family, but Paige, this does go against my instincts."

"I would keep her on a limited basis," Paige suggested. "There's been… too much with her. She's erratic."

"I know this," Jorge nodded. "Oh, Paige, I feel like it is time to get that house in the country built and move away from this…"

"What?" A sharp voice caused him to jump. He turned to see Maria walking into the room. "*Papá,* you aren't going to make us move, are you?"

"Maria, I did not say that," Jorge confirmed. "I just say that there is always so much going on here that it would be nice to get away."

"I don't think moving will be the solution," Paige replied. "These problems will follow us."

"Why do you want to get away?" Maria asked as she stopped by the table.

"Maria, it has been a long day," Jorge shook his head. "I do not even care to go into it with one more person."

"Paige, did you tell him about today?" Maria asked as she sat down, and Miguel attempted to give her a piece of apple, to which she shook her head. "Gross, you are drooling everywhere."

The baby looked confused and pulled the apple back, his eyes full of suspicion.

"Oh, Maria, you hurt his feelings," Jorge teased as he swooped in and kissed the top of his son's head. "Poor Miguel, no one wants to share your apples today."

Paige smiled, her face still looking tense. Maria shrugged.

"So, today…" Maria started and glanced at Paige.

"Oh yes," His wife jumped in. "Tala had her first shooting lesson. She was a little nervous, but she did well. Is that what you mean, Maria?"

"Yeah, but also the other thing we talked about."

"Maria," Paige sighed. "I am not trying to convince your father to have a sweet 15 party. I didn't even know that was a thing."

"Well, we can make it a *thing,"* Maria insisted. "I don't see what the big deal is."

"Maria, I do not want strangers in the house," Jorge reminded her. "You know this."

"What if I have it at someone else's house?"

"Where?" Jorge probed. "Cameron, his family is religious."

"Maybe Diego's?"

"No, he will say no," Jorge shook his head and laughed. "And do not be asking anyone else."

"Chase could have it at the bar?" Maria suggested. "It is supposed to be *my* bar someday."

"Yes, but now you are minors," Jorge reminded her. "We will not be having a teenaged girl's birthday party there."

"But we don't have to drink and…"

"Maria, please, this here is too much," Jorge reminded her. "I said I would think about it, but if I say yes, it will not be at a bar. It is just day two of July. I think this here can wait till it is closer to your birthday."

"But it's next month," She pushed. "I can't wait till the last minute…."

Jorge sighed and looked at Paige.

He was tired.

It was too much.

Maybe he was the one who needed a break.

CHAPTER 15

Regardless of how defeated Jorge was when he went to bed, he woke the following morning feeling regenerated and alive. Fire ran through his veins as he sat up in bed and glanced over at his sleeping wife. Rising, Jorge quickly showered, dressed, and slipped out of their room, glancing into his son's bedroom before going downstairs. He loved early in the morning when everyone was still asleep, and he was ready to start his day. It was so peaceful.

Glancing at the time, he made some coffee and checked his phone while he waited. There were no messages or emails of concern, making it a good start. Looking through the news, social media, all seemed calm. Maybe it would be a better day.

Of course, this notion was a bit premature. Perhaps it was that the rest of the world hadn't awakened yet.

The gurgling sound of the coffee maker finishing its duty grabbed his attention. After preparing a cup, Jorge considered going outside to sit by the pool. However, he decided instead to go to his office to check a few things. As soon as he sat behind his desk, the secure line rang.

Letting out a loud sigh, Jorge answered the call.

"Athas, you make me regret coming to my office so early," Jorge complained as soon as he answered. "What's going on?"

"Good morning to you too," Athas said, showing no concern for Jorge's abrupt nature. "I'm meeting with some people from Health Canada today and hope I can find some solutions for this…issue we have."

"You mean the one where big companies can use everyday people as pigs?"

"Guinea pigs," Athas corrected him. "And it's legal because…"

"I don't care," Jorge cut him off. "The point is that these companies have no liability if they sell a product that causes a disease. Why are there no criminal charges?"

"Well, the problem is…"

"You know what, Athas," Jorge cut him off again. "I am not interested in hearing political talk. What is it you call me about today?

Athas took a deep breath before he continued.

"Just to tell you that I'm meeting with Health Canada to see what can be changed," Athas replied. "Since this story has now hit international media, I have reason to put the pressure on them because the public is outraged."

"Sadly, so much noise has to be made before the public wakes up," Jorge commented. "This here is not news."

"You're right," Athas agreed. "However, most people are compliant and don't pay attention until something affects them. There's a lot of powerful people who prefer it that way."

"Yes, it is true," Jorge said as he glanced at his coffee. "If that is all…"

"If this pushes me up in the polls, I want to call an election for the fall."

"Is this so? I thought this was already the case?"

"I wanted to put it off," Athas continued. "But if I can make some changes with Big Pharma in light of this recent concern, then this will help me get a majority this time. I can spend the summer going to festivals, traveling throughout the country. I think it might work."

"It will work," Jorge insisted. "People, they do not know what they want. *You tell them* what they want. Just put on your pretty boy smile, fix your hair and kiss some babies."

Jorge ended the call and sat back in his chair. Reaching for his coffee, he glanced at the picture of Juliana and the children. He quickly looked away.

There would be justice.

Jorge enjoyed his coffee for a few more minutes before his phone started to beep. He reluctantly reached for it. The message was from Diego.

I was thinking, can you, me, and Jolene get together sometime to talk?

Jorge cringed. Diego's attempts to make the meeting sound so casual only managed to annoy him. He ignored the message.

Finishing his coffee, he rose from his seat and headed out of his office. He could hear the shower running upstairs, indicating that his wife was up, but decided he had to leave before traffic got too hectic. He needed to take care of a few things before his day filled up with distractions.

Jumping in his SUV, Jorge headed for Hernandez Productions. He had some ideas, a lot of plans that he was working out as he drove along. Traffic was still relatively light, the quietness allowing him time to think. Sometimes at home, this was next to impossible. He loved his children, but they always were creating noise in one way or another. Especially now that it was summer and Maria was home.

Arriving at the production house, Jorge noted vehicles were already there. It was good to see that he wasn't the only one who had an early morning.

Walking in, he found complete stillness. Concerned, he started to move slowly down the hallway and reached for his gun. Silence could be a bad sign. He was relieved to find the small group together in the conference room. Jorge opened the door.

"May I join?" He asked, checking the faces of those around the table. Makerson was the only one that seemed surprised, but that was consistent with his nature.

"Sure," Tony said as he gestured for Jorge to sit down. "We were talking about today's news update."

"Lots of shit going on," Andrew lazily shook his head as he reached for his coffee. "Big Pharma is striking back."

"What does this mean?" Jorge asked as he sat down.

"It means that they're attacking Makerson," Andrew replied. "Saying how he works for you and shit…"

"Of course he works for me," Jorge shook his head. "You *all* work for me."

"What he means," Makerson jumped in. "He's more or less saying…"

"Makerson's your puppet," Andrew cut in.

"Oh, is this so?" Jorge showed no reaction.

"They're saying," Makerson attempted to explain. "That we worked closely together when I was at the paper, you gave me exclusive interviews, and of course, I wrote the book about you too…"

"That does not come out till the fall," Jorge reminded him.

"Right," Makerson continued and cleared his throat. "But basically that you're behind this story, and I'm just reporting on it."

"Again, I do not argue," Jorge shook his head. "Why is this here a problem?"

"They say you got a vendetta with Big Pharma," Andrew jumped in while Tony shot him a dirty look.

"I wouldn't say vendetta, exactly," Tony attempted to explain. "They're saying that you like to attack Big Pharma because you want people to instead shop at *Our House of Pot* for more minor medical issues."

"Also not untrue," Jorge nodded.

"They're slanting it," Makerson continued to explain. "They're making it sound like you're exaggerating because you have an ax to grind."

"This here," Jorge shook his head. "This does not bother me, and Makerson, it should not bother you either."

"He doesn't mean an actual ax," Andrew shot out, pretending to bludgeon someone with the weapon.

This caused Jorge to laugh, while the others appeared annoyed with Andrew for his comment.

"They're trying to lower our credibility," Makerson attempted to explain.

"Why are you telling me?" Jorge asked and pointed toward the closed laptop in the middle of the table. "Tell the people. Shoot back. Let them squirm."

Makerson considered his words and nodded.

"That is the only way to deal with them," Jorge insisted. "And you know that I never have a problem with a fight."

The four men went on to discuss the topics for that day's news program. They also touched base on a few other items. Jorge quickly grew tired and glanced at the clock.

"I must go," He finally said. "I have some other things to look into today."

The three men continued to discuss things as Jorge rose from his seat and left the conference room. He wanted to keep one foot in but not immerse his whole body. They would be fine on their own. They had to know that they had no limits.

Jorge was almost at the exit when he heard his name called out. Turning around, he saw Ricardo walking toward him.

"Mr. Hernandez," The young Mexican approached him. "I was hoping to catch you before you leave today. I wanted to thank you again for this opportunity. I am enjoying learning about the process of acting, as well as this new show. I am quite excited."

"This is good," Jorge nodded with a smile. "I figured you would. I do have something else to talk to you about."

"Did you need something?"

"No," Jorge shook his head. "I spoke to Diego yesterday, and to make a long story short, Jolene, she wants to return to the family."

Ricardo took this in stride.

"Now, considering how things ended," Jorge went on. "I know that no one is happy with that idea. I only consider it because of Diego. I wanted to let you know that it is a possibility and also if you have any thoughts."

"Mr. Hernandez," Ricardo hesitated a moment as they both remembered a particular scene in Jolene's living room the previous winter. "I would be cautious with this one. I do not trust."

Jorge didn't reply but nodded. His thoughts went in every direction.

"But sir," Ricardo continued. "This here, it is your decision, not mine."

"I will think about what you said," Jorge replied as he started to walk away. "We will be in touch."

Once outside, he turned his phone back on. Another message awaited him from Diego.

It doesn't have to be all or nothing. We need to talk.

Jorge ignored this too and headed for his SUV. He stopped halfway there and sent a message to Marco.

We gotta talk about Jolene.

Before Jorge would reply to Diego, he had to see what Marco found out. It was important to air out a room before you invited a guest.

CHAPTER 16

"This better be good, Jolene," Jorge sharply spoke as he walked into the VIP room of *Princesa Maria.* The Colombian wore a modest dress rather than the usual skintight outfit. Her presentation was somewhat morbid. Her face drained as if she had been crying. Jorge hesitated before sitting across from her and an equally nervous-looking Diego. "You look like you are about to go to a funeral. Then again, if you try to bullshit me, Jolene, you *might* be."

She accepted the warning and glanced down at her hands.

"Look, she knows she…" Diego attempted to explain. He was quickly cut off by an irritated Jorge.

"I do not want to hear from you," Jorge bluntly instructed. "You are here, yes, this is fine. Jolene, she is your sister, I understand. But her and I will do the talking. You are here only to make sure she does not leave in a body bag."

Jolene sniffed.

"And Jolene," Jorge switched his attention to her. "This here, it is not completely out of the options. Do you understand?"

"But what she did," Diego attempted to explain but stopped when Jorge shot him a warning look. He nodded and looked down.

"Now," Jorge turned his attention to Jolene. "What is it you have to say?"

"I want to say," She spoke slowly, carefully, as if evaluating the situation. "I miss being in the family, and I wish to return."

"This here, I know," Jorge shook his head. "Jolene, tell me why I should *let* you."

"I just….I feel like you were too harsh…"

Jorge shot her a look.

"I mean, yes, I lied to Ricardo and…"

"Jolene, you know that this is not *just* about that," Jorge reminded her. "You have a long history, and I cannot trust you. Last year, when I hear that someone is writing a book about me, who is the first person I suspected might be involved? It was you. Why is it that when something sinister is going on behind my back, my first suspicion is that it is you working with someone against me?"

Her face seemed to age before him; each line grew deeper, the skin below her eyes sagged as she bit on her lower lip.

"It is because you have before, must I remind you?" Jorge continued to speak with a sharpness in his voice. "I know you say you were threatened one time but, you should have come to me. And when you teach Maria to shoot? It is the things you do behind my back that concern me. The things you tell people outside the *familia* that concerns me. You act like a teenager that never grew up, and somehow, I became your father. But you know what, Jolene, I already have children, and I do not need another teenager to keep an eye on. That is the problem here. You do not listen or respect my authority. I cannot trust you."

"I understand."

"Do you?" Jorge asked. "Do you *really,* Jolene? Because I hear this from you before and yet, we come back to the same place again and again."

"I can prove…"

"Can you?" Jorge shot back. "Can you *really,* Jolene?"

"I would like to."

Jorge thought for a moment.

"How are you a benefit to me?" He finally asked. "Why do I need you around? Give me a reason because the way I see it, you are only here for one reason."

Jorge looked toward Diego, who gave him a pleading look.

"This man," Jorge continued. "He has worked with me for many years. He is one of the people I am closest to, and I trust him with my life. We have been through a lot together over the years. He is my brother in many ways. If it were not for Diego, I would have killed you long ago, Jolene. I think we *all* know this."

Tears formed in her eyes, and she nodded.

"But you are his sister," Jorge continued as he leaned back in the chair and thought for a moment. "And for this reason, you are still here. And that is the only reason. And yes, you have done good work for me too, but you know how I feel about loyalty."

"Loyalty above all," She spoke in a small voice as if the words could barely come out.

"*Si,"* Jorge nodded. "This is correct."

"I can do…whatever you need."

She gave him a look that he felt travel right to his groin. This caused Jorge to look away, then back.

"There is nothing you have, Jolene," Jorge insisted. "That I want."

She looked away.

Diego noted the exchange, and his forehead wrinkled as he glared at his sister.

"Jolene," Diego shot her a look. "I didn't bring you here for this! You told me…"

"Ok, enough," Jorge cut his friend off. "I do not have time for this here. I have another meeting to attend, and honestly, I do not care to talk about this any longer. Jolene, I do not know if I feel any differently than I did before."

"Can I speak?" She asked and cleared her throat. "Let me tell one thing before we end this meeting."

"Keep it short, Jolene."

"I want to say," Jolene started and cleared her throat again. "I will do anything, *anything* you need. If you have something, even last minute, dangerous, I do not care. I cannot live like this. I need to be back in the *familia."*

Jorge took a deep breath and exchanged looks with Diego.

"I will think about it, Jolene," Jorge said as he pushed his chair out. "And that is the best you will get from me today."

"*Gracias,"* Jolene said as Jorge walked toward the door. He didn't say another word as he left the room, closing the door behind him.

He found Chase at the main bar. The two shared a look, and Chase gestured toward his office, and Jorge nodded. Neither of the men spoke until they were behind the closed door.

"I'm surprised you met her at all," Chase admitted as he walked behind his desk.

"I had Marco check her out," Jorge admitted as he sat opposite of Chase. "*Carefully,* and she was fine. There was nothing to send off alerts."

"She knows to be careful," Chase reminded him.

"She knows to be careful, but she is not smart enough to cover her tracks from Marco," Jorge reminded him. "No one is."

"True."

"So, I decide to think about it," Jorge confessed. "You never know when you might need someone to do the dirty work that you do not want to expose your valuable people to."

Chase nodded in understanding.

"But I do not know," Jorge shook his head. "I will never trust her."

"Then don't let her completely in the loop," Chase advised. "She's in a powerless position. Keep Marco on her to make sure she doesn't do anything stupid."

"You have learned well," Jorge smirked as he turned his phone back on. "This is exactly what I think."

"I know how you roll," Chase reminded him. "And so does Jolene. So that should be enough to reassure you."

Jorge's phone jumped to life as messages showed up.

"Things, they never end," Jorge shook his head as he looked at his phone.

"Need help with anything?"

"Not unless you want to talk to Athas," Jorge referred to the Canadian prime minister.

"Not particularly," Chase made a face.

"That makes two of us," Jorge shook his head. "And it will only get worse because he is thinking of calling an election for the fall."

"Oh really?"

"Yes, so this summer, he will be sucking hard to get the people to love him," Jorge raised an eyebrow, a grin on his face. "You know, being a politician."

"Hey, you know what he should do?" Chase suggested as he pushed his chair forward. "Fix the fucking water in indigenous communities. When Maria and I were going to these communities to teach women self-defense last winter, so many of them had shitty fucking water that they couldn't drink. The government keeps promising to help, but..."

"They do not have a large enough voting demographic," Jorge finished his sentence.

"I was thinking more that they just don't care."

"Well, there is that too," Jorge nodded. "I will mention this to him. He will be a hero, which is what he wants."

"Literally," Chase nodded. "They told us not to drink the water or even use it under any circumstances in some of those places."

"This here is fucked up."

"Yup," Chase relaxed back in his chair and nodded.

"I must go," Jorge said as he stood up. "We will talk more later."

Once outside, Jorge noted that Diego's Lexus was gone.

Driving home, Jorge attempted to push the entire meeting out of his head. He had a bad feeling about Jolene returning to the group. He was exhausted by her constant bullshit. Perhaps it was time to feed her to the wolves without making it seem like he was doing so on purpose. It was an option. It was always good to have a sacrificial lamb.

By the time he got home, Jorge was ready for his conversation with Athas. It was the last dragon he planned to slay that day. Glancing toward the patio, Jorge saw Paige, Tala, and the children by the pool. That's where he should be too. But first, he would call Athas and see what he wanted.

Entering his office, he let out a heavy sigh as he closed the door and crossed the room. Reaching for the secure line, he made the call.

"Hello?"

"You sound surprised to hear from me," Jorge commented. "For a man who has sent me about 100 fucking texts today."

"I got to meet you in person."

"Is this here necessary?" Jorge asked as he glanced around.

"I'm on my way back to Toronto," Athas replied. "I will stop in when I get there."

"Wonderful," Jorge spoke sarcastically. "This here is *exactly* how I wanted to end my day."

"Look," Athas spoke regretfully. "This meeting with Health Canada was a fucking shit show. It was a mess."

Jorge said nothing but glanced toward the framed photo of Juliana and the children.

"This runs much deeper than I originally thought," Athas continued. "Big Pharma, they own us."

CHAPTER 17

"Can I join your meeting?" Maria boldly asked as she curiously eyed Alec Athas. Snuggly pulling a towel around her body to hide the pink bikini underneath, she spoke like an adult while still looking like a child. Jorge couldn't help but notice that she stood tall, with a sense of confidence in her voice. "*Papá,* you know I want to move up in this family."

"Maria," Jorge started but noting the horrified look on Athas' face, almost conceding to her wishes. "I do not think this is necessary today. Go back to the pool and enjoy the sunshine."

"Are you sure, *Papá?*" She boldly asked. "I want to learn."

Jorge grinned as pride filled his heart. His daughter didn't give two fucks if this ruffled Athas' feathers and this impressed him. Leaning forward, he kissed her on the top of her head. "No, Maria, this here is fine. You go back outside. This will not be long."

His final comment was sharp, meant more for Athas, as he glanced in his direction.

"It won't be long," Athas confirmed. "I promise."

"Well, ok then," Maria continued to ignore Athas, giving her father a side look as she started to walk away.

Winking at his daughter, Jorge couldn't contain his brief moment of joy.

"Let us go speak," Jorge pointed in the direction of his office as he began to walk, with Athas in tow.

It wasn't until they were behind closed doors that the Canadian prime minister finally said something.

"Your daughter?" He asked while he made his way toward the desk.

Jorge chose to ignore his question. Athas needed to recognize that he was not in the position to ask anything.

"So, what do you want?" Jorge snapped as he went behind his desk to sit down. Athas sat on the other side. "Other than to come here and question my choices as a father?"

"I wasn't questioning anything," Athas confirmed. "I meant…you know, never mind. It's probably better that I don't know."

"It is," Jorge confirmed. "Let us focus on this here meeting with Health Canada."

"A total fucking shitshow," Athas shook his head. "I swear, the longer I am the prime minister, the more…"

"I hope your phone is turned off?" Jorge cut him off. "Because we are not discussing any of this otherwise."

"You know it is," Athas pulled it out of his pocket and threw it on Jorge's desk.

"You are learning, Athas," Jorge confirmed. "And it sounds like you have had a blind eye to much in the time you were in office."

"You might be surprised how little I do know," Athas confirmed. "It's a haunted house built long before I moved in, and I'm still discovering all the secret doors."

"They do not want you to know because you are only the talking head," Jorge reminded him. "Just as you are mine, but at least we established this long before you got in."

Athas appeared disgruntled but nodded.

"So, Health Canada and Big Pharma, they got a big romance going on?" Jorge asked as he leaned back in his chair. "Is that what you are about to tell me?"

"Try more of a torrid affair," Athas replied. "There's a lot of secrets."

"You know, Athas, I do enjoy divulging other people's secrets," Jorge grinned as he rubbed his chin. "But this here, it does not surprise me. Health Canada is the puppet for Big Pharma. Except, it sounds like Health Canada enjoys having a hand rammed up its ass."

Athas shook his head and shrugged.

"But you got the fucking power here," Jorge reminded him. "You can dismantle this mess."

"Not really," Athas confirmed. "It's deeply entrenched. Like, to do so would expose decades of collusion and corruption. We could be sued to hell and back for misleading the public."

Jorge had a rare shot of sympathy for Athas. As much as he viewed Athas as his nemesis, Jorge recognized his need to do the right thing. And although that usually exasperated him, in this case, as he glanced at the picture of Juliana on his desk, he gave a sympathetic smile.

"They don't care," Athas shook his head. "There's a lot of money flowing. Lots getting rich. They justify it by saying that we have a health care system for people to fall back on, and Big Pharma saves the day."

"Ah yes," Jorge quipped. "Just like a superhero, they solve all our problems."

"Fuck," Athas shook his head. "What did I get myself into?"

"Well, the good news," Jorge moved his chair forward and leaned on his desk. "Is that they may have won the battle, but they won't win the war."

"How?" Athas shook his head. "Like, how can I do that when they have such a tight hold on us?"

"I did not say *you,*" Jorge shook his head. "Let me figure this out."

"What are you going to do?" Athas said as his body leaned ahead.

"What would you like me to do?" Jorge replied as he moved more in Athas' direction, and they shared a look. "It would be such a shame if the same people who have caused so many to die, they also die but not peacefully in a hospital, attached to a morphine drip."

"I don't want these guys to go out peacefully," Athas confirmed, darkness swept over his eyes, and for the first time, Jorge saw something that told him everything he had to know.

"You give me names," Jorge spoke slowly, pausing for a moment. "And they will suffer for the misery they have brought to others. And Athas, you know, this here, I can do."

Athas nodded with no response.

"You tell me what you need."

"And in return?" Athas boldly asked

"It was brought to my attention," Jorge's tone slightly changed as he pulled back a bit. "That there are many indigenous communities with poor drinking water. I think it would be beneficial if you start working on them immediately, before the election campaign. Show some real results."

Athas sat up a bit straighter, a look of surprise on his face.

"This…this is what you want?"

"Yes," Jorge nodded. "It is, you know, important to Chase. It is important to my daughter, so yes, this is what I want."

"It's just that…"

"I don't care," Jorge cut him off. "And if you wish, my company, it can help in some way. It would be a joint project. Maybe I give money, volunteers, whatever you need to help solve this problem."

"It's a massive project to take on."

"That is why we must do it."

"Ok," Athas thought for a moment. "I…ok…"

"Athas, this here, it is the kind of thing you said you wanted to get in to do," Jorge reminded him. "Let it happen now. It will renew your hope. Fix a problem that should have been fixed long ago. This here shows you are better than all the fucking prime ministers before you who lied, who said they would help or ignored these communities. It will pave the way for after you are elected again to rip Big Pharma and Health Canada apart with one brutal tear. A smart prime minister doesn't get his hands dirty the first time around, but the second, it is a whole other ball game."

"I can't believe that I'm starting to agree with you," Athas nodded as a grin crossed his lips. "But I'm starting to see your point."

"Then this is what we must do," Jorge confirmed. "Announce it on HPC news, interview with Makerson, talk about your plan but first, tell me what you need from me, and we will get the wheels in motion."

"And you can get volunteers for me?"

"*Si,*" Jorge nodded. "My company will put a call out for volunteers and, you know, maybe they will get a bonus on their paychecks. Something to motivate them. Maybe, you know, I send Diego to help."

With this, Jorge threw his head back in laughter at the thought of his Armani-wearing associate getting his hands dirty.

"Well, we will take whoever we can get," Athas nodded. "I do like this idea. And I thank you."

"You know me," Jorge confirmed as he stood up. "I like to solve problems. And of course, I will be resolving your other problem. Just give me your hit list and, it will be taken care of."

Athas appeared uncertain as he slowly stood up.

"Maybe murder is a bit too…"

"Who said anything about murder?" Jorge asked as he walked around the desk. "Maybe these people will have an…unfortunate accident, or maybe, the pressures will be too much, and they will commit suicide. These things they do happen."

Athas nodded as the two men walked out of the office.

Jorge was relieved to be finished with the meeting as they headed toward the door. Paige spotted the men and jumped up to head toward the patio doors. She was wearing a tank top and shorts, something Jorge noticed Athas checking out, causing his anger to simmer. Paige slid the door opened and turned her attention toward Athas.

"Alec, we were about to barbecue," She pointed outside. "You should join us."

"Well, I…." Athas glanced between the couple, getting vastly different reactions.

"Jorge," Paige caught her husband's expression and gave him a look. "Be polite."

"I did not say anything," Jorge reminded her.

"You know, I was going to…" Athas started, but Paige quickly cut him off.

"You got to eat," She insisted. "And Maria wants you to stay. She's doing a project for school and has lots of questions."

Jorge glanced behind his wife and noted Maria was excitedly nodding and pointing toward Tala, who was standing behind the barbecue, flipping burgers.

"I…well, I guess I can stay," Athas was hesitant. "Thank you."

Jorge took a deep breath and exchanged looks with his wife as Alec passed Paige to meet the others outside.

"Be nice," Paige whispered.

"Paige, I am always nice," Jorge grinned and leaned in to kiss her. "You know me. I am a pussycat."

CHAPTER 18

"You worry too much," Paige whispered as she cuddled up to him later that night. "Alec is not the enemy."

"Paige," Jorge turned around and adjusted his pillow. "I did not say he was my enemy. I said that he is my nemesis. He still wants you, and I do not like him hanging around."

"Well, first of all," Paige spoke slightly more sternly. "I'm married to you, not him. So clearly, this isn't a concern other than in your mind. I see him as an old friend, nothing more."

"And he sees you as the, what do they say?" Jorge thought for a moment. "She who got away?"

"The one who got away," Paige corrected him and shook her head, looking into his eyes through the darkness. "I don't think so. He just... he's lonely. He doesn't have a lot of friends. That's the problem when you have such a high position."

"Paige, he wants you," Jorge countered. "I can see it in his eyes. I could see it in how he look at you tonight. He wishes to get you back. He is single because he is still in love with you. Why do you not see this here?"

"Jorge," Paige suddenly sat up in bed and turned on the light. "That is not true."

"Paige," Jorge sat up and looked at her as she adjusted her ponytail. "I know this here man, and I tell you, he wants you. He gets these, you know, puppy dog eyes around you."

His wife appeared humored as she tilted her head and listened.

"Paige, you are a smart woman," Jorge assured her. "But sometimes, you can be a little naive, and this here is one of those situations. I *know* men, and I *know* how they think. I saw how he looked at you. Trust me. I know these things."

"I think you're wrong."

"You can think what you wish," Jorge reminded her. "But Paige, I am not wrong. I promise you. That is why I do not want him around. What we talk about tonight, him and I, we could have talked about on the phone. He wanted to come here for a reason, and Paige, it was not to see me."

"You won't let this go."

"I would be happy to let this go," Jorge reminded her. "But I cannot. I see what I see. I do not want to see this, but this is how it is."

"You're misinterpreting the situation," Paige looked into his eyes. "I can't believe we're even talking about this."

"It was you who brought it up."

"I said you were rude to him."

"I do not care," Jorge shook his head. "When it comes to my family, I will never apologize."

Paige shook her head, turned off the light, and laid back down. Jorge continued to sit up.

"Tell me this then," Jorge asked. "Why is it he never has relationships that last? His wife, she left him. His girlfriends, they never stay. I mean, he hired a hooker once, remember?"

"He didn't hire a hooker," Paige reminded him. "His staff hired a masseuse, supposedly."

"He did not have to let her suck his dick," Jorge replied. "And besides, everything I say is true."

"Jorge, will you drop it," Paige sounded annoyed. "Alec is a complicated person. That's why his relationships don't work. He overthinks everything, kind of like you right now."

Jorge laid back down and didn't say anything.

"Paige?"

She didn't respond, causing his defenses to drop.

"Paige, I do not know what I would do without you," Jorge quietly confessed.

Slowly turning around, Paige's demeanor softened.

"I know you are committed to me," Jorge spoke logically. "But Paige, Athas is the angel, and I am the devil. *El diablo,* he can take you on a wild ride, but the angel, he brings you peace. He brings you calm. He is my opposite in every way."

"Maybe I like the wild ride," She whispered as her hand moved down his chest and slid into his boxers.

It wasn't until he sat alone in his office the following morning that Jorge thought about their conversation again. At the time, the physical ecstasy had sidetracked his thoughts; but had she done that so he would stop overthinking or because he was on the right track? There was something there. Maybe not on his wife's side, but with Athas.

Jorge's phone alerted his attention. Reaching for it, he saw Diego was attempting to talk to him. Knowing what he wanted, Jorge took a deep breath and sat his phone aside. Running a hand over the stubble on his face, Jorge needed to get out of the house before everyone woke up. He needed to change his thoughts.

Heading outside, Jorge jumped in his SUV and started driving with no destination. He hated the fact that he was jealous of anyone, let alone Athas. It wasn't logical, but that was what made him the most nervous of all. That meant it came from another place. And that was the place that saw things and stored them away.

He found himself outside of Marco's place. Staring at the house, he finally messaged him to see if it was a good time to drop by.

Good morning, Marco. I know it is early, but I'm outside. Can I talk to you?

Sir, yes, good morning. Come in!

Before Jorge could even get out of his vehicle, Marco was at his door and waving him in. Dressed casually in a pair of shorts and a t-shirt, his smile was genuine as Jorge approached.

"I am sorry," Jorge shook his head. "I did not think where I was going..."

"Sir, this is fine," Marco smiled as Jorge entered the house. He could hear children chattering upstairs. Overall, there was a peaceful feeling in the home. "Please, I do have some things I would like to discuss with you. Would you like some coffee?"

"Yes, actually," Jorge said after a moment's thought. "That would be wonderful, but I do not wish to take too much of your time on a Saturday."

"No, my wife, she is getting the kids ready to go to a playdate," Marco shook his head. "Whatever that is, sir."

Jorge laughed.

"Marco, I do not know," Jorge spoke honestly. "I think this is something white people invented."

To this, Marco laughed as he poured Jorge a cup of coffee.

"I do not know of such things until I move to Canada," Marco confessed.

"Exactly," Jorge said as Marco passed him a cup of coffee and pointed toward the basement. "Let us go to talk."

Jorge nodded and followed him downstairs to a clutter-filled basement.

"Be careful of the toys," Marco shook his head. "My wife, she is trying to get rid of some, but I'm afraid it's a mess.

"That is fine," Jorge said as he looked around the cramped surroundings as the two men found a small room in the back.

"My office, it is not as nice as yours," Marco grinned as they entered the room and closed the door. "Please make yourself comfortable."

Jorge sat down on the older-style chair and looked around. It was small but somehow cozier than his own office. There were plants, photos of his family on the wall, and pictures his children had drawn. It made Jorge smile.

"So, sir," Marco said as he sat behind his desk and reached for his laptop. "I continue to look up Jolene, but I am not finding much. She spends a lot of time on social media."

Jorge rolled his eyes.

"But that is all," Marco shook his head. "She has been researching different places in the country to live."

"She wishes to return to the family," Jorge shook his head. "But I would rather keep her at a distance. But this here, it means a lot to Diego as well."

"Sir, if you do allow this," Marco shook his head. "I will continue to monitor her."

Jorge nodded and took a drink of his coffee.

"I have been helping a lot with the news channel," Marco said as he turned his monitor around to show Jorge some graphs. "It seems that Big Pharma has been keeping tabs on the number of deaths associated with the pill we exposed, long before we caught them. Now they are monitoring how much money they are losing and figuring out ways to increase propaganda. But they do not call it propaganda, sir. They refer to it as the 'SOS file' and hire people to attack anyone who attacks them online."

Jorge rolled his eyes.

"They are evil, sir."

"I talk to Athas yesterday," Jorge said and grimaced. "It goes deep between Health Canada and Big Pharma. They work together."

Marco nodded with concern on his face.

"Sir, this does not surprise me," he finally replied. "But it is…disturbing just the same. I can look into them as well."

"That would be perfect."

"And Athas, he cannot do anything?"

"He said things are strongly entrenched," Jorge shook his head. "And an election is coming up…"

"Ah, I see," Marco nodded. "This here, it could be a problem."

"So, for now," Jorge thought for a moment. "We must take care of it ourselves."

"The man," Marco pointed at the screen. "That was pushing drug trials despite reports of it causing cancer…"

"Ah yes, Marco," Jorge perked up. "Do you have something for me?"

"There is one man connected to all the cases. He encouraged their reps to push it on doctors."

Jorge nodded.

"Even when he knew it was potentially killing people," Marco added.

Jorge didn't say anything but nodded, his face growing darker.

"His name, sir," Marco continued. "Is Louis Downs."

CHAPTER 19

"What?" Chase shook his head and grinned. "I think you're worrying about nothing. You know that's never gonna happen."

"I know," Jorge confirmed as he glanced around the empty *Princesa Maria* before sitting at the bar. "I know, this here is all in my head, but I know what I saw. And what I saw was how Athas looked at her. It did not make me happy."

"But just because he looks at her whatever way," Chase reminded him, "It doesn't mean anything. Did Paige look at him the same?"

"No," Jorge shook his head and thought for a moment. "But Paige, she would know to be careful."

"Or maybe," Chase reminded him. "It's because she has no interest. I mean, not to get personal, but your marriage…is it ok?"

"Yes," Jorge nodded. "It is just not the same as it used to be. You know, kids, Juliana dying, everyday life, it takes some of the excitement out of things."

"You know, maybe Juliana dying is what's really going on here," Chase suggested. "I mean, it kind of shakes your foundation and makes you see that nothing is forever. It's scary."

Jorge thought for a moment and nodded.

"You could be right."

"I just know," Chase went on to explain as he reached for the coffee pot. "That when my ex told me that the kids wanted to be adopted by her new man, it shook up my whole world. It made me feel like nothing would last forever. You assume when you become a father, you're always going to be a father, and when that disappears, who's to say what's next? Who's leaving next? I had nightmares that you threw *me* out of the family."

Jorge's head fell back in laughter as Chase passed him a cup of coffee and reached under the counter for the cream.

"Ok, so we both know that there will not happen," Jorge insisted. "And for the record, those are still your kids. I don't give a fuck what your ex says, they are your blood."

"I wish I shared your confidence," Chase shook his head. "The boys check in from time to time. I get some reports on how they're doing in school, that kind of thing, but that's it. It's been a minute since I've heard from either of them. I try to talk to them, but it's a dicey situation."

"So much with family," Jorge shook his head as he stirred his coffee. "It is what you call a dicey situation. Who knows how to act or what to say, to do, for that matter. I can run an entire organization. But when my daughter comes crying to me because she didn't get a part in some school play, I do not know what to say. It is difficult."

"Well, regardless of what you think," Chase leaned against the counter. "Paige is loyal to you. Athas, well, who gives a fuck what he thinks or wants. You've even said he has a purpose. That's all he's there for."

"He better win that next fucking election," Jorge tapped his finger on the bar. "Or his purpose, it is gone."

"So, you're spying on him?"

"I got Marco on it," Jorge confirmed. "His text messages, this kind of thing. I think it's probably beneficial to keep one step ahead."

"And the election?"

"It is coming," Jorge nodded. "I gave him your suggestion about the water in indigenous communities. I think he is going to do it. I said, this here will make him a hero to the people. This is what you must do. Then after he's in again, we can crack heads with Big Pharma."

"I suspect you'll be cracking heads before then," Chase grinned. "Do you think he's going to do it? Fix the water situation?"

"I think so," Jorge nodded. "There are lots of communities in need. So, it will take some time, but at least it is more than they are doing now. Also, I said that my company would help if we can, like a joint project. If he needs volunteers, money, whatever, it's a good look for us too. It helps your people. I think everyone will be happy."

"Not everyone," Chase reminded him. "There's a lot of people who hate the indigenous and would rather see their community burn to the ground than to help them."

Jorge solemnly nodded. Chase referenced a couple of years earlier when forest fires were rampant due to dry weather, and one of its victims was an indigenous community. They later learned that Mother Nature hadn't worked alone in that particular situation.

Before they could continue, the door opened, and Diego walked in.

"About time you give me a key to this place," He sniffed as he fixed his tie and walked across the room. "Instead of waiting like a dog to get in."

"Well, Diego, I have heard rumors that you *can* be a dog," Jorge grinned as his associate approached the bar. "Is Ricardo on his way?"

"*Allegedly* a dog." Diego corrected him. "And you made a superstar out of Ricardo, so he don't got time for us now."

Chase grinned as he poured Diego a cup of coffee and passed it across the bar.

"*Gracias,*" Diego said, then turned to Jorge. "Where's Paige?"

"You know," Jorge shook his head. "She is going somewhere with the children today, so it is just us. I will tell her everything when I get home."

"Was Clara in today?" Diego turned to Chase, who nodded in response. "Well, we may as well have the meeting here."

Diego sat next to Jorge while Chase leaned against the counter adjacent to the bar and crossed his arms over his chest.

"So, what's going on?" Diego asked but quickly switched gears. "I see Athas was at your house last night. You call him over for a barbecue, but you don't invite *me?*"

"Diego, none of this was my idea," Jorge shook his head. "I did not know about the barbecue, and I certainly did *not* invite Athas to join us."

"Oh, that doesn't sound good," Diego observed as he turned to Jorge. "What's that about?"

"Don't ask," Chase suggested and shook his head.

"Hey, you don't like the guy," Diego twisted his mouth and nodded. "I get that. He's your wife's ex. I mean, it was like 20 years ago, but you can never be too careful."

Noting the sarcasm in Diego's voice, Jorge shot him a look.

"Anyway," Chase said and cleared his throat. "I think there's other stuff going on we should probably get to."

"There is a few things," Jorge said. "I do not know where to start."

"I was going to ask about Jolene…" Diego started.

"Nope," Jorge shook his head. "That is *not* where we are starting with, so please, do not bring up her name."

"Fair," Diego pulled back and nodded.

"Jorge is pushing Athas to clean up the water in indigenous communities," Chase offered. "I think that's great."

"Very good," Diego nodded in approval. "It's your people, Chase. I assume you'll be involved."

"I would like to be."

"Contact Athas," Jorge suggested. "This here seems like something you can work on with him. The man is fucking clueless on his own."

"Most politicians are," Chase muttered.

"So, yes, we have this going on," Jorge jumped in. "And well, it seems that Health Canada is in deep with Big Pharma, so this here is a problem. Unfortunately, we might have to wait until after the election to do anything, although it does not sound like Athas thinks he can do much."

"Does he ever think he can do much?" Diego countered. "The man is spineless."

"Well, that we can agree on," Jorge grinned. "But yes, so there is a man on the top of the Big Pharma food chain who pushed for the drug that killed Juliana to be tested on people. They had reps pressure the doctors to try this new medication on patients and the more they pushed it, the more money they got."

"Fuck," Diego shook his head. "They'll feed us any poison to make a buck."

"Yup," Jorge said as he looked into his coffee and took a deep breath. "The more they got the pill out there, the bigger his bonus. This here is according to Marco, who is continuing to look, but that was all I had to know."

"We got a name?"

"Louis Downs," Jorge replied. "Marco, he is learning more on this here man, but I can promise you one thing. He will not live long enough to enjoy this money he made killing people."

Both Diego and Chase gave Jorge a sympathetic look, which he ignored.

"Anything else?" Diego asked.

Jorge thought for a moment.

"HPC News is growing fast," Jorge added. "Lots of subscribers, but we make a lot of enemies too. Makerson is the target, but this here doesn't bother him."

"I saw the news was talking about how he was working on your book," Chase said and shook his head. "Saying that you two are as thick as thieves, that he's doing your dirty work."

"They can throw stones all they wish," Jorge replied. "Because I throw a motherfucking cannon. We continue to mock the channels getting corporate and government money to run them. They are puppets. We have not dropped that narrative, and we won't. We are taking away their viewers, and that's the real problem here. They do not like that. Advertising is going down. People are walking away, and you know what? They will continue to walk away. Fuck them. Let them talk. Only the old people watch them anymore."

"True," Chase nodded. "My generation doesn't even have cable. Forget about the news. The world is changing, and they're the dinosaurs."

"So that it?" Diego asked as he fixed his tie. "I got a date later."

"Diego, it is still early," Jorge shook his head. "What time is your date?"

"Six, but I gotta do other things before then."

Chase laughed.

"Go, Diego, you know what you need to know," Jorge grinned. "Go get ready for your date."

"Keep me posted," Diego slid off the barstool. He grabbed his coffee and drank the rest in one gulp. "I'll talk to you later."

Jorge and Chase exchanged looks as Diego rushed out the door.

"He is so dramatic," Jorge shook his head, and Chase laughed.

CHAPTER 20

"Mr. Hernandez," Clarence walked into Hail's kitchen wearing a shirt and pants that were outdated but still managed to make him look distinguished. "Thank you for meeting with me again. I know a man like you is very busy."

"This here, it is not a problem," Jorge studied him as the old man slowly sat down, while Hail stood back as if unsure of whether he should join the two. That was until Jorge pointed toward an empty chair, beckoning him to sit down. "I was told you wished to speak to me again. Is this because you have some new information you would like to share?"

The senior shook his head, his eyes watered slightly, but he managed to regain his composure. Hail glanced at him as he sat down, immediately looking away.

"I wanted to make sure you took me seriously," Clarence confirmed as he seemed to diminish in size. "For some reason, the older you get, the more invisible you are to everyone. After a while, they stop hearing you too."

"I assure you," Jorge leaned in, his eyes growing dark. "I hear you. This here situation, it also affects my own family. I understand."

Satisfied, the old man nodded, his eyes full of curiosity.

"It is better," Jorge continued. "If I do not tell you much, but I can assure you that this situation is being looked after."

"These big pharmaceutical companies," Clarence shook his head. "They always get away with what they do."

Jorge wasn't sure what to say. He wanted to appease the old man, but he couldn't reveal too much information.

"There are no details that I can share," Jorge continued. "But I can promise you that when this day comes, you will find some information that satisfies you. Maybe Hail will see an article that he will share with you."

Hail nodded in understanding.

"But I assure you," Jorge continued. "We do share an enemy."

"That is all I ask," Clarence seemed to understand the suggestion. "Then, I can one day die in peace, but not until someone pays for what they did."

Jorge didn't respond, but the two men shared a knowing look while Hail stared at the table.

It was after Clarence left that Hail asked Jorge the blunt question.

"So, will I be dealing with a body or a missing person case?"

To which, Jorge studied him and shrugged.

"Ah, but is it not more fun when it is a surprise?"

Hail said nothing as Jorge headed out the door.

Once in his SUV, he jumped back on the highway. Jorge was on his way to the bar, where he was meeting with Marco. Hopefully, he had the information needed to get the revenge that both he and Clarence wanted. It was time for Louis Downs to die.

Arriving at the *Princesa Maria,* Jorge noted Paige was there. Although he had casually mentioned his meeting with Marco that morning, Jorge preferred his wife not to join them. She was more than capable of helping out, but he preferred she kept away from any potential danger. After seeing her shot in the past, he grew much more protective.

Jorge parked the SUV and slowly got out. Checking his phone, he noted no new messages and turned it off before entering the building. Chase was behind the bar watching Jorge as he walked into the empty room.

"I saw Athas making his announcement earlier," Chase commented, his face lit up, "About the water in the indigenous communities."

"Oh yes, that was today," Jorge nodded as he approached the bar. "How did it go over?"

"Great," Chase nodded. "I mean, there are all sorts of naysayers, but that's normal."

"There always will be."

"He said he's starting right away."

"Did you end up calling him?" Jorge asked.

"Yup," Chase nodded. "He asked where we should start. I said with the communities that have waited for the longest. There's some from back in the 90s, still waiting to get their water fixed."

"That there, it is not right," Jorge confirmed what he suspected Chase was thinking. "But at least, we are now working at it."

"Thank you again," Chase said. "For....doing everything you do."

"You know me," Jorge commented as he headed toward the VIP room. "I like to swoop in and play God whenever I can."

Chase laughed as Jorge walked away, reaching for the door of the VIP room.

Inside, Marco was showing Paige something on a tablet.

"You made it," His wife commented as she and Marco looked up from the screen.

"Sir, I have found everything you need," He jumped in, pointing toward the device. "This man, he will be easy."

"I even have a plan," Paige added as Jorge sat across from them.

"You must tell me everything," Jorge said, glancing between the two. "I am curious."

"He travels a lot," Paige said. "So, if he went missing, it wouldn't be such a stretch."

"This week, though," Marco added. "He is talking to pharmaceutical reps to encourage them to push another new drug that seems to replace the one they just took off the market for causing cancer."

"Do I even want to ask if this one is safe?" Jorge asked as his body grew heavy. "What does this one here do, make your dick fall off or something?"

Marco laughed, and Paige shook her head, causing Jorge to shrug.

"What you got, Marco?"

"Sir, I did some investigating," Marco continued. "it seems like this drug may be no better than the last. It may even be worse. The thing is that they use their words carefully. They say it may cause 'stomach interruption'. I do not know what this means, but it sounds questionable."

"It all is more carefully worded," Paige jumped in. "But basically, it's not better."

"Does it cause cancer?" Jorge got right to the point. "Or is this something they will not say in documents?"

"They do not say it directly," Marco confirmed as he scrolled through a document. "It does say, *may cause stomach interruption that has a slight link to cancer.*"

"Are you fucking kidding me right now?" Jorge shook his head. "So, they do this again?"

"Sir, did you think they would stop?"

"And that's not the worst part," Paige added. "Because they warn of this in the findings, officially, I don't think they are libel if anything happens because it was in fine print somewhere. It's very dubious. I'm sure people can sue, but they'll turn it around and say, 'they were warned and took the chance'."

"Sir, that is what I think too," Marco said and took a deep breath. "If they admit it is a possibility early on, then if people die, they have clean hands."

"Well, except for the blood on their hands already," Paige muttered. "But that doesn't appear to be a concern."

"Unfortunately for them," Jorge replied. "Getting blood on *my* hands is also not a concern."

"Sir, this company, it is evil," Marco shook his head. "They must be stopped."

"We may have to wait until after the election," Jorge replied. "But for now, anything more on this Louis Downs? Where does he live? Where can we find him?"

"Sir, it seems that he has a pretty wild life," Marco shared looks with Paige. "This man, he likes to party. He likes drugs."

"Could be an overdose?" Paige suggested.

"I would rather make him suffer," Jorge shook his head. "What you got, Marco?"

"He is a womanizer…"

"Paige, I know what you are thinking, and no," Jorge shook his head. "You are not doing this…"

"We do not have a lot of options," Marco sheepishly suggested. "Normally, he lives with his sister, and she is always there. The only other way we can get this man, sir, is in public places."

"But he meets with women either at their place or hotels," Paige continued. "Especially while traveling."

"Where does he meet them?"

"Online, mostly, apps," Marco replied.

"Paige, I know what you are thinking…." Jorge repeated. "But I do not want you to get involved in this here. I want…"

"I know I could do this," Paige replied then glanced at the screen. "Although, it doesn't look like I'm his type."

Marco's eyes widened as he looked at the screen.

"Why, he don't like blondes?" Jorge shrugged. "Or is he into men that dress like women, what?"

"He likes women who are…" Marco seemed to be searching for the correct words.

"He likes women with big boobs," Paige replied, glancing down at her modest chest. "So, maybe we could ask…"

"I know what you are thinking," Jorge shook his head. "But Paige, if we bring Jolene back…."

"I know," Paige nodded and put her hand in the air. "But she fits the bill, and you know she'd do this."

Jorge thought for a moment and exchanged looks with Marco, then his wife. His eyes went toward her chest. He didn't want her involved, but he also didn't want to get Jolene's help either.

"What if we get one of those bras, you know, that makes them look bigger and…"

"He needs to be tantalized by the real thing," Paige informed him.

"Yes, he likes to see them before he meets the lady," Marco replied. "He is…not exactly a gentleman, sir."

Jorge sighed and looked away.

And that was how Jolene slithered back into their lives.

CHAPTER 21

"It will focus on the more… unpleasant people in our country," Makerson explained to Jorge. Across the table sat both Tony and Andrew in the boardroom at Hernandez Production Company. "People who are leaders in business, politicians, celebrities, whoever it is that falls in this category that does something nefarious in nature."

"What he means," Andrew was quick to jump in. "The assholes who are the big shots around in Canada, and there are *lots.*"

Jorge grinned at the comment and raised an eyebrow without saying anything.

"What we want to do," Tony added as he leaned on the table. "Is have a segment that focuses both on current and past…personalities who have done things that are questionable, but maybe something the media didn't give enough attention to, but we will."

"Let's highlight those motherfuckers," Andrew spoke excitedly "Fuck them up!"

This caused Jorge to laugh, even though Makerson and Tony both cringed at Andrew's explanation.

"Ok, I see," Jorge finally replied and shrugged. "Whatever it is you think we should do, then do it. This here, you know I have no problem with."

"We wanted to run it by you since," Makerson hesitated. "Sometimes, there may be specific people you might prefer to target."

Jorge nodded in understanding.

"Like in the pharmaceutical industry," Tony continued. "I'm willing to bet that anyone is fair game there."

"You better fucking believe it," Jorge nodded. "Burn those fuckers to the ground."

"YEAH!" Andrew threw a fist up in the air. "Rage against the machine!"

"Isn't that what we've been doing all along?" Tony shrugged.

"I don't think anyone can argue with that," Jorge nodded. "Maybe we should call the segment *'Raging against the Machine'*?"

"I was thinking more like," Makerson hesitated. "Everybody wants to rule the world."

"I like that too," Jorge nodded. "Let us go with *'Everybody wants to rule the World'* and Andrew..."

Jorge turned toward the young man beside him, who was casually leaning back in his chair, a skeptical look on his face.

"Save that rage title," Jorge suggested. "I have something I am thinking for you."

"For me?" Andrew raised an eyebrow.

"I see that title as more for younger people," Jorge considered. "I would like to see you and someone else, someone perhaps very different from you, doing a show together to debate recent news stories. I saw something like this online recently, and I liked the concept."

Jorge noted that everyone around the table appeared intrigued by the idea.

"Oh yeah, who would I debate, Makerson?" Andrew smirked as he glanced at the man across the table, who showed no expression.

"Actually, no," Jorge shook his head. "I have an idea. I want to give it more thought."

"Is it a lady?" Andrew leaned in, suddenly very intrigued.

"Just wait, you will see," Jorge decided not to give too many details. "It is someone you know. That is all I say for now."

"That might work," Makerson nodded.

"But you can't go too crazy," Tony quickly warned Andrew. "Modestly entertaining, but not your usual circus act."

"Wow, all these limitations…" Andrew shook his head, appearing defeated.

"We will talk more on this another day," Jorge insisted. "I have to leave shortly to meet with Jolene."

Everyone around the table reacted to the news. None of which were good.

"Trust me," Jorge shook his head. "This here is not something I am happy about."

"Is it because of Diego you got her back?" Andrew asked as he made a face.

"No," Jorge answered honestly. "There is some work we need her to help with, and unfortunately, she is the best person for the job. It is not without some hesitation that I allow this return."

"But last time," Andrew shrugged. "I mean, she was a hoe bag, but it wasn't like she did something super disloyal, did she? I mean, you thought she was behind the book about you, but she wasn't, so I gotta be fair."

"Look, no offense," Tony shook his head and put a hand in the air. "I respect your decisions, but does she have to come back *here?*"

"She will need a job," Jorge said and took a deep breath. "I know this is the place she wants to be, and really, it would be good to have her working on the cartel show. She does know her stuff, so it is a good fit. Believe me, I am not doing cartwheels over this, but we will make it work. I will make sure that Jolene understands that she is not management, so she has no say in any meetings or tries to give orders."

"Did she try to give orders before?" Makerson asked as he raised an eyebrow.

"Yeah, she tries to take over everything," Andrew jumped in and shook his head. "So, be warned!"

"She's not going anywhere near HPC news," Jorge shook his head. "Or I will put her back at the crematorium, which she hates."

"Ok, well, I guess it is what it is," Tony let out a sigh.

"So, if that is all," Jorge stood up.

"There's one more thing," Makerson said and glanced around the table before continuing. "Some people here…some staff want to know if we can get a safe space."

"A safe space?" Jorge repeated as his forehead wrinkled in confusion.

"Not your kind," Andrew automatically answered the question floating through Jorge's mind. "Not like a room where your family hides while some maniac comes into your house with an AK15. He means a place where pussies go to cry when you say mean shit to them or whatever."

"Well, it's not exactly that," Makerson attempted to explain. "We had one at the paper…"

"I am confused," Jorge sat back down. "What is this?"

"There's this thing," Tony attempted to explain. "A lot of businesses have it. It's a room where employees can go if they feel….uncomfortable with a comment made to them, or a topic, somewhere they can get away from everything."

"What?" Jorge shook his head. "This here is their *home.* That is where you go to get away from people you work with."

"Nah," Andrew shook his head. "It's this new fucking thing where people who can't handle anything go and hide. They got like coloring books and pillows, stupid shit. They go there and cry or like, whatever. It's fucking bullshit."

Jorge exchanged looks with the three men.

"Is this here a fucking joke?"

"No, he's kind of right," Makerson shrugged. "I think it started on university campuses for students who heard something that made them uncomfortable. It would allow them to go to this safe room, which is supposed to be calm and peaceful, to reflect or…"

"Get in the fucking fetal position and call their mommy," Andrew continued and laughed. "Like a fucking pussy."

"Again, is this here a joke?" Jorge asked and watched all three shake their heads.

"Oh, fuck me!" Jorge stood up. "This here is what is wrong with the world now."

"It certainly isn't helping us," Tony replied. "So, that's a no?"

"This here is a production company," Jorge shook his head as he reached the door. "We deal with some insane things, so if you cannot handle this, then you probably shouldn't be working here."

With that, he walked out as the three men laughed at his final, abrupt comment.

Back in his SUV, he turned on his phone to find a message from his daughter.

I think we should have a pool party.

I don't want a bunch of kids at my house.

I mean the familia.

This here is fine. Maria, do you know what a safe room is? Where people go if they are uncomfortable or something like that?

Yes, we have one at school.

Jorge let out an exasperated sigh.

Like if you hurt someone's feelings or question their opinion and it upsets them, they can go to the safe room.

Sitting his phone aside, Jorge started the SUV and headed to the club.

It was still early, and already he was irritated.

Arriving at the bar to see Diego's Lexus, he let out another heavy sigh. He wasn't looking forward to this conversation. Then again, didn't he always know that Diego's sister would eventually find a way back into the *familia*. Didn't she always?

Turning off his phone, Jorge headed inside to find Chase standing behind the bar while Jolene and Diego sat on the other side, both enjoying a fancy drink.

"Is this your lunchtime cocktail?" Jorge asked as he walked across the room. He noted that Chase raised an eyebrow. "Who's running my company while you're hitting the bar, Diego?"

"Don't worry," Diego turned around and put his hand in the air. "I only had one drink, and that's it. Everyone does it."

Jorge didn't reply but exchanged looks with Jolene.

"I might have something for you," Jorge informed her, then turned to Chase. "Was Clara in today?"

"Yes," Chase nodded. "We're good."

"Ok, Jolene," Jorge continued. "I am going to keep this short. We need you to take care of a man. I have a specific way you have to do it, but unfortunately, you're going to have to use some T & A to get his attention."

"Ok," Jolene nodded excitedly. "I can do. Whatever you want. Just tell me."

"There is a man called Louis Downs," Jorge continued. "And this motherfucker, he's got to suffer."

Jolene nodded in understanding.

"And Jolene," Jorge continued. "If you do this right, you are back in the *familia.*"

CHAPTER 22

"This guy!" Andrew stopped suddenly in the conference room doorway at the Hernandez Production Company. Tony was in his tracks and almost ran into him but caught himself in time. "*This* guy? This is the guy you want me to debate news topics with on a show? Is this a *joke?"*

"I could say the same thing," Sonny McTea muttered under his breath as he sat up straighter and adjusted his tie.

"Ok, this here is enough drama," Jorge shook his head and abruptly pointed toward the chair beside him. "Sit the fuck down, Andrew, and listen to what I got to say."

Outside the door, a young employee was walking by and nervously rushed past.

"That's the safe room guy," Tony muttered and titled his head. "He's kind of sensitive. Should I be…checking on him or something?"

Jorge let out an exasperated sigh.

"What does this man do here?" Jorge asked. "Is he important?"

"No," Andrew shook his head as he walked in and sat down. "just an intern."

"Then why are we worrying about what he thinks so much?" Jorge shook his head and turned his attention to Tony, who was closing the door behind him. "What did he expect when he got involved in a production house?"

"I did a whole show on safe spaces," Sonny suddenly spoke up, dramatically swinging his hands around. "There are some people who had to go on stress leave from their jobs because the vibe was so negative, so that's why safe rooms come in handy."

"Oh my God, *this* is who you want me to work with?" Andrew grew angry again. "I mean, *really*?"

"This here is good," Jorge shrugged as the rest of them took a seat. "Very different personalities and different opinions, this is good. We need to debate more. According to my daughter, we need safe rooms because people no longer want to debate anything and get upset if people have different views. But this here, it is not reality."

"I didn't say I *agreed* with safe rooms," Sonny went on to say, pushing his dark-framed glasses closer to his face. "I was just stating that some people are a little more sensitive than others. There are some terrible environments that people work in. I guess that's kind of my point."

"It's stupid," Andrew shot back. "Like really, a room to cry and color or whatever?"

"Well, that is a bit extreme," Sonny nodded. "But yeah, I think it's nice to have a place to get away from everything. Workplaces have become very stressful and so, like, zen room with candles or something is kind of nice."

"Isn't that called a staff room in most places?" Tony asked.

"Well, not really," Sonny wrinkled his nose. "Staff rooms can be pretty toxic too. I think with safe rooms, people are encouraged to be quiet, to respect each other's right to sit in silence and..."

"Ok, this here is enough," Jorge cut him off. "I did not come here to discuss safe rooms, and I got somewhere I have to be soon, so I want to get right to the point."

"Of course," Sonny nodded as his position stiffened.

"Whatever," Andrew shook his head. "You really think me and this guy can do a show?"

"Well, you just kind of did a debate right here," Tony pointed out. "It would be the same thing except live. Less swearing, Andrew, but basically the same thing. Of course, you'd have to research your topic and be fully prepared."

"Like, why him?" Andrew shook his head and gestured toward Sonny. "This is a guy who was trying to say shit about you on his podcast last year. Remember? We paid him a visit?"

Jorge grinned and nodded. At the time, he had made a strong argument for Sonny to change his opinion on the subject at hand.

"Yes, but you know, that worked out," Jorge shrugged. "I liked his show. I watched it since and thought he did quite well."

"He's ultra *woke* in his views," Andrew pointed out. "It's annoying."

"And you tend to take a more…old-school approach," Tony added as Andrew rolled his eyes. "That's why we think this will work."

"At worst, we try and don't like," Jorge shrugged. "If this is the case, Sonny can return to his show, and you can return to…whatever it is you do all day."

Andrew shot him a look, and Jorge grinned.

"I think it would work," Sonny said and exchanged looks with Andrew. "I mean, I'm willing to give it a try. I would love the opportunity."

"Then, I will leave this in your hands," Jorge said to Tony. "You can figure out the format, the ground rules, whatever it is you need to do."

"I will talk to Makerson more," Tony nodded. "But I like the energy between these two."

"Well, if that is the case," Jorge stood up. "Then I have somewhere I have to be."

"Thank you again for this opportunity," Sonny said as Jorge headed toward the door. Turning around, he noted that Andrew was rolling his eyes while the other young man gave a sincere smile.

"Do me a favor, Sonny," Jorge said as he pointed at Andrew. "Make him dress better. We can't have one of you looking professional, and the other look like he is homeless."

"What?" Andrew looked down at his faded black t-shirt and ripped jeans. "You want me to wear a fucking suit or something?"

"Just look presentable," Jorge insisted. "And by the way, this is the *Raging Against the Machine* show that I was talking about. So make sure you both do a lot of raging, and Tony knows the machines you must fight."

On that note, Jorge left the building and started home. Feeling pretty calm as he drove, Jorge was surprised to see a familiar car in the driveway.

Going into his garage, he got out of the SUV and walked into the house. Paige met him at the door.

"He's in your office. Don't worry, I was watching him on my phone."

Jorge didn't reply but made his way through the house. The sound of Maria singing along to something upstairs helped to lighten his mood. Feeling slightly annoyed, he walked into his office to find Mark Hail waiting for him.

"I did not expect to find you here," Jorge commented as he closed the door and crossed the room. "What can I do for you?"

"I see you took care of Clarence's problem," Hail commented.

"I hope your phone is turned off."

"It's off," Hail shook his head. "And in my car and nothing on me, I promise."

"Ok, so yes," Jorge nodded as he sat behind his desk. "We had a common enemy."

"I shared what I could with him," Mark went on. "He wanted me to give you this."

Reaching in his pocket, Mark pulled out an old, sterling silver flask and set it on the desk.

"He said he figured you were a man who'd appreciate this."

Jorge's head fell back in laughter. He reached for it, inspecting it, he nodded.

"This here, it looks like it cost some money at one time."

"It did," Hail replied. "That's why he wanted you to have it."

"Well, tell him the gift, it was not necessary, but I do thank him."

"He was very relieved and appreciative."

"And we can trust him?"

"He's good," Hail assured him. "That's not the only thing. I got something else for you."

"Oh?" Jorge was intrigued.

Hail reached into his pocket and pulled out an evidence bag, and handed it to Jorge.

"What is this?"

"An earring was found on the scene," Hail replied. "Your girl needs to be more careful. I caught it before any of the other investigators. It was the only evidence I could've used against her."

"She is not *my* girl," Jorge shook his head as he reached forward to get it. "Just a solution to a problem, and she knows to be more careful."

"Rule number one of murdering someone is to not leave any evidence," Hail shook his head. "But I wanted to let you know."

"Thank you," Jorge nodded. "I will bring this to her attention."

"She was pretty brutal."

"That is what I wanted."

"An eye for an eye?" Hail replied. "He gives people stomach cancer with his pills, so you have someone stab him, quite ferociously, I might add, in the stomach. There was a lot of blood. He didn't die peacefully. I tell you that."

"I'm sure a lot of his victims didn't either," Jorge retorted.

"Fair enough," Hail shook his head. "Hey, I'm not saying he deserved better. I saw Clarence's great-granddaughter many times. She was young and vibrant. There was no reason for her or the many others to die."

"Maybe this here will be a warning to Big Pharma," Jorge said as he leaned back in his chair.

"If you ask me," Hail shook his head. "You started a war."

"Death comes to those who ask for it."

"There's a lot of that around you," Hail said as he stood up. "I gotta roll but wanted you to have that… well, both those things."

"The rest of the place, it was fine?" Jorge asked as he stood.

"Yup," Hail assured him. "I was the lead investigator. She was clean."

"I appreciate it," Jorge said as he started to walk toward the door. "I will talk…"

His words were interrupted by the sound of his secure line.

"What the fuck is that?" Hail turned with a grin on his face.

"I gotta take this," Jorge replied.

"I know my way out," Hail said as he continued to walk away.

Jorge closed his door and rushed back. Answering the call, he was somewhat annoyed.

"We might have a problem."

"*We* have a problem?" Jorge asked. "You were up in the polls. Everything was going great."

"The problem isn't my poll numbers," Athas continued. "Do you know anything about this Big Pharma rep that died?"

"I think it…..was on the news?" Jorge innocently replied.

"Yeah, well, he was strongly connected in government, and someone approached me today to say there's talk of creating a censorship bill that would specifically target independent or 'unofficial' media. And guess who's their main target?"

"They have approached you with this?"

"They started to work on it when HPC news had the report that pulled them through the mud," Athas replied. "They didn't tell me about it until today. They think you're connected to Louis Downs's death but can't prove it, but they plan to force the bill through as soon as possible."

"Does this not go against the Charter of Rights and Freedoms?"

"It's supposed to discourage disinformation, online attacks, and essentially is propped up to make people feel safer on the internet," Athas reported. "You've rattled some cages."

"I'm gonna rattle a lot more than fucking cages if they think they're going to silence me."

Jorge felt his blood boiling as he glanced toward his bulletproof window.

CHAPTER 23

"I give you *one* job!" Jorge raised his voice as he hovered over Jolene in the *Princesa Maria* boardroom. At the head of the table, Paige sat and silently listened. "One job, and you cannot manage to get out of there without leaving evidence? If it was not for our friend Constable Hail, your fat, Colombian ass would be in jail right now!"

"I am *not* fat!" Jolene shot back, then automatically looked regretful. "I mean, I did not mean to do this. I was very careful. You know this about me."

"In fairness," Paige cut in. "She hasn't worked with us in months."

"You banish me!" Jolene reminded him with tears in her eyes. "I do my best, and what difference? If they find earring, you control the police, no?"

"This here is not the point," Jorge shook his head. "It does not mean we get sloppy, Jolene."

"Can we…" Paige started, but Jorge cut her off. His focus was on Jolene, who began to shake as tears ran down her face.

"Do not bother crying, Jolene!" Jorge snapped at her. "This here is not going to help you. It is *always* something with you. This is the problem."

"I will do better, I promise," Jolene insisted. "I make mistake. I am sorry."

"You always are making mistakes, Jolene."

"Ok," Paige raised her voice this time. "Jorge, please, can we let this go? I agree that was a serious error, but it was caught. We are fine. Screaming at her isn't going to change anything. The bottom line is Louis Downs is dead, as he deserves to be. His death was brutal, which is what you wanted."

"I promise, it will not happen again," Jolene assured him. "I be careful."

Jorge didn't say anything but continued to glare at her as he sat down.

"We need to move on," Paige quietly commented to Jorge, who, this time, was listening to her and slowly nodded. "It was a serious mistake, but it *was* a mistake. We have other things to deal with now."

"I guess….we can bring the others in," Jorge finally replied as he looked away from Jolene.

"I will get them," Paige said as she stood up and headed toward the door.

"But Jolene," Jorge gave her one final warning. "No more mistakes. If you are caught, *we* all are caught. And jail, it would look like a luxury hotel beside what I would do to you."

"I know," Jolene wiped away another tear. "I understand."

"Well, she's not on the floor bleeding out," Diego made the snappy remark as he walked in the room. "So, I guess Jorge let her live. We could hear your screaming from the bar."

"I was so looking forward to burning her body too," Andrew showed no compassion to the broken woman who sat awkwardly at the table. "I guess not every day can be Christmas."

"In all honesty," Chase reminded them. "It was a mistake. Chances are most of the cops wouldn't even have found it and would fucking lose it if they did."

"They'd lose it all right," Jorge insisted as he began to relax as he glanced at Marco closing the door. "If I had to burn the whole department down to get it."

"See, this is what I say," Jolene spoke up. "Even if they had…"

"That is not the point," Diego cut her off. "Jolene, you know that! Your biggest worry was that the news didn't report the gory details."

"Gory details?" Andrew automatically jumped in, turning toward Jolene. "Well, bitch, don't hold back. I wanna hear!"

"She stab him with scissors," Jorge shook his head and gave Andrew a look. "Of course, it would not be pretty."

"Most murder scenes aren't," Paige added.

"No, but this one, it was so bad," Jolene spoke up, her usual confidence returning. "There was a lot of blood…I took picture."

"What?" Jorge yelled as he turned toward Jolene, who was reaching in her purse.

"Oh no, sir, there must not be pictures," Marco shook his head. "If she is hacked…"

"Jesus Christ, Jolene!" Diego snapped. "The first rule of murdering someone is don't take fucking pictures."

"But I…."

"Wait, hold on," Andrew leaned in closer to Jolene. "Let's calm down. Maybe an independent source leaked the photos, and we can use them on our show…"

"Probably too graphic for Canadian television," Paige muttered.

"Maybe you know, blur some stuff or whatever," Andrew continued to look intrigued. His entire face opened, and his eyes widened when he finally saw the snapshot. "Holy fuck, Queen, you got this one."

"What?" Diego made a face.

"Don't worry, Diego," Andrew glanced down at the table. "You're still a queen, but Jolene here, she's *the* queen. That is one bloody murder. I think I see his stomach oozing out. Yeah, we gotta use this picture…"

"I think that might be pushing it," Paige shook her head while Diego did the same.

Jorge reached for her phone and studied the image. Having committed many atrocious attacks on people in the past, it barely caused him to flinch. There was a lot of blood, but the only thing he saw was the horror in the eyes of the victim.

"I would say," Jorge contemplated it for a moment. "That maybe a witness of the scene reported that it was quite….gruesome in nature. What do you think, Paige?"

Glancing at the picture, she shrugged. "I would say it was *very* brutal and maybe state that it was one of the worst crime scenes the investigator ever witnessed. Something like that."

"Oh, fuck yeah," Andrew nodded enthusiastically. "I'm gonna get this to Makerson for tonight. He can say we had an exclusive interview with someone on the scene, but we can't reveal our sources."

"Will that help your ego, Jolene?" Diego spoke condescendingly toward his sister. "To have the world know it was a bloodbath."

"In some small way, yes, this make me happy," Jolene humbly admitted.

"Ok, well, I think this here would be ok," Jorge deleted the picture, turned off the phone, and passed it back to her. "I am in enough trouble with these government motherfuckers. I do not need more."

"Our channel is barely launched and in shit already," Andrew shook his head. "We knew it, though. Big media don't like the competition. Their numbers are sliding into the shitter. No one be fucking watching."

"Then who will give them advertising dollars?" Diego sniffed.

"So, what's going on?" Chase asked suspiciously. "Are they still attacking Makerson on their show? Saying you bought and paid for him?"

"Actually, it's a bit more serious," Paige commented and glanced at her husband.

"I spoke with Athas yesterday, and he tell me that some MP is creating a bill that would censor independent media, saying we give false information."

"What?" Andrew shot back. "Are you fucking serious?"

"Yes, this here," Jorge shook his head. "It started as soon as our news channel began. We caused a lot of people to ask questions that they were not prepared to answer. This upset the media, Big Pharma, and of course government, and they are all connected."

"Like one sweaty, dirty fucking orgy," Andrew shook his head. "Is the bill passed or what?"

"It can't pass that quickly," Paige shook his head. "It has to be introduced, passed, then go to the senate. But if they want it to work, they can do it."

"Wait, what the fuck is Athas doing?" Andrew complained. "He's the fucking prime minister. Can't he stop it?"

"He can't stop a bill," Paige attempted to answer. "But he can pressure the MPs to go against it. Still, they're going to try to find a way to push it ahead. There's a lot of power and money behind it because Big Pharma wants it, and the politicians will insist it's to discourage disinformation by any, random, fly by night group that calls themselves independent media."

"The usual, government bullshit," Chase shook his head. "*This is for your own good* bullshit."

"So we gonna report on this or not?" Andrew asked Jorge.

"Sir, if it's there, I can find it," Marco insisted.

"Find it," Jorge insisted. "Then we will expose them before they have a chance to get it off the ground."

"Doesn't this go against the charter?" Chase asked. "I mean, freedom of expression? Isn't that still a thing in this country?"

"That's why they're trying to say it's disinformation," Paige reminded him. "That way, they can justify having it removed."

"So who gets to decide what is true and not true?" Chase countered.

"That's a good question," Paige nodded. "Who gets to oversee the news and decide what's correct and what's not?"

"Yeah, but you got like, tabloids that lie all the time," Andrew shook his head. "No one gives a fuck about them."

"My guess is they're planning to create a board to oversee it if they're talking about a bill," Paige said. "Marco, could you look into this too?"

"Yes, of course," Marco nodded and jotted something in a notebook. "I do not understand why Athas cannot control his own government."

Jorge raised an eyebrow and shared a look with Paige, who didn't reply.

CHAPTER 24

"....sources have said that it was one of the most brutal crime scenes they had ever witnessed," Makerson spoke soberly and took a deep breath, as if in contemplation of what he had just reported. *"For those who forget, Louis Downs was connected with the recent scandal involving the medication..."*

A knock at Jorge's office door pulled him out of his moment of satisfaction and back to reality.

"Si?" He called out in a casual tone, assuming it was Maria there to tell him that the barbecue with his *familia* was about to start. He had hidden away in his office to have some quiet time before the whole gang arrived, once again enjoying the video clip that was now trending on social media.

"Jorge," Paige stuck her head in the door. "You're not going to like this..."

"Oh no," He shook his head. "What is it now, Paige? What did Jolene do? Come wearing a thong bikini?"

"Well, it *is* a pool party," Paige reminded him, and he rolled his eyes. "But your daughter is the only person walking around in a bikini, but that's not what I mean. Alec just showed up and..."

"Are you fucking kidding me right now?" Jorge cut her off as he started to stand up. "What the hell is he doing here?"

"He claims Maria invited him," Paige said as she stepped into the office, her voice low. "But he wants to talk to you about..."

"Oh God," Jorge loudly sighed and sat back down. "Send him in…I guess…"

"Be nice," She spoke in an lower tone but was met by Jorge's glare. She grinned and left the room.

Another knock caused Jorge to stiffen.

"What you want, Athas?"

The Canadian prime minister opened the door. He was dressed casually in shorts and a black t-shirt.

"Thank you for inviting me…"

"I didn't invite you," Jorge automatically cut him off. "What you want?"

Closing the door behind him, Athas made his way across the room.

"I was looking more into that bill…."

"The censorship bill?" Jorge snapped as Athas sat down. "You must explain to me, Athas, how this shit seems to pass by you all the time. You are like the cat who don't know a mouse is walking on top of you. You continue to sleep. How do you not know what is going on in your government?"

"They don't tell me," Athas shrugged. "This might surprise you, but the prime minister is…"

"Just the face of the government," Jorge replied in a bored voice. "I figured this out a long time ago. So, what you got for me?"

"It's not exactly like that, but…" Athas hesitated before going on. "I looked into it more, and it seems that there's been talk for a while. Even before your channel started. They have an issue, in general, with some of the things being brought up online as well in your docuseries like *Eat the Rich*. They've had some pressure from powerful people."

"More powerful than me?" Jorge shook his head. "Perhaps these people in your government that do not like such things as freedom of speech, they should move to a communist country."

"That's the thing," Athas countered. "They want to control the narrative, and they want to do it here. You have hit a lot of nerves. They're worried about what else you might expose."

"They should be."

"You caused a lot of people to lose a *lot* of money with the recent Big Pharma story," Athas moved closer. "They're not going to back down."

"*I'm* not going to back down," Jorge leaned ahead. "And if they keep pushing me, I will push back *harder.*"

"I don't disagree with you," Athas shook his head. "The problem isn't what you are saying. The problem is that too many people are listening. That's what worries them."

"Athas, again, this here is your government," Jorge pointed out. "Why do you not tell them to fuck off? Why do you not kick them out? Why do you not expose them? Why do you not remind them that you are the prime minister? Why do you not do *something?*"

"It's not that easy, I..."

"Enough," Jorge stood up, and Athas nervously did the same. "You know, if I knew you would end up being such a fucking pussy, I would have run for prime minister *myself* instead of backing you. Because you know what? These fuckers wouldn't even *try* this shit with me. I would destroy them, not hide under the bed."

"But there are certain procedures and..."

"Yes, there are certain procedures and public bullshit that you say in speeches and to answer the questions," Jorge shook his head. "I am not talking about the public prime minister. I am talking about the private one. The one who tells these pieces of shit to get the fuck out of his office. Just like I am about to do with you! Enough is enough, Athas. I am tired of fixing your problems. Be a man or at least pretend you are a man and deal with these assholes or, you know what? I will slit their fucking throats myself. Do you understand?"

"I....yes, I mean...." Athas attempted to take it all in.

"Now, my daughter, she has a pool party out there," Jorge pointed toward the window as he walked to his door. "That I plan to enjoy, despite the fact you are here. I am going to eat a big fucking steak and have some Mexican beer, and you, you can go drown yourself in the pool, for all I fucking care."

With that, he swung the door opened and walked out, leaving behind a stunned Greek Canadian.

Heading toward the patio, he could see that there was a small group already gathered. Chase was standing behind the barbecue, a skeptical look on his face. Miguel appeared content on Jolene's lap at the patio table. Paige was beside her, looking at her husband as he reached the door, with

Athas in tow. Then Jorge noticed Maria in a string bikini talking to Chase, and his blood began to boil. Aggressively swinging open the door, he was about to call his daughter out, when out of the corner of his eye, he noticed Diego, who appeared to be telling a story.

"....told him that I got on *this* ship with no kids, and I'm not leaving with them *either!"*

Jolene gave her brother a confused look while Paige grinned.

"Maria, I need to talk to you," Jorge pointed at his half-naked daughter while glancing around at the others. "Where is everybody?"

"Marco is with his family," Paige replied as she fixed her sunglasses. "They had something planned already with relatives. Andrew is on his way, and so is Tom. Tony is busy with the production house. I think that's it."

Jorge nodded and noted that his daughter was slowly approaching him.

"We gotta talk," Jorge glared at her as Athas passed him to join the others. The smell of food seeping in caused his stomach to growl. "Come with me, Maria."

She obediently followed him inside, closing the door behind them.

"Are you mad because I invited Alec to the barbecue?" She asked in a small voice. "I thought...."

"Maria, I am not happy that you invite him," Jorge shook his head. "I do not like that man hanging around here."

"You make it sound like he's dangerous."

"I do not want...anyway, Maria, this is not about Alec," Jorge switched gears as they entered the kitchen area. "This here is about you parading around in your underwear in front of guests."

"It's a *bikini, Papá,"* Maria shook her head. "It's completely normal for a woman to wear a bikini."

"You are not a woman," Jorge shook his head. "You're a teenager."

"So?" She complained. "It's not like I have a figure like Jolene!"

Jorge glanced at her skinny little body and looked away.

"This here, it is too much," Jorge complained. "You need to put on a tank top and shorts or something, but you need to wear more clothes."

"What next? Do you want me to cover my *hair* or wear a niqab?"

"Maria, do not be ridiculous," Jorge snapped. "I did not say you should cover yourself completely, just cover *more..."*

"No," She shot back and rushed toward the patio door.

"Maria...."

Jorge called out, but she was already furiously swinging the door open, and in doing so in such fury, his daughter didn't realize that she had also caught hold of the string of her bikini top, unaware she was untying it at the same time. It took a moment for her to realize, to her horror, that one side of the flimsy material had fallen. Frantically pulling up the material, Maria tearfully turned and ran upstairs, leaving behind her stunned *familia.*

Chase looked up from the barbecue.

"What happened? Where did Maria go?" He was asking.

"I do not think this is a big deal," Jolene shrugged. "We have all seen this before."

"She's embarrassed," Diego was attempting to explain to his sister while Paige stood up, heading toward the patio door.

"This is fine," Jorge put up his hand to stop his wife. "I will go talk to her."

"Are you sure?" She seemed skeptical.

"Yes, this here is fine," Jorge insisted as he turned. "It will be fine."

Heading upstairs, he felt remorseful. It was because he had given Maria grief over the outfit. Chances were she wouldn't have had a wardrobe malfunction had she not been so angry when grabbing the patio door and ripped it open. He felt awful for his *hija.*

Knocking on the door, he waited for a moment.

"Maria, please, let me come in."

He could hear her crying on the other side.

"Maria, I am coming in..."

He eased the door open and found Maria on the bed, her head buried in a pillow as she cried hysterically.

"Maria," he gingerly closed the door behind him. "This here is ok..."

"No, it's not!" She snapped. "I've never been so humiliated in my life. I could *die!"*

"Maria, you are dramatic," Jorge attempted to reason with her as he sat on the side of the bed. He noted she was now wearing a hoody. "This is your family. You should never be embarrassed in front of them."

"It's easy for *you* to say! It's not *you!"*

"Maria..."

"It happened in front of the *prime minister!"* She started to cry harder, as she curled up, hiding her face. "In front of Diego and Jolene…in front of *Chase!"*

Jorge paused for a moment as he thought about what to say.

"You know, Chase, he did not see," Jorge finally countered. "He was looking down at the barbecue. Athas was getting a beer and had his back turned."

"You're just saying that."

"No, Maria, I am *not* just saying that."

"You wanted this to happen because you were mad I was wearing a bikini."

"Maria, you know this is not true," Jorge attempted to reach out and touch her shoulder but she flinched. "Trust me, the only people who see is Jolene, Diego, and Paige. And maybe Miguel, I am not sure. Diego is gay. Jolene and Paige are women."

"It's still embarrassing," Maria continued to whine, although she had stopped crying.

"Of course it is," Jorge admitted. "I understand this, Maria. But your world will not stop because your bikini top fell down. You are dramatic! Is it not better you have this happen here, now, with family, not with, say, a group of your friends at a sweet 15 party?"

"I thought you said I couldn't have that?" Maria seemed to perk up slightly.

"Maria, I say we can discuss it," Jorge replied. "Please, come downstairs…"

She shook her head no.

"Ok," Jorge nodded. "I hope you change your mind. Are you hungry?"

"A little bit," She admitted.

"I will send up some food."

She fell silent as he left her room, closing the door behind him. He stood in the hallway for a few minutes. His chest felt heavy.

He worried about his daughter. He worried a lot.

CHAPTER 25

The sun seemed to be shining brighter that morning as Jorge made his way toward the patio. With a coffee in hand, he was looking forward to enjoying a quiet morning by the pool before rushing out the door to start his day. Paige and the kids were still in bed. There was something about early morning silence that somehow put Jorge in the right frame of mind to start his day.

Sliding the door opened, he walked onto the patio. A sharp chill ran up his spine. Clouds suddenly began to roll in as the wind picked up. He was about to slide the door shut when he saw something out of the corner of his eye. His heart began to pound as Jorge realized that someone was in the pool. It took him a second to realize that it was Alec Athas floating in the water.

Sitting down his coffee, Jorge glanced around the area before gingerly walking toward his pool. He stared at the lifeless body for a moment before grabbing a nearby toy baseball bat that belonged to Miguel and poked him with it. The body sunk momentarily but quickly rose again.

"Jorge?" Paige's voice was soft, gentle.

He turned toward his wife in the doorway and realized how this would look. As she rushed out to see Athas's body floating, she gasped in horror, her eyes filled with tears, and she abruptly turned and ran away. Jorge attempted to follow her, but his feet were like lead. He couldn't move.

"Jorge!" Paige's voice continued. "Jorge…"

Opening his eyes, he suddenly realized that it was only a dream. And yet, it gave him a shot of very realistic joy.

"Jorge, your alarm went off," Paige tiredly said. "I don't think you heard. You must've been in a deep sleep."

"Paige," Jorge yawned. "I was having the most beautiful dream."

"Oh? What was it about?"

He gave her a mischievous smile before shaking his head.

"I will tell you later," Jorge decided it was better to avoid the subject. "I have to get ready to meet with Marco at the club."

Slowly getting out of bed, he noted that his wife nodded and closed her eyes, snuggling up to her pillow.

Twenty minutes later, Jorge was showered, in a suit, and leaving his driveway when his phone rang. It was Makerson.

"*Buenos dias,*" Jorge answered the phone.

"Good morning," Makerson said. "Sorry I didn't make it to the barbecue yesterday. I was planning on it but got tied up at HPC and ended up ordering in pizza."

"This here is fine," Jorge paused for a moment. "Anything I should know about?"

"No, just some equipment issues," Makerson replied. "I wanted to take care of it right away before another week started."

"Sounds like a good idea."

"I also wanted to tell you that our publisher contacted me," Makerson went on. "They're talking about the release date for the book. I think they want me to do a tour and stuff, but with the HPC news and everything here…"

"We will cross that bridge when we come to it," Jorge shook his head. "We will hire more people and make sure they are fully trained and capable before that time."

"I know, but I think they want *you* touring too," Makerson went on. "Talking about your life, the book…"

"Ughh," Jorge frowned. "This here does not appeal to me. I must see if I can get out of it."

"Maybe that's another 'cross that bridge when we come to it' situation?"

"I think so."

"I will talk to you later."

"Sounds good."

Jorge ended the call and frowned. The last thing he felt like doing was touring all over the place, meeting people, and speaking about his life. He had only done the book to appease the interested parties and discourage anyone else from writing an unauthorized version that might be much less pleasant and with much more truth. However, the interest seemed to have worn off. He hoped the book wouldn't flame the fires when it was released that fall.

Arriving at the club, he swung into his usual parking spot, noting that Chase was already there. He checked his phone quickly before turning it off and entering the bar.

"Anyone here?" Jorge called out as he locked the door behind him.

"In here, sir," Marco replied.

"I'm in my office," Chase's voice came from another direction.

"Marco, I will be in shortly," Jorge replied. "I must have a brief discussion with Chase."

Walking behind the bar, Jorge stuck his head in the office. He leaned against the doorway.

"How's Maria this morning?" Chase asked with concern in his eyes.

"I did not see her before leaving the house," Jorge admitted. "I was in such a rush, but she seemed better last night. She didn't *die* of embarrassment as she thought."

Chase grinned and shook his head.

"I guess it is that age," Jorge went on. "I do understand, but at the same time, she has to realize that there are much worse things than your bikini top falling."

"She's a teenager," Chase attempted to explain. "Everything embarrasses you at that age."

"I have not been one in over twenty years," Jorge reminded him. "But I do not recall much embarrassing me. But then again, I walked around with a gun at her age, so there is that."

Chase laughed and shook his head.

"But you cheered her up," Jorge reminded him. "You always do."

"I just took her some food and told her I didn't see anything," Chase reminded him. "Because I didn't. I told her it wasn't a big deal. She thought people would be laughing at her. I said no, but they were concerned."

"I still am concerned," Jorge admitted. "Again, I understand that she is a teenager and this here, embarrassment over everything, it is normal. However, I worry sometimes. She gets so upset over these here things. She is very emotional at times."

"She's dramatic," Chase sat back in his chair. "That's just Maria."

"I hope you are right," Jorge said as he started to walk away. "Thank you again, Chase."

"No problem," He replied.

Jorge headed to the VIP room.

"Was Clara in?" Jorge called out behind him.

"Yes," Chase yelled back.

Jorge entered the room to find Marco furiously tapping on his keyboard.

"I will be a moment, sir," He said as Jorge sat in his usual place.

"No rush."

Marco finished what he was doing and closed his laptop.

"So, Marco, what you got for me this morning?" Jorge got right to the point.

"Sir, I have been looking into what Athas is saying regarding this censorship law," Marco began to speak. "He is right. They did not tell him much. It is after I checked out the people he told you about that I did some deep research to learn that they were going behind his back because they knew he would never approve."

Jorge nodded with interest.

"He also does not know that they are forming a board to oversee these things," Marco continued. "A few names are floating around. None of them, sir, will disagree with what they want. They will be very bias."

"Marco, my goal is to stop them before they even start," Jorge admitted. "I do not want this here."

"Oh sir, once they start," Marco was shaking his head. "It will never end. It will be more and more, as much as they can push."

"That is my fear," Jorge took a deep breath. "This here is a free country. You know, many say things about me that I do not like, but unless I see it as a concern, I do not care. These here companies do not want the truth coming out about them because they have gotten away with so much, for so long."

"Especially Big Pharma, sir," Marco shook his head. "They have knowingly hurt people for many years with their products, but this is not their concern. Their concern is their shareholders and profits. That is all."

"And good media coverage," Jorge added.

"Yes, sir," Marco nodded in agreement. "That is the bottom line with them."

"So, how will this look?"

"It would be primarily on social media," Marco replied. "A lot of censorship on specific topics, I believe. I think these powerful people are paying off social media companies to make sure they police for them. Removing articles that make them look bad, that kind of thing. Kicking people off that don't abide by their rules. That will happen regardless of any censorship bills. Actually, it's already started."

Jorge nodded but didn't reply.

"There are some people kicked off permanently for saying too much," Marco went on. "Suspended for shorter times."

"Just like children in school," Jorge raised an eyebrow. "This here is interesting."

"That is one way to put it, sir," Marco shook his head. "But if this censorship law goes through, it would be even scarier. They make it sound like it is for people's own good because it will stop racism and hate, misinformation, but who decides what falls in this category, and we already know it will be slanted to fit their agenda."

"I will not let this bill get through," Jorge reminded Marco. "We will be giving coverage on HPC news every goddam day until the people know what is going on."

"That is the thing," Marco shook his head. "They plan to slander HPC and make it sound like you are extremists. They're trying to get Athas on board to let the public know that this bill is great, but he's not playing ball, and they have already indicated that it is a problem."

Jorge thought briefly about his dream the previous night.

"Is there any word on what they plan to do?" Jorge inquired. "To make him go along with them."

"They plan to blackmail him, sir."

"Is this so?"

"They plan to..." Marco hesitated for a moment. "They want to make it seem like Athas is having an affair with Paige so that you kill him."

Jorge twisted his head and raised an eyebrow.

CHAPTER 26

It was always Paige that answered the door when he went to the house. And always with a smile on her face, a welcoming demeanor that vastly contrasted that of her husband. Although she was nothing like the woman he had dated 20 years earlier, sometimes Alec saw a glimmer still in there, and it gave him hope. There was a spark that she had carried with her in those days, something special that made her stand out against everyone else. He sometimes mourned the woman she used to be, even though it wasn't realistic to expect her to be the same. Life happened. Life had changed them all.

"What…what is this about?" Alec quietly asked her as he walked into their enormous house. "He never calls me over here."

"Come on," Paige attempted to brush off his comment. "You make it sound like you're never here. You were here the other day…"

"Because Maria invited me to the barbecue," Athas rushed to explain. "Trust me, I knew right away I shouldn't have come."

The two shared a look, and Paige appeared uncertain on how to respond.

"He hates me," Alec curtly reminded her. "And he doesn't exactly go out of his way to hide it either."

"That's just his way," She attempted to explain. "He comes across as…"

"Blunt," Alec cut her off and shook his head. "Paige, please don't try to sugarcoat. He's pretty clear about how he feels."

Her expression fell.

"So, what's this about?" He repeated his earlier question.

"I don't know."

Alec gave her a look. Tilting his head slightly, he studied her face. He couldn't tell if she was lying. She had changed so much.

"Really…I don't," She finally added and gestured toward the office. "You may as well get it over with."

Alec said nothing but followed Paige as she escorted him to the office. It was an unnecessary gesture but appreciated just the same, as she turned back to smile at him. A whiff of a vanilla scent flowed his way, once again taking him back to a much simpler time. How had things got so incredibly complicated?

Once outside the office, she tapped on the door and waited for Jorge's approval before entering the room. As soon as Hernandez saw Alec on the other side, he automatically grimaced while gesturing for him to come in.

"Sit down, Athas," Jorge grumbled from behind his desk, where he sat like an oligarch overseeing his empire. "Paige, can you come in too?"

Alec noted how Jorge's tone changed when talking to his wife. It was a minor flicker, a softness in his voice that almost was unnoticeable. Alec pretended to not notice as he entered the room and sat in his usual spot. Jorge's attention returned to him, his focus was strong, his eyes boring through him.

"So, what's going on?" Paige asked as she closed the door and crossed the room to sit beside Alec. "Does this have something to do with this censorship bill that you were talking about?"

"You might say that," Jorge said and took a deep breath. "It is, how you say, quite unfortunate that these people decide that we should censor our speech in a free country, but here we are."

"It's because your production company has exposed a lot," Paige reminded him. "Especially in the *Eat the Rich* series. I can imagine there's a lot of powerful people worried about what you will do with a regular news program."

"I can do much," Jorge pointed out. "And already have."

"This censorship law," Athas decided to intercept. "I think it was in the works for a long time though. I'm not even sure it wasn't before your series came about."

"Yes, this here is a fair comment," Jorge nodded as he sat back in his chair. "However, it is the things I have done that have made them more nervous. And when rich men get nervous about losing money, they tend to move quickly to regain their power."

And you would know.

"Yes, well, that seems to be the nature of the beast," Paige reminded him. "But we can fight back."

"We are," Jorge assured her. "We will continue to talk about issues that need addressing while talking about this current bill that they are trying to push through. Unfortunately, it does not look like Athas has as much power as we thought because he cannot stop his party from voting for it."

"I can....encourage them to toe the party line," Alec reminded him. "But there are no guarantees."

"But what about what constituents want?" Paige directed her question at Alec, but it was answered by Jorge.

"Paige, this here does not matter," He shook his head. "The people, they do not know what they want. They do not even know what is going on in government half the time."

"But that's in part because so much is hidden by the regular media," She attempted to understand. "Once people know that they could be censored, surely..."

"Paige, it does not matter," Jorge shook his head. "People, they do not pay attention and assume that their country would never turn on them. How ignorant they can be."

"He's right," Alec jumped in. "The reality is that they will spin it like the bill is a good thing to stop online bullying and racism, and obviously, we don't want these things. They won't explain how we will do this by censoring them and that the lines in the sand can be...insecure."

"The rules, they will keep changing," Jorge nodded. "And who gets to decide what is and isn't racist? What is and isn't bullying? If you go online and attack a local business because they did not fulfill their contract or their product makes you sick, is this here online bullying? Is anything against the powerful people now considered bullying? It is concerning."

Alec nodded while wondering to himself what was in this for Jorge Hernandez. He assumed his primary concern was freedom of speech at his production house, not to mention his ability to remain powerful by bringing others down. Did Jorge even care about the average person's freedom of speech? He was difficult to understand. However, it was necessary to try to work with him.

"So it's to protect the powerful?" Paige asked.

"I would say, yes," Jorge nodded. "But that is not why I bring Alec here to talk to me."

"It's not about....just this?" Alec was confused, perhaps a little concerned. "Please don't tell me there's more."

"As it turns out," Jorge replied as he glanced at his wife before returning his attention to Alec. "These here people know you have me on your side, and this concerns them. They also are trying to find a way to make you go along with their plan to make censorship sound sexy to the regular voter."

"I've already been clear that there's no way I'm going along with this," Alec assured him.

"They plan to blackmail you," Jorge spoke bluntly.

"Me? With what?" Alec waved his hands in the air.

"They plan to say that you're having an affair with my wife," Jorge spoke bluntly, causing a chill to run up Alec's spine as he sat up straighter, unsure of what to say. "With the threat of telling me if you don't comply. They believe if I believe this is true, I will kill you myself."

"That's outrageous!" Paige threw her arms in the air.

"Not really, Paige because if I did think that you two were having an affair," Jorge gave Alec a warning look. "This might be his fate."

"Wait, nothing is happening here," Alec attempted to sound calm even though his heart was pounding furiously. "They can't make up what they want and have no proof."

"And they can't have proof if it's not happening," Paige jumped in. "Give me the name of the person who came up with this, and I will kill them myself!"

"Ok, let us settle down," Jorge spoke in an almost bashful manner. "Let us not throw out the baby and then the bathwater..."

"I don't think..." Paige began to speak.

"At any rate," Jorge cut her off. "I know this here is not true. I think they plan to make a picture look like it is so or some nonsense. They think I will overreact and murder Athas. This here is what they want because they can take care of both problems. He is dead, and I will be in prison."

"They *really* think you'd go to prison?" Alec couldn't help but ask and automatically wished he hadn't said a word.

"Well, it does seem this way," Jorge shrugged casually. "These people, they are clearly out of touch with reality."

Alec didn't reply.

"I can't believe they think this would work," Paige shook her head. "It sounds incredibly naive."

"Blackmailing prime ministers and presidents, it is a common thing," Jorge went on. "But usually, they are easy because they do have unsavory things in their past. But with Alec, they could not find much. At any rate, this clearly will not work."

"So what's the plan?" Alec decided to get right to the point. "Why did you call me here today?"

"You need to call these here people in your office and tell them to remove the bill."

"And they will say no," Alec reminded him.

"Then you blackmail the fuckers yourself," Jorge said as he reached into his desk and pulled out an envelope. "As it turns out, you beat them to the punch."

"You have pictures of them doing something unsavory?" Alec asked as he reached for the envelope.

"No, Athas, this here is not an 80s drama," Jorge shook his head. "It is pictures of their *children* doing some *very* unsavory things. And trust me, they do not want this here stuff getting out."

"Like…" Paige glanced toward the envelope.

"Some, bullying online," Jorge nodded. "Which I admit is minor but still goes against the bill they want to introduce."

"That's it?" Athas reached into the envelope to pull out a stack of pictures, the first being a young woman snorting cocaine. He noted that each image included the name of a person behind the censorship bill and that person's relationship to the subject in the picture. "Oh….I see."

"Those pictures," Jorge pointed at the envelope. "They get worse as you go along, not better. I would not want that to be my children."

"I don't know if I feel comfortable using someone's kids to…."

"Athas," Jorge shook his head. "I do not feel *comfortable* making parliament hill look like something out of a horror movie, but I fucking will if I have to…so, it is your choice. Because me? I don't got a conscience, but this might be the easier way to shut these fuckers up."

Athas didn't reply but glanced at Paige.

One look in her eyes told Alec he should stick with the first option.

CHAPTER 27

"The first show should be about how people identify," Sonny McTea suggested as he pushed up his dark-framed glasses and looked from Jorge to Tony, ignoring Andrew beside him. "I have a lot of friends who are *struggling* with this lately. I have one friend who identifies as otherkin and..."

"Wait," Jorge put his hand up in the air and shook his head. "What the fuck is otherkin?"

"It means you identify as like dragon, demons, animals," Sonny attempted to explain in a very matter-of-fact manner, while beside him, Andrew rolled his eyes. "I have one person who identifies as a cat..."

"Wait, what the *actual fuck?"* Andrew finally broke his silence. "A cat? Does this idiot lick his own ass too?"

To this, Tony groaned. Beside him, Jorge's head fell back in laughter.

"Well, it's not exactly like that," Sonny went on to explain, showing no concern for the reactions around the table. "I mean, she wears a tail and ears."

"It is interesting to me," Jorge cut him off. "That your generation enjoys taking on these identities, but do not seem to like to deal with the less pleasant side. For example, I am sure a cat would love to not have to lick their own ass and use a litter box, but the tail and ears are just...."

"Some weird, fucked up sexual fantasy," Andrew cut Jorge off. "Maybe licking their own ass is part of the intrigue."

To this, Jorge's head flew back in laughter again.

"No, you don't understand," Sonny grew flustered as he attempted to explain. "It's not like that. She deeply, in her *soul,* feels like a cat."

"Well, you know, deep in my soul, I feel much like a devil," Jorge sat forward and gave Sonny an intimidating look. "But I do not walk around with horns and a tail. I do not like the attention. Perhaps, your friend, she likes the attention."

"Well, she doesn't really identify as a *she* either," Sonny picked his words carefully. "I…"

"If I gotta talk about this fucked up shit," Andrew cut him off. "Then I'm not doing this motherfucking show. These people he's talking about need to be locked up in a padded room. They don't need attention. In fact, that's all they fucking want. Attention."

"Actually, my friend who identifies as a cat is quite bashful about it," Sonny attempted to explain. "She *used* to hide her tail in public because of society shaming her, but now she wears it with confidence. I'm quite proud of her."

To this, Andrew rolled his eyes, and Jorge's head fell back in laughter once again.

"It is….an *interesting* topic," Tony attempted to smooth things out. "But, I think this is more of a *political* show."

"Yes, unless Athas or one of these assholes in parliament starts walking around with cat ears and a tail," Jorge jumped in. "I do not see how it is relevant to this here show."

"Fair," Sonny nodded. "However, maybe in the future…."

"Let us hope not," Jorge shook his head. "Me, I think that your generation has too much time on their hands to think about such ridiculous things. If you had real problems, then you would not spend time on this nonsense."

"It's very *real* to some people," Sonny attempted to argue.

"It's fucking stupid, that's what it is," Andrew shook his head. "Can we talk about something relevant on our first show?"

"I have a topic for you," Tony jumped in, appearing happy to change the topic. He reached in a folder and slid a short report to both the young men while Jorge watched their reaction. "It's about an upcoming censorship bill that the government is trying to sneak through."

"Like fuck they will," Andrew shook his head, automatically rejecting it. "We live in a free country, don't we?"

"I don't know," Jorge countered. "Do we?"

Andrew thought for a moment and shrugged.

"Well, it says here," Sonny said as he examined the sheets. "It's to prevent online bullying and racism. I would think that's appealing to most people."

"Nah Nah," Andrew shook his head. "Because *who* decides *what* is racism and bullying? The goal post will keep fucking moving."

"Well, I don't know about that," Sonny said with a shrug. "I mean, I don't in general trust the government, but this seems to make sense. It even uses an example here about people and how they identify. I mean, I have friends who are bullied online, and even me, I've been bullied online. It's not necessary. And my friend who identifies as a cat...."

"Deserves to be fucking bullied online," Andrew complained. "For being stupid."

"No one deserves to be bullied," Sonny attempted to correct him. "I think you think that way because *you* are a bully."

"I think people are way too worried about being politically correct," Andrew continued. "You know what? That's real life! Being bullied happens. People need to be stronger and look after themselves instead of crying about it. There are bullies *everywhere.* At school, at work, in the subway, in stores, at the DMV, I don't care where you go, there's always a bully, and you gotta learn to deal with them."

"But this here society," Jorge jumped in. "It does not want that. They want us all holding hands and crying in a safe room."

"That reminds me," Tony turned to Jorge. "There's an employee asking...

"No," Jorge answered. "This here is a busy, fast-paced environment and very stressful. That is the nature of the job. We cannot have the entire staff in a safe room all day, or I do not have a business."

"In fairness, it will probably just be that loser," Andrew muttered.

"You are so mean and cynical," Sonny observed. "Maybe *you* need some psychiatric help, not my friend who identifies as a cat."

"No, your friend that thinks she's a cat," Jorge shook his head. "Needs psychiatric help. If my daughter came home today and thought she was a cat, I would hire the best fucking psychiatrist in Toronto. But I did not bring up my daughter to indulge in fantasy and silliness."

"See, I feel differently," Sonny spoke in a condescending tone.

"Can we get back on track?" Tony kindly suggested. "The first episode of *Raging Against the Machine* has to be on this censorship bill. Tom is going to talk about it in the news beforehand. You guys will follow up. I need you both to read all this carefully, then talk about it. Argue about it. You have to be like you are today, except maybe…you know, tone it down a tad."

"Why you looking at me?" Andrew observed that Tony's eyes were resting on him. "I'm an expressive guy."

"Just tone it down a *bit,"* Tony suggested. "I'm not saying you sedate yourself."

"Although that wouldn't be such a bad thing either," Sonny muttered.

"Hey, don't you worry about me," Andrew snapped. "I am fine how I am."

"Good, so we are all on the same page?" Tony asked.

"I think this here will be fine," Jorge nodded. "I think this will be a good show. I think people will like it. The regular HPC news is already doing very well."

"So, we will do a topic weekly," Sonny asked. "Whatever is going on at parliament hill?"

"Whatever we decide ahead of time that we will talk about," Tony nodded. "This week, it will be this, and hey, you know, we might be talking about it regularly while bringing up whatever else is in the news at the time. It's an hour for you two to duke it out and say what you think. But keep it professional."

A knock at the door was a welcomed interruption for Jorge, who was growing bored.

"Come in," He called out.

The door opened, and Diego stuck his head into the room.

"What are you doing here?" Jorge asked his associate, who examined who was sitting at the table, his eyes landing on Sonny.

"Who's this guy?" He pointed at the new edition. "Ain't that the guy…

"That I did an interview with last year," Jorge finished his sentence. "*Si.*"

Of course, Diego knew about the interview that was at gunpoint. Word got around.

"Oh yes," Diego nodded, giving Sonny another long look.

"Diego, what is it you need?" Jorge asked, quickly wishing he had worded his question differently. "Why are you here?"

"I gotta talk to you," Diego grew serious as he leaned back.

"I am done here," Jorge stood up and headed for the door. "Tony can take care of the details."

After they were out of the room and down the hallway, Diego's questions began.

"What is that guy's name again?" He asked. "So, he's working with us? Can we trust him? What's his background? He's cute. How old is he?"

"He knows better than not to be trustworthy," Jorge answered one question and decided to ignore the rest. "What you doing here, Diego?"

"I gotta talk to you about something."

"What?" Jorge shook his head. "You left work on a Monday morning to find me?"

"I was out anyway," Diego shook his head. "I stopped at the bar…"

Jorge gave him a look.

"I wasn't drinking," Diego insisted. "I had to talk to Chase about something and thought you might be there. And he said you were but came here…"

"Ok, I see," Jorge nodded. "What's up, Diego?"

"I got something kind of important that I stumbled on."

"Ok," Jorge said as the two headed toward the main exit. "What you got?"

"Jolene," Diego started, and Jorge was already rolling his eyes. "She got married."

CHAPTER 28

"Sir, that did not show up when I was checking on her," Marco appeared hesitant to believe the news as he leaned back in his chair. "I checked her emails, text messages, everything and there was absolutely nothing indicating that Jolene was married."

Jorge remained silent but let out a loud sigh as he glanced around the VIP room at *Princesa Maria*. This was a drama that he did not need.

"I'm positive!" Diego went on to explain to a flustered Marco, who was shaking his head. "I'm telling you, she is staying at my house, and there's a couple of times I overheard things, but then I thought I misunderstood. You know, because Jolene, she talks loud when she's on the phone. I'd have to be *deaf* not to hear her."

"Can we get on with this here?" Jorge shook his head. "I have other things I would like to do today, and to be honest, Diego, unless she is married to a cop or someone she is going to tell our secrets to, I do not care what Jolene does."

"That's the thing," Diego shook his head as frown lines formed on his forehead. "We don't know, and the fact that she hid it from us makes me suspicious."

"Sir," Marco continued to shake his head as he scanned through something on his laptop. "I am not seeing anything to indicate that, but I am hacking into government records to see what I can find out."

"Diego, ok, let us step back," Jorge attempted to calm the room. "And go through this again."

A knock at the door interrupted them. Chase stuck his head in.

"Chase!" Jorge gestured for him to come in. "We just got here. Diego has an emergency that he wants us to address."

"I saw your cars when I got back…" Chase started to speak but was quickly cut off by Diego.

"Jolene's married!"

"Wh…what?" Chase appeared surprised as he entered the room and closed the door behind him. "To who? When did this happen?"

"I overheard her talking about being married on the phone," Diego rushed to explain. "I was gonna confront her but decided to talk to Jorge first."

"Sir, I think I found something," Marco's face turned red as he shook his head, causing Jorge to worry. "Sir, she got married during the time she was separated from the group."

"Wait? What?" Chase attempted to catch up to speed as he sat beside Marco and looked over his shoulder "Why would she hide it?"

"Why does she hide anything?" Diego ranted. "It's Jolene!"

"I would not have known," Marco shook his head. "There was nothing when I was investigating her at all. Maybe she knows we were spying on her?"

Jorge said nothing, his mind racing.

"Who's the guy?" Diego pushed ahead. "Anyone we know?"

"I am about to get to the name," Marco shook his head. "I'm in the government records. I must confirm something first."

Jorge watched with mild interest as Marco furiously tapped on his laptop, his eyes scanning the screen before hitting more buttons. Looking away, Jorge considered what this might mean to the group, as well as Jolene.

"Why don't we get her over here and make her talk?" Diego suggested. "*Make* her tell us what she's hiding."

"She will not talk," Jorge shook his head. "And the fact that she hide this, makes me worry what else is hidden away."

Jorge and Diego exchanged looks.

Marco stopped tapping and took a deep breath.

"You got something for us?" Jorge asked.

"I do, sir," Marco said in a defeated voice. "But you may not like it."

"I am used to not liking most of what Jolene does," Jorge replied in a tired voice. "What is it now? Does it involve the police?"

"No, sir," Marco shook his head. "At least it is not that. Just give me a moment to make sure I'm right."

Everyone fell silent.

"Sir, it looks like she is married to Enrique Blanco," Marco turned the laptop around to show Jorge the proof. "I guess when in Mexico, he divorced his wife, and when Jolene left the group, she got in contact with him again. It looks like they have an apartment in both their names."

Jorge took a moment to process the news.

"So tell me what I won't like," Jorge finally said as the others seemed to process the information. "Other than they both hide this from me."

"Sir, it's not that you would necessarily have a problem with the two of them being married," Marco went on. "It is the fact that she must have another phone, probably another email, so much she has hidden from us. That is the part that makes me suspicious. The fact that she made this effort concerns me."

"It concerns me too," Jorge said as he glanced at the screen.

"Jolene is *married,"* Diego seemed stuck on that fact. "And to that guy? They fought all the time!"

"Remember the fight here?" Chase pointed toward the door, indicating the club. "I thought they were going to destroy the whole bar!"

"They certainly tried," Marco said as he made a face. "What a mess!"

"I do not care about that part," Jorge insisted. "As you said, Marco, it is the secretiveness that concerns me. It could just be that she was no longer a part of the group and wanted to be private, but I do not have a good feeling about this."

"How would she even know that we were watching her at all?" Chase wondered.

"Because she knows me," Jorge insisted and took a deep breath, his thoughts racing in a million different directions. "Ok, well, Marco, maybe you and Chase can look into this. It may be nothing, but it does concern me. See if there is anything that alerts your attention. Diego, you do not let on anything. Just keep an eye on Jolene. See what she says. Is she talking about moving to Toronto?"

"She hasn't said anything one way or the other," Diego admitted. "I assumed..."

"Also, no one tell me that Enrique left Mexico," Jorge considered.

"Sir, it looks like he is back and forth. That might be why," Marco let him know. "I do not see issues from his side of things. He seems worried in his messages to his brother that you will find out. Let me see if he has messages to another phone used by Jolene."

Jorge bit his bottom lip and nodded.

"She wouldn't have another email and phone unless she got something to hide," Diego insisted, his lips twisting together.

"It may be because she did want me to know her private life," Jorge repeated his earlier thought. "Let us not jump ahead of ourselves. She would take these measures, so I do not learn about Enrique, but just in case..."

"We will look into it, sir," Marco insisted.

"You know," Chase shook his head. "That's probably all it is."

Jorge wasn't so sure.

He left the bar shortly afterward, deciding to head home to discuss it with his wife. She took the news with her usual poised manner.

"Of course, she's going to hide it," Paige calmly replied as she sat beside him on the couch. "She's terrified of you."

"But if she has nothing to hide," Jorge paused for a moment. "I do not understand."

"You just let her back in the group," Paige said with a shrug. "I'm sure she wanted to tread lightly."

"But new email and phone number?"

"That's probably because she was mad when you kicked her out," Paige considered. "So, she wanted to make sure you couldn't track her or what she was doing. It's not that surprising."

Jorge nodded but didn't reply.

"I don't *think* you have anything to worry about," Paige said, then paused for a moment. "But if she turns out to be clean, maybe it's time to let her go."

"I did, and she is back."

"No, Jorge, let her go," Paige leaned in and touched his arm. "With your blessing. Let her go. Let her live her life. Maybe her time with us is over."

Jorge didn't comment but watched his wife.

"She did a lot of work for you over the years," Paige continued. "Let her retire in peace. And speaking of retiring, I think it's time you slow down. I know I sound like a broken record, but you need to spend time here. You need to guide Maria into the future if you both still want her to lead the family. Miguel hardly sees you. It's time you slow down too."

"Paige, I need to keep busy," Jorge reminded her. "I want to keep on top of everything that goes on."

"Do it out there," Paige pointed toward the table beside the pool. "Have them come to you sometimes. Talk to them on video. Jorge, you work hard, and you never get to enjoy your life."

He considered her words.

"I'm not saying sit at home all the time," She continued. "But if you want Maria to lead, this is the summer to start working with her. This fall is going to be crazy with the book coming out, and if there's an election, I know you'll be tied up with Alec. Take the summer. Just this summer."

"Paige," Jorge reached out and touched her hand. "You make a good point. I worry..."

"Just dip your toes in," She leaned in. "Don't jump in with both feet. Even today, when you talked about this drama with Jolene, you couldn't have been less interested. That's Diego being dramatic, but chances are Jolene isn't doing anything wrong. Let Tony run the production house. Makerson is competent in the news section. Diego has got *Our House of Pot.* Someone's managing the crematorium. Everything is fine. Step back. If something comes up, we will figure it out. But for now, focus on your daughter. It's a crucial time even if she wasn't taking over the family someday."

Paige was right. It was time to put his attention where it really mattered.

CHAPTER 29

"I do not understand why she does not want a *quinceañera*?" Jolene slowly spoke as she shook her head. "I mean, you know, rather than another party. I do not understand.

Jorge didn't reply at first; he instead looked around the VIP room and avoided his wife's eyes. The discussion of the traditional party had surfaced a few times with no luck.

"Well, she's at that age," Paige calmly replied. "Teenagers can be unpredictable."

"And whatever you do," Jorge shook his head, attempting to act natural even though he didn't want to be having this meeting. "Do not bring it up to her. When I did, she yell that we are 'not in Mexico anymore' and rushed out of the room."

"This is sad," Jolene shook her head. "It is her culture. She must not forget where she come from."

The room fell silent, and Jolene's position stiffened.

"What did I do?"

"What?" Jorge was surprised by her question. "I did not say..."

"I know you talk to me before the group for a reason," Jolene pointed toward the door, where Diego and the others waited on the other side. "You are mad at me."

"Jolene, we know you are married," Paige jumped in. "We just don't understand why you hid it from us."

"I did not mean to hide," She looked away as tears formed in her eyes. "Please do not hurt Enrique! It is not his fault."

"That wasn't..." Paige started, but Jorge quickly cut her off.

"Why?" His voice was loud. "What did he do?"

"He is not always in Mexico like he tell you," Jolene said in a small voice as one tear ran down her cheek. "He still do his job. Please do not be mad at him."

"Is that it?" Paige asked. "Is there anything else?"

"This is your only chance to tell if it is," Jorge quickly followed up. "No more games, Jolene."

"There are no games," She shook her head as tears continued to fall down her face. "I promise. We start talking when you made me leave the group. He and his wife parted after he return to Mexico, but I did not know. He come to see me, and it was a beautiful time. We decided that we want to be together. I did not tell because I was scared how you would react."

Jorge took a deep breath. He did not want to have this conversation. He wanted to be home, by the pool, playing with his son.

"Please," Jolene suddenly grew hysterical. "Please do not kill me! I promise I did nothing wrong."

"Jolene, calm down!" Jorge snapped.

"Jolene, we aren't saying that," Paige was quick to add.

"I was upset when you make me leave," She continued to cry. "I was so hurt. I felt so alone. I thought you might spy, so I got another phone and..."

"Jolene," Jorge put his hand up in the air, indicating for her to stop. "Enough! Please! This here is enough."

"We know about the email and phone," Paige confirmed. "We know you didn't do anything wrong."

"You do?" Jolene appeared surprised. "Then why this meeting?"

"Jolene," Jorge spoke slowly, attempting to be calm. "We think that it is time that you retire from the family."

"But I did not do anything wrong!" Jolene started to cry hysterically once again.

"No, Jolene, you aren't being forced out of the group," Paige corrected her. "This isn't like last time. What he means is you've done a lot of great work for us, and we thank you, but we see that your life is taking a different turn, and we respect that."

"Oh…" Jolene appeared shocked as she processed their words.

"We want you to leave *peacefully*," Jorge added, unsure of the correct wording. "So you can continue your life with Enrique. You can still reach out to us for help, and maybe, from time to time, we will do the same. But for the most part, you have no obligation to us, and we have no ill feelings toward you."

"Yes," Paige agreed. "It's just time."

"I, myself, will be stepping back too," Jorge added. "So, this here, it is not just for you."

"Stepping back?" Jolene asked as she wiped a tear away. "Why?"

"I must focus on my children," Jorge replied. "I will get more into this when the others join us."

"Oh," Jolene appeared dazed by the news as she glanced between Jorge and Paige. "I did not expect this."

"Things, they are changing," Jorge replied. "This, we must accept."

Shortly after, once the group gathered at the table, Jorge took a moment to observe all the faces. The strongest of members, like Diego and Chase, appeared worried. He then casually glanced toward Andrew, Makerson, Tony, and Marco. It was rare that everyone was together in one meeting. There was a sense of concern that filled the room.

"I wanted to get everyone here together today," Jorge said as he looked briefly at Jolene, who appeared calm, relaxed, with a sense of peace in her eyes which made him wonder if he could feel the same way. "Because I have an announcement, and then later, Jolene also has something to share with you."

"This seems…serious," Chase observed as he seemed to sink in his chair.

"I would not say this, no," Jorge shook his head.

"Nothing's wrong," Paige quickly picked up on the vibe of the room.

"No, it is not like that," Jorge agreed with his wife. "I call you together because this summer, I will be spending a lot of time at home with my children. I want to continue teaching my daughter how to one day lead my family. I want to spend time with my son. I, of course, will still be available to everyone, but I will not be running from place to place every day, as I usually do. I will still be available to you for help or questions, but I want to conduct as much business as possible beside my pool, enjoying the summer."

The table fell silent.

"Are you like, dying or something?" Andrew finally broke the silence. "Like, because that's not like you."

"No, at least, I do not think," Jorge said and laughed. "But I think that maybe it will be a busy fall, so it is good that I take some time to relax this summer."

"With the book coming out," Makerson jumped in. "Our publisher will keep us busy."

"This here is for sure," Jorge agreed. "And if there is an election too."

"Do I even want to know what you're teaching your daughter?" Andrew boldly asked.

"Everything I know," Jorge replied as he raised an eyebrow, causing Andrew's eyes to widen.

"So, nothing's wrong?" Chase showed concern.

"No," Jorge assured him. "It is just me, finally listening to my wife, that is all."

There was some laughter around the table.

"This ain't gonna last long," Diego smugly predicted. "I give you two weeks."

"We will see, Diego," Jorge admitted. "I have not spent much time relaxing over the last 20, probably 30 years. So it will be different for me."

"It's needed," Paige insisted. "We all need a break sometimes."

Jorge noted that Paige and Jolene shared a look.

"I think we can run things pretty smoothly on our end," Makerson said as he glanced at Andrew, who nodded. "We'll continue to send you previews, that kind of thing if you want?"

"Oh yes!" Jorge insisted. "I want to see those."

"I got one for you today," Andrew casually spoke as he sat back in his chair. "For *Raging Against the Machine.* I gotta give you credit, I didn't think me and Sonny would be able to pull this show out of our asses, but it's working. We went live to tell people about it and got a lot of attention."

"Likes, shares, retweets," Tony jumped in. "And they have good onscreen chemistry. They play off each other in a way that makes it entertaining and draws people in."

"I wouldn't go so far to say *chemistry,* but we got something," Andrew nodded. "I predict things might get heated when we run into certain topics."

"People are subscribing to their channels," Tony continued as he pointed toward his closed laptop. "The numbers keep going up."

"Let me see what you got," Jorge said.

"Sure," Tony opened his laptop and started to hit buttons. "I'll start with the teaser video that we put out…."

"Is there anything else that I need to know while he finds it?" Jorge glanced around the table. "Anything?"

"Business is good at my end," Diego nodded.

"Same," Chase added with some emotion in his eyes. "It will be weird you not stopping by all the time."

"I will be, sometimes," Jorge replied. "Just not every five minutes, like I do now."

Chase grinned and nodded.

Jorge glanced toward Jolene to see if she wanted to say anything, but he could tell by the look in her eyes that she was still processing everything, so he left it alone.

"Here it is," Tony turned the laptop around and pulled it back so the whole table could see. "Or should we hook it up to the big screen?"

"Nah," Jorge shook his head. "This is fine."

Hitting the button, Andrew came to life on the screen.

"Check out our debut on July 20th," Andrew spoke into the camera. Sonny stood back, wearing a shirt and tie. He was nodding as his costar continued to talk. *"Your online rights are being taken away! Are you going to stand for it?"*

A loud, aggressive song began to play as Andrew spoke faster, erratically, continuing to rant into the camera.

"If the government has their way, you'll give them away. Is that what you want? Is that the kind of country you want to live in? Do you want to be the government's bitch? Cause it's not going to stop there!"

This was when Sonny moved in, his face right in the camera.

"Know your rights! Know what's really going on. Don't stick your head in the sand. You need to take a stand now!"

The screen went black and the music suddenly stopped as the words *Raging Against the Machine* appeared in white letters.

"Wow, this here, I like!" Jorge nodded in approval. "This here is perfect!"

Andrew nodded with pride.

"And we've only just begun," Makerson said while Jorge glanced around the table again. Truer words had never been spoken.

CHAPTER 30

"So, the bill has been blocked?" Jorge asked for confirmation as he pushed his sunglasses up and tilted his head to look at Paige. "This here censorship will not happen?"

"For now," Paige reminded him as she sat down beside him and glanced toward the pool. "But the problem is that it will return in the fall."

"Unless Athas, he calls an election," Jorge added as he reached for his coffee, ignoring his phone when it buzzed. "This is what you mean?"

"Well, the problem is that people assume it was Alec's idea," Paige reminded him as she leaned in Jorge's direction. "So they will hold it against him."

"But it was, you know, those shit stains in his party," Jorge nodded. "It was not him that decide we should censor things on the internet. As *if* he has that kind of power."

"But that's the problem," Paige added. "People assume the prime minister has all the power, when in fact, he's often clueless about what his people are doing."

"Paige," Jorge shook his head. "He *chooses* to be clueless. He does not keep on top of things. If I did not keep on top of things in my organization, it would be the same. But I do, and I make my people aware of this, but Athas, he's a fucking pussy who lets everyone else run the show. Then he turns around and shrugs his shoulders like he does not know anything happened."

"I don't think…."

"Paige, you must stop defending this man and see him for who he is," Jorge reminded her. "He is a pussy, and he does not want to deal with anything. This is the real problem, and I am starting to have second thoughts about him running in the next election."

"But, if he doesn't run…" Paige stopped mid-sentence.

"Paige," Jorge shook his head. "This is part of the reason why I rest now. I may have to be the next prime minister and clean up his messes."

"Jorge!" Paige's eyes widened as she leaned in, her voice full of tension. "We talked about this before, and you can't do that…plus, you can't just step in and…"

"Paige, I may have to," Jorge shook his head. "If Athas does not want to be a man and take care of things, then I must do it. And I assure you, this here party knows I can win, and that is all they care about. They will make it happen."

"But if you're in the public eye…"

"Paige, I know how you feel about this," Jorge shrugged, and he pulled his sunglasses back down and looked away. "But it may have to happen. It seems impossible that so many things happen right under his nose, and he does not see. I am sure some things are hidden, but come on! It has been so much!"

"But why do you have to be involved at all?" Paige shook her head. "Is this just about the power?"

"Paige, if the wrong person gets in there," Jorge shook his head. "They will make trouble for me. I have a lot of enemies, and Big Pharma owns most of these here politicians. I need to keep someone with my interests in that position, and who is better than me to do it?"

"Someone who knows the political system better?" Paige suggested.

"You!" Jorge turned to his wife and lifted his sunglasses. "You can do it!"

"No," Paige dramatically shook her head. "There is *no* way!"

"Well, then, there is just me," Jorge lowered his sunglasses again. "Unless Athas, he can get his shit together. I must talk to him."

"You know, maybe he's simply telling the truth," Paige reminded him. "He may not know everything going on in his party."

"Paige, I used to believe this too," Jorge shook his head. "But this time, I do not. He would know about this bill, and he could've spoke up, but he did not. They know they can walk over him."

Paige didn't say anything but looked away.

"I do not know," Jorge took a deep breath and leaned back on his chair. "But it is a possibility."

"Let's hope not," Paige muttered as she stood up. "Because we don't need this attention on you. Think long and hard about it."

"I will," Jorge smiled at her, and she seemed to lower her defenses. She leaned in and gave him a quick kiss before walking toward the patio doors and going inside.

In truth, the idea of getting mixed up in politics wasn't exactly exciting to Jorge, but winning was another story. And he would win. There had been rumbling on social media that an election was around the corner. And even more, rumblings that he would be throwing his hat in the race. This was what got him thinking, and yet, the task seemed pretty enormous to take on. But there was something about saying it out loud that brought it to life.

A shuffling noise alerted him, and Jorge looked up to see a crow sitting on the back of the chair across from him. He looked at the crow, who looked back at him, tilting his head slightly. Jumping on the table, the bird boldly walked toward Jorge's plate that had been pushed aside and grabbed a piece of bread before rising into the air and flying away.

"Take what you want," Jorge grinned as he relaxed again, reaching for his coffee. "That is what I always say."

He glanced at his phone and saw messages waiting for him. They weren't of importance, simply the others touching base. He would get to them later, or maybe not at all.

The sun was growing warmer as he finished his coffee and considered laying on the lounge chair and taking a nap. It was 8:45 in the morning.

The patio door slid open, and Maria walked out with a cup of coffee in her hand.

"*Papá,* it is so weird seeing you sit out here."

"Well, Maria, it is my house, so it is not weird," Jorge teased her.

"You know what I mean!" Maria insisted as she walked over and sat beside him. She placed her coffee on the table. "You're usually gone before I even get out of bed."

"It is the summer, Maria," Jorge insisted. "I plan to enjoy it for a change."

"I thought you were taking it off to work with me."

"That too," He agreed. "There are many things that I wish to do. I want to look at the property where we are working on the safe house. I want to prepare for the fall when I have my book coming out. And of course, to spend time with my family. You know this here is important to me."

"I know," Maria dramatically swung her hand in the air. "I mean, you always talk about slowing down, but you never do."

"Things come up," Jorge replied. "But Maria, it is important to take time to ourselves."

"That doesn't sound like you at all," Maria insisted, causing Jorge to laugh.

"Well, you know, I am getting older, Maria," Jorge reminded her. "Sometimes, this here gives us perspective."

"I don't know if that's true," Maria shook her head. "Some people have a mid-life crisis. Look at Diego!"

"Oh, well, Diego is another situation altogether," Jorge reminded her. "And we do not know."

"He's dating a *much* younger guy," Maria reminded him. "Unless it's just a casual fling, but Chase said he probably wants to be a sugar daddy. That's gross."

"Well, Maria," Jorge shook his head. "People always want power and in many different ways. Let that be your first lesson this summer. For Diego, this imbalance of power makes him feel more in control. That is why you see much older men with much younger, well, women, men, whatever they choose."

"I thought they were just old perves," Maria flatly commented, causing Jorge's head to fall back in laughter.

"Well, this here, it could be true too," Jorge continued to laugh. "But it is a power move. Do not let anyone try to tell you otherwise. They may not know, but it is for power, for control."

"But not always," Maria pointed out. "Like say, I don't know when I get older if I were to date….Chase, for example…"

Jorge kept a straight face, knowing about his daughter's ongoing crush on Chase Jacobs. It was innocent, but it sometimes concerned him.

"Well, Chase," Jorge cut her off. "He is only, maybe 10 years older than you. So, Maria, that is not quite the same. Diego, he is a man in his forties dating someone who is around 25. So that is a huge difference. That is a man's lifetime in the difference."

"It is, isn't it," Maria considered. "He's *literally* old enough to be his father. That's kind of gross."

"But Diego, he is young at heart," Jorge reminded her. "And he has money."

"Where did he meet that Sonny guy, anyway?" Maria asked with interest as she reached for her coffee. "Oh wait, he works for you, doesn't he?"

"He is on a show with Andrew," Jorge reminded her. "And Diego, he see him at the production house, and that is where it began, I guess. But Maria, the point is that it is a power game."

"Because he's so much older," Maria nodded and took a drink of her coffee, continuing to hold it close to her lips.

"Everything is a power game," Jorge reminded her.

"Even like, dating relationships?" Maria asked.

"Well, not the successful ones," Jorge replied. "As you can see with Paige and me, we are balanced, and that is one of the reasons why it works."

Maria nodded.

"But this is often not the case in relationships," Jorge went on. "Whether it be dating or otherwise because people are mostly weak and weak people, they seek out people who are strong."

Maria nodded as she took in his words.

"That is why," Jorge continued. "You must be the strong one. The weak seek out the strong to lead them. If you don't do it, someone else will and trust me, Maria, that's usually not the best idea. In the end, it is always beneficial to be the powerful one. It is always beneficial to take control.

After a while, people automatically look to you, even if you are, say, sitting by the pool after telling them you are taking a break."

Maria glanced at the phone as the constant alerts popped up.

"And that is what you want," Jorge reached for his phone while grinning at his daughter. "For them to know that they *need* you."

Her brown eyes watched him with interest as she took in the information.

It would be a life-changing moment for her.

CHAPTER 31

Her father taught her so much, and she was eager to learn.

Even as she sat across from him that morning, Maria listened carefully to his wisdom. While many kids her age scoffed at the idea of hearing what their parents had to say, let alone listen to it, Maria knew better. In her eyes, Jorge Hernandez was not only her *Papá* but the most powerful man in the world. She had seen it. She knew it was true. She wanted to be like him.

But as much as she took these lessons and attempted to apply them, she was clumsy at best. She could walk confidently through the hallways of her school, but once under the powerful eyes of other kids in the classroom, Maria felt herself turn to mush. Even though she had a lot in common with them, it was during these times that she saw the differences. Maria struggled to keep afloat in a world that was trying to drown her with their eyes. In essence, nothing had changed since she lived in Mexico. The kids here also heard rumors about her father. They knew how he made his money.

Maria was proud of her *Papá*. She wished people recognized the good things he did rather than listen to the rumors. Maybe the book that Tom Makerson wrote would set the record straight. Although she knew that Paige worried it might open a pandora's box, her father remained confident that it would set the record straight. Maria wasn't so sure.

"But *Papá*," She nervously fidgeted in her chair as she glanced toward the pool, in order to avoid his eyes. "I don't understand how to be strong. I try...."

"Maria, this here, it does not happen overnight," Jorge admitted as he leaned in as if they were about to share a secret. "Do you think when I was young, that I always felt strong? That I always felt confident?"

"Well," She began to answer. "I mean, yes, I thought that you..."

"Not at all," Jorge cut her off as he leaned back in his chair, and they shared a smile. "We are clumsy when we are young. We are brought up to feel powerless, weak. My parents, you know, they did not want me to be powerful. They wanted to control me. They wanted me to feel shame when my brother died. But it was their contempt, their hatred for me, that made me stronger."

"Did they really hate you?" Maria asked, but automatically thought about when her grandparents were alive. There was no love in their eyes when they looked at their son. "I mean, how does that make you stronger?"

"Because, Maria, when someone pushes you," Jorge reached out and gently tapped her arm. "You have a decision to make. Will you allow them to keep pushing you until you fall to the ground, or do you stand powerfully? Do you push back? It is a decision you make, and it is a decision that can change your life. If others see you pushed around, they will do the same."

She thought about his words. He was right. He didn't know how many times kids at school had attempted to pick a fight with her, but she decided to walk away. They hadn't stopped, but it escalated. Maria wasn't sure why she could take on an adult man who once broke into their house, but not kids her age. She couldn't tell her father.

"Maria, I promise you," Jorge continued. "That it is true, what they say. They say that you teach others how to treat you. You cannot let anyone push you around. You must stand firm. You must be the powerful one. One slip and this here can change everything."

Not knowing what to say, she nodded.

"Maria, this is why I put you in self-defense," Jorge continued to speak. "This is why I tell you how powerful you are, and it is not just words. I say it because it is true. But Maria, you have to believe it, or it does not matter how many times I say this here."

She nodded and fought the tears on the verge of breaking through.

"If you think with a powerful mind," Jorge said as he reached for his coffee. "It will change your entire life."

He was right.

It did.

The first time was minor. It was a response to a nagging message from a relative, back in Mexico, who continued to harass her that she had to have the traditional *quinceañera* to mark her change to womanhood. Maria had kindly attempted to tell her that she didn't wish to have such a party, that it was too old-fashioned and didn't appeal to her. She was told repeatedly that this would be a regrettable decision since it was such a wonderful ceremony, that was a part of her heritage.

I'm not having one. Don't ask me again. This is my final decision.

Maria felt her heart race as she completed the text and set the phone on her bed. She nervously waited for an argument, unsure how to react. It was one thing to make one strong statement, quite another to back it up, to hold firm to what you believe. This was the part she hated. This was the same anxiety that swept over her entire body every day at school.

When the response finally arrived, Maria peeked nervously at her phone.

Ok, Maria. I understand.

That was it? No more nagging?

Blinking rapidly, Maria looked in the mirror, noting the surprise on her face.

Maybe her father was right.

Maybe she was stronger than she thought.

The next day, she decided to text Chase. Maria had avoided him since the *incredibly* embarrassing moment when her bikini top fell off at the barbecue. He had come to her room after the fact to try to cheer her up, but that only made the entire thing even *more* humiliating. She canceled her work shifts because Maria couldn't look him in the eye. It didn't matter that he didn't see anything. That wasn't the point.

She had felt powerless, vulnerable in the moment. It sunk her to a whole new level. Her anxieties kicked in on high alert, and her thoughts flew about like erratic birds chased by a vulture. Her mind wouldn't stop screaming at her.

Hi.

Hi, Maria. Are you feeling better?

Thank you for not telling Papá that I haven't been coming to work.

I keep my promises, but Maria, you have nothing to be ashamed of.

I know that now. I want to return. I'm sorry, I was just very embarrassed.

You have nothing to be embarrassed about.

Did you ever have any embarrassing moments like that?

Maria, you have no idea how many embarrassing moments I've had like yours. Some way worse, especially when I was a teenager.

Really?

She felt a weight lifted off her chest, but a thought threw her off track again.

You're not just saying that to make me feel better?

No, Maria. I promise you. Everyone does.

I bet my father doesn't.

I bet he has. But he doesn't let it bother him.

I will be back to work tomorrow.

That's good. I missed having you around.

Maria's heart lit up as she read the comment over and over again. He missed her!

Taking a deep breath, she stood up and looked in her mirror. If only she wasn't so skinny! How could she be a *Latina* and have no curves? She was practically a *boy!*

Closing her eyes, she decided she couldn't think like that anymore. There were lots of pretty celebrity girls that was as skinny as her. Everyone loved them.

Opening her eyes again, Maria decided to go to the mall. She wanted to buy some padded bras. Why not? By the time she went back to school, the kids would think she filled out during the summer. Of course, that was weeks away, but she wanted to get used to it now.

Going downstairs, she noticed her father was talking to Paige by the pool.

"*...it's because you never had a chance to feel before because you never stopped...*" She was saying, but neither of them noticed her passing the patio door.

Quietly sneaking out the door, Maria felt excitement pass through her as she headed toward the bus stop, clutching her purse like a vigilant lady, as she stood tall.

Fuck everybody! She was going to go shopping!

Usually, she kept her head down, but Maria noticed that no one seemed to pay attention at the bus stop, nor later when she got on the bus. Everyone was staring at their phone. She found this fascinating. Didn't her father always say that people were so wrapped up in themselves that they barely knew what was happening around them? How pathetic. Maria considered this as she waited for the bus to arrive at the mall.

It was a long drive, too many stops, but Maria didn't care. It was an adventure. She'd slip in and do some shopping, then go home. Her parents wouldn't even notice she was gone. It wasn't like she was a *child.*

The bus turned a corner, and finally, the shopping center was in full view. People were waiting outside for their own bus, while Maria stood up with the others, preparing to get off. She was nervous as she did but pushed this emotion aside. What was the big deal? She was going shopping. Lots of people did this all that time.

Once in the mall, she took in the familiar sights and sounds: music blasting from various stores, inviting signs, and colors, images of models in the windows. Everything was so pristine, so inviting. She could smell an array of delicious scents from the nearby food court, causing her mouth to water. Maybe she'd get something to eat, but first, Maria wanted to get her new bra.

On her way to the store, which felt like miles away, she decided to stop at the washrooms. She was feeling a little warm and wanted to make sure she wasn't sweating. Her phone hadn't beeped, but eventually, her father would be looking for her and would text. Hopefully, she could get back before he did.

After going down a long, dark hallway, Maria entered a washroom full of a group on their way out. Relived when it cleared out, she wasn't so relieved when she spotted who was left behind.

"Maria Hernandez?" Teresa, a Latina girl from her school, was standing in front of the mirror. "What? Your big, rich *Papá* allows his little *Princesa* to leave the house without security?"

She heard laughter and noticed Teresa's Asian friend giggling as she came out of a stall and stopped to wash her hands. Her heart began to pound furiously, as heat swept over her body. This girl *hated* her. She considered running, but her feet wouldn't move beneath her.

A glance toward the stalls showed her they were alone in the washroom. She shouldn't have chosen this particular bathroom, but it was usually the least busy because it was out of the way. Her father warned her to avoid getting in a vulnerable situation. This was what he meant.

"Your narco father," Teresa continued as she walked toward her, and Maria wanted to cry. "Everyone back in Mexico knows what he is about. He's *El diablo,* but you, you are nothing. I am not scared of you..."

Teresa lurched forward and gave her a shove. It was at that moment that something snapped in Maria. She felt a fury like never before as her father's words flowed through her mind, while her self-defense caused her to instinctively swerve then, with all her strength, grab Teresa, twisting her arm, she knocked her to the ground. It was as if she were taken over by an animal when she stomped on the girl's hand, causing her to cry out. It happened so fast, Maria couldn't believe what she had done.

The Asian girl let out a gasp, and Maria looked in her direction.

"You say anything," Maria pointed toward Teresa's friend. "And I'm coming for you next."

Teresa attempted to get up, and Maria stood back and pointed at her.

"And if *you* say anything," She said as their eyes met, but Maria didn't finish the sentence, but sent her a warning look.

There was an understanding between them.

Maria walked out of the bathroom. Her heart pounded, and she suddenly felt exhausted but exhilarated at the same time.

She decided to go home.

She'd buy her new bra online.

CHAPTER 32

"Maria, what would possess you to go to the mall without telling us?" Paige calmly asked her step-daughter while Jorge watched his Maria's reaction from across the kitchen table. "One of us would've dropped you off. You have to let us know what you're doing."

"I know," Maria nodded but showed no shame. "I wanted to do my own thing. I wasn't doing anything wrong."

"Maria," Jorge's voice seemed to startle her slightly, but she quickly regained her composure. "You know that this is not an average family. We must check in with each other to make sure we are always safe."

"I know," Maria nodded. "But, *Papá,* I was fine. Even when the girl from school tried to attack me..."

"What?" Paige cut her off, while at the same time, Jorge sat ahead in his seat.

"Maria, someone, they attacked you?"

"Well, she kind of tried," Maria spoke sheepishly. "But *Papá,* I fought back!"

Paige exchanged looks with Jorge.

"Maria, you mean you..." Jorge attempted to understand the situation.

"I fought back," Maria replied and sat up straighter. "She started to attack me, so I did my self-defense thing and knocked her on the floor."

Maria went through the motions as if she were reliving the moment.

"Then I stepped on her hand," Maria continued. "And told her to leave me alone."

Jorge was stunned.

"That's good…I mean," Paige hesitated. "Were there cameras around? People? Anything?"

"No," Maria shook her head. "It was the public bathroom at the back of the mall. I didn't see any cameras. They shouldn't be allowed in there, and no one except Teresa and her stupid friend was in the washroom."

Impressed, Jorge nodded.

"No one saw a thing," Maria continued, noting the expression on her father's face.

"They still could go to the police," Paige considered.

"They *won't,"* Maria insisted, causing Jorge's chest to fill with pride.

"Maria, this is a new side of you," Jorge observed. "I am quite proud that you stood up to these girls, but you still must be careful. You should not be going to these bathrooms that are out of sight, I've told you that before."

"I know," Maria nodded as she got up from the table. "I will know next time."

It was after she was back upstairs that Paige and Jorge shared a look.

"Do you believe this here?" Jorge spoke in a low voice. "I talk to her about being strong, and I am such a good motivator. I have changed her life!"

"Oh my God," Paige laughed. "What next? Do you want to start a motivational speaker business?"

"Well, Paige, let's face it," Jorge shrugged. "I could do this here."

"Maybe let this business idea slide," Paige suggested as she stood up from the table. "I worry that this will come back to bite her."

"I do not think that will happen," Jorge replied as he turned his phone back on. "My daughter, she is like a baby goat finding her feet. I am so proud."

Glancing at the messages popping up on his screen, Jorge reluctantly scrolled through them. Only one caught his eye.

"Paige, have you heard the phone in my office ring today?"

"The secure line?" She replied while opening the fridge door. "No, but I've been on the patio with you and upstairs too."

"It looks like Athas wants something," Jorge shook his head. "Does he not always?"

"Hopefully this doesn't mean more problems," Paige said as Jorge stood up and headed for the office.

"Is it ever anything but problems with him?" Jorge replied over his shoulder.

Entering the room, he sent a quick text message to Athas. Within minutes, his phone rang. Jorge abruptly answered.

"What the fuck do you want now, Athas?"

"I wanted to let you know that the pictures worked," Athas replied. "They backed off on the censorship bill, but I don't think we're out of woods yet."

"Are we ever?" Jorge complained. "Athas, you need to take a lesson from my *teenaged* daughter on how to be strong with people. Even she stands up more powerfully against her enemies than you."

Athas let out a loud sigh, and Jorge rolled his eyes.

"Look, what is it this time?" Jorge snapped. "What you got for me?"

"While it's true that they have backed off for now," Athas reminded him. "This is temporary because we're done for the summer, but there are hints it might be 'revised' and brought back up this fall."

"Did we not talk about this before?" Jorge asked. "This here possibility?"

"I think they have other things going on," Athas informed him. "I'm told, by a reliable source, that they want to create propaganda against HPC news and your production company in general. If they can discredit you, then people won't take anything you do seriously."

"Did they say how?" Jorge asked. "What we report is right, so I do not understand."

"I don't know," Athas replied. "This is second-hand information. But I get the sense that maybe it has to do with a source giving information that is bullshit. They will make sure it comes out that you reported it, as a way of showing that Hernandez Production Company produces tabloid type shows."

Jorge thought for a moment.

"I couldn't find out much…"

"You never can," Jorge reminded him.

"I know, but the sources I have are limited," Athas admitted. "I don't trust many people in my office."

"I wouldn't trust anyone in government," Jorge insisted. "Especially if I was you."

"It's funny," Athas said. "I thought the prime minister had the most power, but the longer I'm here, the more I see that I'm just the face representing the country."

"Athas, you are the mascot," Jorge said, then threw his head back in laughter. "I am sorry, but this here, it is true. They want you to look pretty, make the little speeches, which I assume someone else writes, then 10 other people approve, then do a few photo ops and call it a day. It's *not* a real job, Athas. Just something you get paid way more than you should, doing a lot less than you expect."

"I wouldn't exactly say..."

"You can say whatever you want," Jorge cut him off. "It does not matter."

"I might need help with something else."

"And what is that?"

"I think I got myself in a....precarious situation," Athas spoke nervously, causing Jorge's attention to be alerted, "With a woman."

"Oh, is this right?" Jorge grinned as he sat back in the chair. "Did you hire another hooker to *meditate* with you?"

"As I mentioned in the past," Athas attempted to explain. "She was supposed to help me with stress..."

"From the sounds of it," Jorge cut him off. "She helped you with a lot of stress. Who knew she would have to crawl under your desk to do that?"

"I...I thought, I mean, I was told she was supposed to teach me meditation," Athas attempted to explain. "I didn't know, and then..."

"Anyway, Athas, I do not wish to go through this again," Jorge cut him off. "So, it is not a hooker this time? Don't tell me you fell for that trick again? You know, you need to fire a lot of your staff, if you haven't already. I do not think I should have to mention that, but clearly, I *do.*"

"The staff involved in that situation was fired at the time," Athas assured him. "It was done discreetly."

"Sure, whatever, I do not care."

"This is a very different situation," Athas went on to explain. "There's a woman that I met at a function. We've been having an intimate relationship for the past few months."

"Is this so?" Jorge was slightly interested, but not really.

"She's kind of well known in my circles," Athas continued. "She's also in politics."

"So what?" Jorge rolled his eyes.

"The problem is she's married," Athas continued. "And her husband may have found out."

"Oh fuck," Jorge shook his head. "First, you tell me that you hook up with someone you more or less work with…have you not ever heard that expression, do not shit where you eat?"

"Well, that's where I meet the most people…."

"And also," Jorge cut him off again. "You pick a *married* woman. Are you not at least discrete about these matters?"

"It wasn't supposed to go this far," Athas insisted. "I thought it would be a one-time thing."

"I think I like it better when you hired a hooker," Jorge shook his head.

"She's with the opposition party…"

"You know how to fucking pick them, don't you, Athas?" Jorge continued to complain. "What else? Is she also a minor? Transgender? Did you get her pregnant? Give her a sexual disease of some kind?"

"Look," Athas spoke up, ignoring Jorge's harsh return. "I just need for this problem to go away."

"What you want?" Jorge asked. "For me to kill her husband or her?"

"No, of course not!" Athas replied and lowered his voice. "Everything isn't always about murder, Hernandez."

"Then what you want?"

"I need your people to spin the story," Athas sounded defeated as he spoke. "To get her husband off my track."

CHAPTER 33

"I had this here dream that Athas was dead," Jorge informed Chase as the two sat in the VIP room of the *Princesa Maria*. "He was floating in my pool. I cannot lie. I was a little bit disappointed to wake up and learn that this was only a dream."

Chase's response was to look down and laugh.

"But you know," Jorge continued as he looked around the empty room. "Perhaps, this was a sign. I know, the more I work with the Athas, the less helpful he seems to be, but he sure brings me a lot of problems."

"I would hold off on killing him just yet," Chase recommended in his usual, good-natured way. "Plus, his replacement could be even worse."

"You know, Chase, it has crossed my mind that I could easily run for prime minister," Jorge said and took a deep breath. "Things would be very different if that were the case."

"I thought you considered it once and changed your mind," Chase reminded him. "You sent Athas in to do the dirty work."

"Well, unfortunately, it is only his personal dirty work that he seems to be doing," Jorge shook his head. "He is not doing enough for me, and quite frankly, I am getting frustrated."

"But would you seriously want the job?" Chase asked him as he sat back in his chair, watching Jorge. "I mean, really? And Paige, you know she'd hate the idea."

"I make her come around," Jorge insisted, then hesitated. "Eventually, I might. But the way I look at it, Chase, is I ran a successful cartel for years and managed to stay alive. I can do any fucking thing I want. Running this country, it cannot be much different."

"Sometimes I wonder," Chase muttered and grinned.

"This is why Athas, he is not that good at what he does," Jorge reminded Chase. "He is not a criminal. To run a country successfully, you must be able to present a certain image to the public while being a fucking gangster when the people are not looking."

"That sounds about right," Chase nodded. "Well, you got all that."

"And more," Jorge nodded. "And more."

Their conversation was interrupted when a knock came from the outside door. Chase rose from his chair to answer it, first checking the camera nearby. He let in Makerson and Tony.

"I thought you were spending your time by the pool," Makerson teased as he walked into the room with Tony in tow.

"These things, they do not always work out," Jorge replied as he watched the two men sit down while Chase locked the door and returned to his seat. "I have something that I needed to address in person. Some things, as you know, you cannot do over the phone or through technology."

"Speaking of which," Tony took out his phone and turned it off. "I kind of welcome a few minutes without it beeping."

"Mine's off," Makerson said to Jorge as he turned his chair slightly. "So, what's up? Did you get a lead for us? I heard the crew in Ottawa are on vacation till the fall, so I take it the censorship bill is pushed aside?"

"Probably hoping we'll forget about them," Tony suggested as he moved his chair in closer to the table. "Or shift them around a bit in the fall and slide them through."

"Well, this here, it might happen," Jorge shook his head. "But there may also be an election this fall, and if this here is the case, a lot could change very quickly."

"Do you think Athas could get back in?" Tony asked. "He's going down in the polls again."

"The polls, they mean nothing," Jorge reminded him. "They are a random group of people asked questions, which are usually slanted, so the answers are unreliable. We have to make sure he is voted in or, if not, a reasonable alternative."

"Any thoughts of who?" Makerson pushed as he leaned toward Jorge.

"Let us not worry about it at this time," Jorge suggested. "We have more pressing issues we must address."

"Ok," Tony nodded. "Does this have to do with HPC?"

"Yes, unfortunately, the wolves are out," Jorge said as he nodded. "And they think they smell blood, but they think wrong."

Tony and Makerson looked confused.

"They dropped the censorship thing for now," Jorge continued. "However, they want to find a way to discredit us, to make it seem that we are merely a tabloid organization, one that has nothing worthwhile to say. So, do not be surprised if you have someone at your door saying that they fucked an alien in a tent and had their love child because they want to make us look unreliable."

"Ah, yeah, that does make sense," Makerson nodded. "Discredit us before we get on our feet, so people stop paying attention before they start."

"The point is to pay careful attention to details," Jorge insisted. "That includes the *Raging Against the Machine* show because Andrew and Sonny, they may seem the most vulnerable. I would suggest you oversee everything carefully and warn everyone what might happen. Do not say where you heard, just that you *did* hear, and also, maybe make it clear that if anyone who works with us is involved, they will be gone."

Tony's eyes widened.

"Fired," Jorge clarified. "That is what I mean."

"Well, in their contracts, there's a section that states they must not knowingly report inaccurate news," Makerson reminded them. "However, we have some freelancers too, who haven't signed anything."

"Perhaps we should have our lawyers look into this," Jorge suggested. "I would pay close attention to what crosses your desk. And if a staff member is involved, I want to take care of it personally."

No one replied, but everyone nodded. They knew.

"Also," Jorge let out a frustrated sigh. "Fucking Athas, once again, he gives me headaches. It turns out he was having an affair with someone in the opposition party, who is also married."

"I did hear a rumor about that," Makerson quickly jumped in. "I figured it was because they publicly rip into each other over policies, so it was probably a joke."

"I do not know her," Jorge said. "He say Sheila something or another..."

"Ah, yeah," Makerson made a weird face and turned his phone back on. "Sheila Proctor-Wade. She's an interesting choice."

"Do I even want to know?" Jorge asked. "What is wrong with her?"

"Well, nothing is...wrong with her," Makerson said while continuing to make a face. "She's pretty aggressive and vocal."

"Do you think she does this to humiliate him?" Jorge wondered. "To turn this into a 'me too' situation or some shit like that?"

"I don't think that would work," Tony disagreed. "He's not really in a position of power over her."

"He's the prime minister," Jorge replied.

"Then everyone in the country could 'me too' him," Chase said with a shrug.

"And she's with the opposition party," Tony shook his head. "And well....

"And well what?" Jorge asked and glanced at Chase, who shrugged.

"I have no idea who this is."

"This is her," Makerson turned his phone to show Jorge a picture of a middle-aged redhead dressed professionally.

"I don't get it," Jorge shrugged. "She looks like a politician. Am I missing something?"

"Well, that's her *professional* pictures," Makerson grinned as he scrolled. "Then there are these pictures involved in a scandal last summer."

He turned the phone around to show the same woman wearing a thin bikini on a beach. Her voluptuous figure was prominently displayed. Even Jorge found himself taking a double-take.

"Ah! Now I see why the affair started," Jorge nodded as he continued to look at the screen. "And maybe why it has continued. I think I remember this here."

Makerson grinned. "It was quite a scandal last summer."

"I guess this lady," Jorge finally looked away. "She likes the attention?"

"Anyone who wears a thin, white bikini in public probably isn't looking to avoid attention," Makerson predicted. "Maybe she *intended* to get caught."

"I can't see this doing much for her political career," Chase suggested as he also gave a long look at the picture.

"That's the thing," Makerson jumped in. "When people tried to shame her, she turned it around. Said it was discriminatory because she was a woman in power. I forget what all she said, but it somehow disappeared from people's minds by the fall."

"Not everyone's mind, apparently," Jorge grinned as Makerson turned off his phone. "Do not tell me that Athas *accidentally* bumped into *that* woman at a function. This here, I do not believe."

"Well, they work in the same building," Makerson reminded him. "But they do have a lot of functions. More like dog and pony shows, if anything."

"Overpriced meals for charity or some crap," Chase added. "I'm assuming."

Jorge raised an eyebrow and nodded.

"So, now what?" Makerson asked. "He thinks it's about to be leaked or something?"

"He thinks the husband is about to find out," Jorge replied. "But you already said that you heard rumors?"

"Yeah, but I hear a lot of things," Makerson shook his head. "There was no evidence to back it up…at least, not that I'm aware of."

"You know," Tony said and thought for a moment. "I thought I heard a rumor too. Are she and her husband divorcing?"

"I do not know," Jorge shook his head.

"Nah, I haven't heard that," Makerson shook his head.

"Athas was concerned that it was about to get out," Jorge said. "He says some reporters were poking around from *your* old paper, Makerson."

"*Toronto AM?"* Makerson made a face. "Yeah, they are becoming more tabloid these days. Whatever sells papers, I guess."

"So, what do we do?" Tony asked. "We can't stop the rumors, can we?"

"We gotta do what politicians always do," Jorge reminded him. "When people start looking in one direction, we start a fire on the other side to make them forget what they saw."

"What kind of fire are we talking about here?" Makerson cautiously asked.

"The best kind," Jorge replied with a grin.

CHAPTER 34

"It's not exactly something you wanna put on your dating profile," Diego reminded Jorge as he leaned in and wrinkled his nose. "If you know what I mean."

"Well, Diego, there is a lot that you maybe do not want to put on your dating *profile,"* Jorge mocked him, briefly lifting his sunglasses and shaking his head before pushing them back down and glancing at the nearby pool. "But tell me this, do you want to be a sugar daddy?"

"I...it's my thing," Diego spoke defensively and pulled back. "I like younger men. I find..."

"You have control?" Jorge asked with interest.

"They have that...I don't know, a slightly naive view that is kind of refreshing," Diego attempted to explain himself, turning his head to glance toward the screen door and then back again. "Someone who is not part of the life."

"Well, Diego, you must remember that just because he is not part of the life," Jorge said and paused for a moment. "He may be close enough to the fire to realize that things get a little bit hot at times."

"Don't worry," Diego shook his head. "I know what you're thinking. He won't learn anything we are doing."

"Diego, Sonny is a reporter," Jorge reminded him. "We must be careful with him."

"But he works for you."

"Yes, but this here, you never know," Jorge shook his head. "People, they can be disloyal."

"I know how you feel about loyalty."

"As I always say," Jorge nodded. "Loyalty above all. There are no exceptions. I teach this to my daughter every day. And this man, he must know this as well, or we will have a problem."

"Like I said," Diego assured him. "He knows nothing. Plus, he's excited to be working for you, not just sitting behind a computer doing a podcast at home. So, why would he fuck that up?"

"Diego, people, they do stupid things sometimes," Jorge reminded him. "But this one here, we will keep an eye on. I have Marco on it. But you must also watch."

"I will," Diego assured him. "Trust me. I know what I'm doing."

"I hope so because Diego," Jorge shook his head. "Do not let your dick rule this situation. I cannot have this here happen. We must always be vigilant."

"You know I'm careful…"

"Diego," Jorge cut him off and shook his head. "I am old enough to remember when this wasn't the case."

Diego closed his mouth and looked down. He was referring to a situation a couple of years earlier. It did not end well for the man in question.

"This is different," Diego finally spoke. "I promise."

"I hope so," Jorge spoke earnestly. "Keep this one in a bubble. Only let him see what he needs to see. You cannot reveal anything."

"As if I would!"

"Diego, I am serious here," Jorge reminded him again. "We cannot have any leaks. None."

Their meeting was about to end when the patio doors slid open, and Marco stuck his head out.

"Good morning, sir," The Filipino smiled brightly, nodding toward Diego. "Would you like me to wait inside?"

"That's fine, Marco," Jorge said as he started to stand. "We are finished here."

"I gotta get to the office," Diego sprang from his chair. "I have a busy morning."

"We will talk later," Jorge said as he followed Diego toward the door, where Marco stood aside and waited. "Just remember what I say."

"I got it," Diego nodded as they walked back into the house. "Don't worry."

After Diego left and Jorge was sitting in his office with Marco, they got down to business.

"So that there," Jorge pointed toward the door. "It was me talking to Diego about his new boy toy. I hope he is cautious when picking his boyfriends, but I guess it would not matter. We must always watch."

"Sir," Marco shook his head as he sat his laptop bag down. "So far, I am seeing nothing that concerns me. I think Sonny is just pleased to have the job, but he finds Andrew annoying."

"We *all* find Andrew annoying," Jorge replied, and Marco laughed. "It is who he is but the people they like him when he does the show. He gets people fired up, and this is what we want."

"Yes, sir, that is for sure," Marco said and took a deep breath. "I would not worry about him at this time, but I am keeping an eye on his emails and text messages. He seems quite taken with Diego."

"An older man with money, I bet," Jorge nodded. "He could live a good life with Diego. That is unless he sees too much and decides to talk."

"I do not have any reason to think this will happen," Marco replied. "At least, not yet."

"So, Marco, what else you got for me?" Jorge asked. "Have you looked into this Sheila Proctor-Wade character, or what?"

"She is a very…interesting character, sir," Marco nodded. "I have much information about her."

"Do tell," Jorge grinned and leaned back in his chair.

"Well, sir, this affair with Athas," Marco said. "It is not her first. I see that she used to be quite overweight, and since losing the weight, she has been more comfortable with her body, I guess you would say."

"I saw the bikini pictures, Marco," Jorge nodded. "She seemed very comfortable."

"Sir, that is one of the…less promiscuous pictures of her that I have seen lately," Marco's eyes widened. "For a woman who is in the public eye, especially in her job, I am surprised that she is so casual taking these pictures."

"Really?" Jorge raised an eyebrow. "You must tell me more."

"It often surprises me that people do not realize how easy it is to hack into their emails, to their text, messages....to their cameras..."

Jorge raised his eyebrow at the last comment.

"I have a video that will take attention away from any stories of this Sheila lady and Athas having an affair."

"Marco, do tell...."

"Sir, I can show you," Marco replied as he reached into his bag, grabbing his laptop. "But this video, it is with her husband."

"Was this here something she recorded or you caught?"

"I caught it, sir," Marco replied as his cheeks turned pink. "But it looks like they recorded it on purpose, so if it is released, it does fit the narrative."

"That she is a bit of a.....what is the word?"

"I think the word you are thinking of is exhibitionist," Marco guessed as he turned on the laptop that was balancing on his knee. "Although you could be thinking of other words, sir."

Jorge grinned as Marco pushed his chair forward and sat the laptop on the desk. A still image of a woman's naked back was on the screen. Marco touched a button, and the short movie came to life. Sheila Proctor-Wade was naked, straddling her husband with great enthusiasm, leaning back slightly, allowing the camera to pick up her breasts bopping around, while her husband's face was in clear view as he lay back on the bed. Marco turned it off.

"There are a lot," He seemed mildly embarrassed. "But this is just a sample."

"Interesting," Jorge suddenly felt his desires simmering. "So, it does look like maybe they recorded a sex tape of themselves. And if it gets out, this gives the impression that maybe this lady is more interested in starting a reality show than being a respectful member of parliament."

"Sir, this is something a young, immature woman would do for attention," Marco suggested. "It is highly inappropriate for someone older, in her position in government."

"And Marco, I have learned that she is one of the people behind this here bill that would create censorship laws," Jorge reported as he leaned back in his chair, his thoughts still on the naked woman in the video. "It was bipartisan, both sides working against Athas, which is interesting."

"Sir, this has been the case all along, has it not?" Marco said as he turned off the laptop and placed it back in his bag. "This does not sit well with me."

"It does not sit well with me either," Jorge confirmed. "But Athas is a pussy, so it does not surprise me either."

Marco laughed.

"We must monitor the rumors and maybe release this little movie at the exact, right time."

"Do you want to release it on your show?"

"No, I do not want us to seem like a tabloid show, which is what they want," Jorge thought for a moment. "I am sure there is somewhere out there that it can pop up and catch on fire quickly."

"This would be easy," Marco assured him. "You just say when."

"How much talk is there of Athas fucking this one here?" Jorge gestured toward the laptop bag.

"There is more, sir, but I would not say at a dangerous level," Marco replied. "But that can happen quickly."

"Let it just get out there a bit more," Jorge considered. "I do not mind humiliating Athas in the process, but then jumping in to release the tape, taking attention away."

"People still might talk about them, sir."

"Is there any proof out there?" Jorge asked. "Other than potentially her word?"

"I could find nothing, and I deleted all texts. Neither will see them on their phone."

"None backed up somewhere?"

"No, sir."

Jorge nodded as he reached for his phone. Turning it on, he sent a quick text to Athas, then turned it off again. His secure line rang within minutes. Jorge hit a button.

"Athas, you're on speakerphone," Jorge spoke curtly. "I am with Marco."

"Hello," Marco said.

"Hi," Athas spoke with caution in his voice. "What's going on?"

"What's going on," Jorge replied. "Is you are going to keep your dick out of the redhead and away from her. No text messages. All the previous messages are permanently deleted."

"I…ok," Athas appeared hesitant, confused, only causing Jorge to grow irritated.

"And," Jorge continued. "Marco has found some amateur porn of your girlfriend with her husband. If the rumor mill heats up, we are going to get it out there."

"I don't want to…"

"Athas," Jorge cut him off. "You wanted this problem fixed. You do not get to pick *how* it is fixed."

There was a pause.

"And further," Jorge continued. "If she says that you were together, there is no proof out there. Nothing. But I guess she will be so humiliated that it will not occur to her to speak of such."

"Actually, about that," Athas slowly responded. "I had a reporter ask my assistant about it today."

Jorge exchanged looks with Marco, who nodded.

"Then this here," Jorge continued. "will be taken care of."

CHAPTER 35

"It is our feeling here at HPC news that this is a private matter and is not something we want to dive into," Makerson spoke earnestly into the camera with gentle professionalism that was almost soothing to the viewer. *"However, we are left questioning why someone in such a powerful role in the Canadian government would put themselves in such a vulnerable position."*

Jorge's head fell back in laughter, and he clapped his hands together, startling Maria, who sat on the other side of his desk. Her eyes widened, and her mouth fell open as she watched the blurred-out still image of Sheila Proctor-Wade's exposed video. Her eyes returned to her father, who continued to look humored, as he watched her reaction.

"My only concern is that this reckless attitude is overlapping into our Canadian government," Makerson continued to speak, showing no expression. *"We aren't sure how this will affect Sheila Proctor-Wade's public life, but we will continue to monitor the story. We felt the need to say something since this scandal has taken over the news cycle for the past couple of days."*

Jorge closed his laptop and shared a silent look with his daughter.

"So, why would she do something like that?" Maria blushed as she asked. "That seems *so* embarrassing!"

"Maria, who knows why people do the things they do?" Jorge said as he sat back in his chair, studying her face. "But we must remember that when we are in a weak or vulnerable position, there is always a chance that it will come back to haunt us. We must make careful and good decisions so that does not happen."

"I…I would be scared of making a bad decision," Maria confessed.

"Maria, none of us are perfect," Jorge shook his head. "We sometimes make bad choices, but it is how we fix them. But a decision like this one that the politician lady made, how could she have thought this here was a good decision?"

Maria nodded her head. She continued to look nervous.

"Now, Maria, I have said that this summer, I would like to work with you," Jorge continued. "This here, I must remind you, is something you asked me to do. So, today is the first day."

Maria sat motionlessly.

"That there book you have in your hand," Jorge gestured toward a red journal that Maria was holding. "This will be your notebook. It is important that whatever you put in it, no one sees."

She nodded again.

"Now, I want you to open it," Jorge instructed her. "What do you see on the inside cover?"

Maria opened the cover and looked at the writing inside.

"It says, *Loyalty above all. There are no exceptions,"* Maria read and looked up. "You always say that."

"Because Maria," Jorge leaned back in his chair. "It is *always* true. The minute someone shows they are not loyal is the minute you must remove them from your life. You can tolerate mistakes, arguments, you can overlook a lot, but a disloyal person has no room in your life, especially in our world. A disloyal person can cause many problems. Once someone has proven they are disloyal, they are gone."

She nodded.

"Now, the second rule," Jorge gestured toward the book. "Is that you must always make sure that people know you are in charge, that you are the powerful one. If you do not do this, people will start to run wild or try to take over. This here, you do not want. I fear that when you that over, you will have challenges because you are a young lady. Some men do not want to take instructions from women, especially if the woman is younger or attractive. I am not saying this here is right. I cannot lie, I have been sexist in my day, that is how I know that this is something you will most likely deal with."

Maria nodded, swallowing hard as if fearful.

"But Maria," Jorge leaned forward on his desk. "Power has no size. It has no sex. As much as these men may try to discredit you, they will still fear you. A powerful man, they know what to expect. A powerful woman, they are never sure. But you cannot allow them to disrespect you, and the moment they do, Maria, you must make an example out of them."

"How do I do that?" Maria spoke nervously.

"This here, it is not for you to worry about yet," Jorge assured her. "It is something to keep in mind. I want you to see it as a challenge you must take on, but I do not want you to overthink it. Now, you must work on your confidence, your courage, and your strength. It will come more naturally if you do."

"Ok."

"But Maria," Jorge continued. "I will not lie. This will be your biggest challenge, and it is the one thing that concerns me, but together, we will resolve it."

"I understand."

"Now, we decided to start today," Jorge continued. "And you will follow me for some days to see what I do. As you know, I have been sticking close to home, but the work never goes away. I will give you some time every day to work with me. Today, this video, this here is your first lesson."

"Ok," Maria continued to listen carefully.

"That there woman in the video," Jorge pointed toward the laptop. "She is married and was also having an affair with Athas…"

"Really?" Maria asked as her eyes widened. "Wow!"

"Yes, Maria, but this happens a lot," Jorge continued. "Right there, what is the first rule she would be breaking if it was in our *familia*?"

"She isn't loyal."

"Someone who cheats like she did," Jorge continued. "Will do it again."

Maria nodded.

"If you one day are involved with a man who cheats," Jorge continued as he shook his head. "You must send him away because a cheater is a cheater."

"Have you ever cheated?" Maria asked with interest. "I won't tell if you did."

"Maria, when I was young, I did many things," Jorge admitted. "But I was often disloyal to women because I did not see them as a committed relationship in the beginning. In my mind, that meant that they had no reason to expect this of me. However, with Paige, I am married and therefore committed."

"I understand," Maria nodded.

"You see, Maria, this is a lesson in itself," Jorge continued. "Unless a man makes it clear that he is loyal to you, do not assume."

She nodded.

"Getting back to this woman in the video," Jorge continued. "I do not care what happens in her personal life. However, as I said, she was having an affair with Athas, and it was starting to leak out in the press. We had two choices. Either we eliminated the rumor, or we diverted attention. In this situation, I decided to divert attention. Of course, having this video that featured her husband made the rumors of her and Athas seem less likely."

"How do you know it was her husband?" Marias asked as she tilted her head.

"I saw the tape before it was released."

"Oh," Maria's eyes grew in size. "So, you…"

"Maria, as you know," Jorge said as he leaned back in the chair. "Athas, him and I work together, which means I help him out, and he, in turn, does what I want as prime minister."

"Ok," Maria looked overwhelmed with everything.

"When he has a problem," Jorge continued. "He comes to me. Recently, he came to me with this here potential scandal. I had to find a solution."

"How did you know about the…video?"

"Marco," Jorge continued. "He works in IT, but he is also very good at hacking."

"So," Maria appeared intrigued. "He hacked a computer?"

"He hacked *her* computer," Jorge replied and thought for a moment. "Maria, I know this here is a lot all at once…"

"I am fine, *Papá,*" Maria insisted. "I just realize that you…like, kind of rule the world."

Jorge's head fell back in laughter. This time, Maria started to giggle with him.

"Maria," Jorge shook his head. "I hardly rule the world, but I do have power over a lot of things."

"So," Maria thought for a moment. "You help Athas so that he helps you, and when he has a problem, he comes to you. Even a personal problem?"

"Maria, I could care less about his personal life," Jorge insisted. "I only help with this one because it affects his political life. This, in turn, could affect me. There may be an election this fall, so we must keep him shiny clean before that happens. People will forgive a terrible government. And they will forgive a government that wastes money or is involved in a scandal with taxpayer money. They will overlook *so* many things, but they will not overlook a man having an affair."

"Really?" Maria seemed intrigued. "That seems weird."

"It is because it is something close to home," Jorge reminded her. "If the prime minister of Canada is having an affair, it makes them angry because they do not want to think that their spouse might also be having an affair. They do not want to make it seem acceptable because maybe *their* spouse will also think it is acceptable. Maria, people are complicated, but at the same time, not really. They are basic, and they are fearful. No one wants their world shaken up and any celebrity having an affair feels personal to them."

"I guess..."

"Maria, it is strange," Jorge shook his head. "Athas, this woman, they can screw around with anyone they want. I could care less. But the average person, they care."

Maria giggled.

"It is our job to solve problems," Jorge continued. "But only to those who are loyal to us."

"Loyalty above all," Maria sang out.

"There are no exceptions," Jorge added. "So, as much as Athas and his life do not matter to me, I am obligated to help him because he has shown me loyalty."

"But what if he stopped?" Maria appeared intrigued, as she reached for a pen and turned the page of her book.

Jorge didn't reply. He merely raised his eyebrow and gave her a look.

CHAPTER 36

"That seems like a lot," Paige suggested to Jorge as he leaned in to kiss her neck as the couple stood over the bathroom sink. "Are you sure that you should be getting into all this with her? She's not quite 15 yet."

"My Maria, she is ready," Jorge said as he moved in closer, breathing in the fresh vanilla scent in her hair as his hands roamed underneath her robe. "As I am *mi amor,* I am ready for..."

"*Mama!*" Miguel's muffled voice was on the other side of the door. "*Papá!*

"Children are the best form of birth control," Paige teased Jorge as he moved away from her and glanced toward the door.

"Try sex control," Jorge muttered as he started toward the door. "This, we will continue later."

Paige winked at him in the mirror, causing him to smile as he reached the door and opened it.

"Miguel!" Jorge leaned in and picked him up. "*Buenos dias!*"

"*Buenos dias, Papá!*"

Jorge carried the little boy downstairs. He teased Miguel, who giggled along the way. At 3, his son was stuttering through his words, with fragmented sentences, but was speaking in two languages. It reminded Jorge of something that he would bring up to his daughter later that morning when she joined him in the office for a lesson.

"Maria," Jorge said as she sat in her usual chair on the other side of the desk from him, the red book in hand. "Something I thought of this morning is that you must make a point of speaking Spanish more often."

"I know, *Papá,* I am losing it…"

"Maria, it is important that you do not forget where you come from," Jorge reminded her. "When I come over here to Canada, I knew I had to improve my English…and in truth, it is still not good. But I also could not forget Spanish. The more you know, Maria, it is power. It always gives you an advantage."

"I get used to speaking English," Maria shrugged. "Everyone speaks English here."

"In this house," Jorge reminded her. "We speak Spanish too. Paige, me, Miguel, we speak Spanish."

"I know," Maria sadly nodded. "When Juliana was here, she spoke it all the time, but now that she's gone…"

"I know, Maria, I know," Jorge nodded. "But we must continue, or you will start to forget."

"*Papá,*" Maria said and paused for a moment. "I miss Juliana."

"We all do, Maria," Jorge gently replied. "She was a part of our family for a long time."

"It is so unfair."

"I know this too, Maria," Jorge nodded. "That is why my news channel exposed the truth about the medicine that she was taking. We publicly shamed and exposed the pharmaceutical company that made it. It is important to respect our dead and their legacy. This here leads to another lesson that I wish to teach you, which is to do good in the world."

Maria nodded and opened her notebook.

"As much as I have caused havoc over the years," Jorge continued. "I have also made an effort many times to do the right thing. Again, this comes back to my lesson on loyalty. Juliana, she was always loyal to me. So when I saw the opportunity to expose those who caused her death, I did so. Their greed has consequences."

"What kind of consequences?" Maria asked.

Jorge paused and wondered how much to tell his daughter.

"Maria, we will not get too much into this here today," He finally replied as he glanced toward the bulletproof window nearby. "But it was publicly exposed, so the world knows the truth. It has affected the company's bottom line, and they are still struggling from this event. Anything beyond this is another matter and a lesson you are not ready for yet."

"I think I am..."

"Not yet," Jorge shook his head. "Not today, Maria, I would rather wait for this one."

She said nothing, but they shared a look.

"Now, I am expecting a call from Athas soon," Jorge pointed toward the secure phone. "But when I do, you must be silent. I do not want him to know you are in the room. However, I want you to hear a real conversation that takes place between us. This here is for two reasons. The first one is because you will see a different side of Athas. I want you to later report to me your impression of what you heard. We will talk about it. Also, I would like you to see how I handle him. Listen carefully. There will be a lot to take in."

Maria nodded.

"Now, meanwhile, I want to discuss what you learned yesterday," Jorge gestured toward her notebook. "Paige, she worries it is too much. How do you feel, Maria?"

"I'm fine," Maria replied in a small voice, reminding Jorge that she was still so young.

"I do not want to overwhelm you," He glanced toward the red book on her lap. It was already full of notes.

"*Papá,* I have already seen so much..."

Jorge looked down, shameful of what his daughter had witnessed in her young life.

"Maria, if it were up to me," Jorge earnestly spoke as he looked into her eyes. "You would not even know who I am. You would think I was the founder of *Our House of Pot,* the production house, and whatever else, but you would never know of my past. That you would not know of what I have done."

"I know," She briefly looked away, then looked back up again. "But eventually, I would have to find out. I'm safer if I know, plus I can prepare if anything goes wrong."

"I know this too, Maria," Jorge nodded. "But still, your *Papá,* he has always wished for a different life for you. I want you to be safe, to be happy, to not have to worry about anything."

"I know," Maria spoke softly. "But I think that's what all parents want, but it's not realistic. It doesn't matter who you are."

Before Jorge could respond, his secure line rang, and he gave Maria a look. She nodded and sat back in her chair, closing her notebook.

There was a brief moment when Jorge answered the call when he considered being more courteous than usual, but that might indicate to Athas that something was up. Also, it was better to show the truth.

"Athas, you got your problem solved," Jorge abruptly spoke as his posture stiffened. "Now, I got something you need to do for me..."

"Look, I appreciate it," Athas cut him off, his voice echoing through the room. "But did you have to do it that way? I mean, Sheila was so humiliated..."

"I fixed your *fucking* problem," Jorge sharply replied as he leaned in closer to the phone. "*That* is what you wanted. You do *not* get to stipulate how I do so. I didn't slit anyone's throat, Athas. I showed her fucking her husband. Maybe, Athas, that is the real issue here? Does that make you uncomfortable? That five minutes after your dick is in her, her husband's is too?"

There was a silent pause, and Jorge noted that Maria's jaw was almost hitting the ground. He ignored both.

"Athas, you wanted the problem solved, and you got it," Jorge continued. "The rumor of you and her, it is gone. People are too busy talking about how big her tits look on screen, but I don't gotta tell you about that. Now, this is where you thank me for solving your problem, and you do *not* try to tell me how I do my job. Is that understood?"

"Yes, I just meant..."

"I don't want to hear it!" Jorge cut him off. "I do not care what you think, Athas. I think you should know that by now. You got your problem solved, so unless there is something else you need fixed, I suggest we end this topic."

"No, it's...it's fine," Athas stuttered through his words. "I understand and I do appreciate it."

"Good," Jorge sat back in his chair and glanced at his daughter, who appeared intrigued. "Now, can we move on?"

"I just wanted to say that she's planning to resign," Athas quickly added.

"This here," Jorge considered. "Is cowardly, but I am sure her party decided for her."

"I think so."

"But this is good for you," Athas continued. "It keeps her out of the limelight, and in turn, it keeps your affair silent."

"I suppose."

"Anyway, I need you to help me with something," Jorge cut him off. "Big Pharma is starting to gain some ground again, and I need this to end."

"Their reputation is slowly improving."

"The people, they forget," Jorge exchanged looks with his daughter. "So, it is time to change the laws."

"I can't change the laws before the election…"

"Talk about how the standards have to be higher," Jorge said, and he thought for a moment. "That laws must reflect this, and it is for the safety of the public. As soon as you say it is for public safety, as if you care about them, you can convince them of anything."

"That's true," Athas agreed. "Ok, I will give it some thought, but for once, we agree."

"Start slipping it into your interviews and conversations," Jorge suggested. "This should be one of the things you run your campaign on."

"Ok," Athas spoke with slight reluctance. "I will."

"We will talk later," Jorge abruptly ended the call and looked across the desk at his daughter.

"You were rude, kind of a bully," Maria observed. "But…it seemed to work."

"This here, it depends on the person," Jorge informed her. "Athas, he is weak, which makes me stronger."

"In life, Maria," he finally continued. "There are bullies. They can talk about how this is a bad thing in schools, but Maria, in the real world, bullies exist. All the shaming in the world will not make them go away. As Diego often says, in this world, you are either the sheep or the wolf.

Sheep are weak, compliant, merely followers but the wolf, he does not follow anyone."

Maria nervously nodded but attempted to look brave.

"In a world full of sheep," Jorge continued. "And believe me, Maria, the world *is* full of sheep, you must always be the wolf."

Maria said nothing, but Jorge could see it in her eyes. She already was.

CHAPTER 37

"*Nos quieren enterrar pero se olvidan de que somos semillas,"* Jorge said to Maria as they arrived at the *Princesa Maria.* Glancing at his daughter as he turned off the SUV, he waited to see if she would be able to translate his words.

"They want to bury us, but they had forgotten we are seeds," Maria finally said, her forehead wrinkled up as she spoke. "What does that mean? I don't understand?"

"Maria, this here means that someone will always try to oppress you if you allow them," Jorge attempted to explain the Mexican proverb as he glanced toward the club. "But you are stronger, more powerful than they can ever know. They can bury us, but we will rise, stronger than ever."

Grabbing her red book, Maria started to write something down, while Jorge thought for a moment. He was never sure how much to tell his daughter and when to hold back.

"Maria, the truth is that we are strong," Jorge continued as she scribbled something in her book. "We are powerful, but we must always be on guard. Right now, our biggest enemy is Big Pharma. If they had their way, they would take over *Our House of Pot* or dismiss it. They do not want people moving away from their drugs because that is how they make their money. Big Pharma feasts on the fat that is misery and sickness. They are the enemy that keeps trying to bury us."

She looked up with concern in her eyes, causing Jorge to reach out and touch her arm.

"But they will not," he assured her as his heart softened and Jorge leaned forward to kiss his daughter on the head. "They will never win."

They got out of the SUV and Jorge attempted to ignore the concern in her eyes as they walked toward the club. Once inside, she stopped and touched her father's arm.

"Papá, you scare me when you say that," She spoke earnestly as her large, brown eyes filled with tears. "Do you think…"

"Maria, no," Jorge pulled her into a hug. "You must not worry about this here. I am not saying they will hurt us. I am saying that they will always be our enemy, but Maria, this is half the battle. Once you know your enemies, you can always stay two steps ahead."

"Are we two steps ahead?" Maria asked as she slowly pulled away from her father's embrace. "I mean, you would tell me if we were in danger?"

"We are not in danger, Maria," Jorge assured her and paused for a moment. "The other guy, I am not so sure about."

With that, he headed toward the VIP room, and his daughter followed.

Opening the door, he found Chase, Makerson, and Tony already waiting. They appeared surprised when they saw the petit 14-year-old following behind Jorge, a red book in hand, however, no one reacted.

"Today, we have a guest here with us," Jorge said as he closed the door behind them and gestured for Maria to sit in the seat usually reserved for Paige. "My Maria, she is learning the business from inside, and I decided to invite her along."

Everyone said their share of hellos and welcomed her, although there was clear tension in the room.

"And I do not want anyone to hold back," Jorge said as he sat beside his daughter. "Maria is learning *my* business, so please talk to me as you would if she was not here."

There was a pause as the men exchanged looks.

"Maria will one day take over for me," Jorge spoke lovingly as he leaned back in his chair and reached out to touch his daughter's shoulder. "But do not feel that because she is young that you must protect her. In Mexico, it is common for young people to learn *much more serious* things at a much younger age. So, please, let us have our meeting as we would if Paige was instead sitting in this chair."

Although Jorge noted that things started slow, it didn't take long until everything fell back in line, while Maria listened attentively to every word. Her eyes studied their faces with interest, only looking away to jot down notes in her red book. Jorge noted this but also listened to what was taking place.

"So, you were right about the fake source coming forward," Makerson informed Jorge, as he looked past Maria to her father on the other side. "It happened, and we almost fell for it."

"Let me guess," Jorge said as he glanced at Tony, then back at Makerson. "It was for the *Raging Against the Machine* show?"

"You got it," Makerson said as Tony vigorously nodded in agreement. "You were right that they'd go for that show. Sonny was going for it but, Andrew smelled bullshit right away."

"What was it about?" Jorge asked with mild interest.

"They were talking about the....a *video* of Sheila Proctor-Wade and claimed they had other stories about her that they wanted to share, stuff from her past..."

"Interesting," Jorge nodded and looked toward Chase. "I can only imagine how colorful her past is."

Chase grinned, then looked away.

"Well, it was something of a different nature," Tony jumped in. "This source was suggesting that she was involved in corruption. Things that would make for a great story, but something seemed off."

"Yeah, Proctor-Wade may be a lot of things," Makerson shook his head. "But her belief in doing what is right for the Canadian people has stood the test for time. She's made some...interesting *personal* choices, but her track record otherwise has been pretty strong. People don't always agree with her stand on things, but they never question whether or not she's sincere and moral in her work."

"So, this here story was bullshit?" Jorge asked as he nodded. "But they thought we would run with it?"

"You know, she spoke to Sonny, and although he believed the source," Makerson paused for a moment. "He did as told, which was to make sure it was 100% before we ran with it. Sure enough, we did the research, and it isn't true. Marco did some digging, and well, it was a scam. We know this for sure."

"Maybe they should go to the mainstream media with this here story," Jorge grinned. "Tip them off."

"Interesting thing," Makerson said with a grin. "They claim to have done that, but they aren't interested. They suggested the mainstream media was attempting to cover it up. I think that's why Sonny got suspicious, because Sheila's name is already smeared, so why would they be reluctant?"

"They never went to mainstream news," Tony interjected. "We checked that out too, or rather, Marco checked it out."

"Marco," Jorge spoke to his daughter. "He is worth his weight in gold."

Maria said nothing but nodded.

"He's saved our asses more than once," Chase added. "There's no question."

"Saved our asses," Jorge repeated and turned his attention back to Makerson. "So, what happened after that?"

"We never got back to the source," Makerson replied. "And we won't."

"I think that is the best way to handle it," Tony added. "But, it showed everyone that we have to be vigilant when getting these so-called tips."

"That was to undermine us," Jorge said and once again turned his attention on Maria, who listened carefully. "If we had reported on this here story, it would be proven untrue, and this would make HPC news look like we could not be relied on. This here is crucial now that our company is new."

"If the stories aren't true," Maria seemed to stumble through what he was telling her. "Then people might not believe anything."

"It is like if I lie to you," Jorge explained. "Would you ever believe me again?"

"I understand."

"But mainstream news channels lie all the time," Chase pointed out. "And no one gives a shit."

"They aren't lying so much as misleading because they could be sued," Tony attempted to explain. "They word things carefully, edit things so they seem different from what they are. There's an obvious narrative."

"And the source?" Jorge asked.

"Bought and paid for through the PR side of a Big Pharma company," Makerson replied. "We got the proof."

"That might be the story we want to report," Jorge suggested. "What do you think?"

Tony began to nod, as did Makerson.

"My only concern is that they will wonder how we got the information," Tony spoke reasonably. "I guess we can say a source sent it to us."

"Maybe let this one go," Jorge said with a shrug. "But it is important that they know that we do not fuck around."

Everyone seemed alarmed when Jorge swore in front of his daughter, however, Maria took this all with ease, appearing unconcerned.

"I have talked to Athas," Jorge continued. "He will be making some comments in the media, suggesting that stricter regulations have to come up against Big Pharma and their ability to get new medications through, especially with the latest one from the cancer-causing pill."

"It's almost like mainstream media reported as little as possible about that story," Tony observed. "Then breezed on through, as if it never happened."

"Yeah, the next week, they were praising them for something else," Makerson laughed. "Then you see an ad for the same company during the commercial break for a non-pharmaceutical product."

"Do not bite the hand that feeds you," Jorge reminded them. "This here is also a lesson I have taught Athas. It is time he starts to pay attention to what his party is doing and take charge, rather than being the puppet on a string. If there is an election this fall, he must win, and then, he must start to be powerful. I am tired of his soft stand in politics."

"Maybe we need to do an interview?" Makerson suggested. "Now that he's taking a bit of a summertime break."

"That man has been on break since he got fucking voted in," Jorge complained. "Do an interview and ask him some questions that boost him up, his pre-campaign boost. He must get back into power this fall."

"Let's see if we can get an interview this week," Makerson suggested.

"Good idea," Jorge nodded. "This is what you must do."

"If there's a problem in the party," Chase jumped in. "We need to find it and take care of it this summer."

"It is time to clean house," Jorge nodded, and the two exchanged looks.

CHAPTER 38

"*…and this bill that promotes online safety,*" Makerson paused as if carefully choosing his words, while across from him, Athas appeared perfectly relaxed. "*A lot of people have concerns that it is a censorship bill that will infringe on our rights, specifically that of the press and smaller, independent media like HPC news. Could you address this?*"

Without missing a beat, Athas nodded, a fake smile on his lips.

"*Well, Tom, this was a bipartisan bill brought forward by some concerned members of parliament,*" Athas spoke slowly as if not even sure what he would say. "*In truth, I wasn't involved with creating it, and I certainly think some major changes have to be made before it could be passed.*"

"Wow!" Maria's eyes widened as she looked across the desk at her father, then back at the laptop.

To this, Jorge merely grinned and nodded.

"*So, you are saying that in its current state, this bill should not be passed?*" Makerson faked surprise in his voice. "*And no one approached you when creating it? That seems rather unusual.*"

"*No, I do not believe that in its current state that this bill should be passed,*" Athas confirmed. "*Regarding how a bill does get passed….*

"So Maria," Jorge started to talk over the interview. "The lesson here is that when you are weak like Athas, people, they run the show from behind your back. If I was weak, it would mean that anyone who works for me could easily undermine me. This sends the message to others, both within or outside my organization, that I am powerless."

"Ok," Maria nodded as she wrote something in her red book.

"It would be like," Jorge thought for a moment. "It would be like if there is a riot. Remember, this has happened in Toronto. If you recall, once someone breaks a window to a store and the security stand back and let them come in and take whatever they want, others see this and do the same. It shows that this man wearing a uniform is powerless so, these people have no issue taking whatever they want. That can happen in all our lives. Once people see you are powerless, they can take whatever they want, but only if you let them. If you start letting them, Maria, you cannot wait to speak up. It is too late once half the store is stolen away to speak up because your voice becomes weaker and weaker."

Maria nodded and continued to write in her book.

"And Athas, he has waited until half the fucking store was taken away," Jorge shook his head. "So, he better grow a pair, or this here country will turn into a circus."

"I don't understand why he let this happen," Maria looked up from her book and tilted her head. "Like, with this censorship bill, why didn't he jump in faster and do something?"

"Because he is a coward," Jorge replied as he pointed to the screen, where Athas was still talking. "Because he is allowing the people around him to run the show. Because he doesn't have the strength or power to stand up to them. That is why, Maria, it is so important that you be strong. You do not want to end up being like Alec Athas."

"I used to think he was so cool," Maria shook her head. "I didn't realize he was weak."

"Well, now you know, Maria," Jorge replied as he leaned back in his chair and glanced at the screen. "And if he doesn't get his shit together, Maria, soon, the country will know too, and they will not respect him."

"…..do not want our citizens to feel like they no longer have freedom of speech," Athas was continuing to speak. *"This is not acceptable."*

"So, what will you do?" Makerson bluntly asked him. "Should the bill be thrown *out?"*

Athas paused for a moment while Jorge and Maria watched him with interest.

"*Well, I wouldn't say it necessarily should be...*" Athas replied, and across from Jorge, Maria groaned.

"This is what you mean," She shook her head. "Now I understand."

"He is weak," Jorge reminded her. "You cannot make everyone happy, and when you try, you create a clusterfuck. Athas, he is creating a clusterfuck."

Maria laughed and nodded.

"This bill will put our media company in a bad position," Jorge continued to explain. "Because we are not mainstream, it will undermine us and make us play by different rules than the big media companies. The big media companies are bought, and paid for by rich, powerful people, like Big Pharma, so only will report what *they* want. But Maria, they try to say that is us being bought and paid for, but we rely on donations to run our company."

"I thought you invested in it," Maria wrinkled up her nose.

"Yes, originally, but Maria, it is for the people, so they must invest to keep companies and government from creating the narrative," Jorge explained. "This is a problem. If I put money into it, they can say that I tell them what to say."

"Why isn't there a bill introduced," Maria thought for a moment. "That makes it illegal for companies to have an influence?"

"Because it is hard to prove," Jorge insisted. "You can suspect, but this here is not something that you can easily prove to be true."

She nodded.

"It is obvious sometimes," Jorge said as he turned to see Athas continuing to talk. "Well, enough of this man."

"*....for your own good...*"

With that, Jorge closed the laptop and pushed it aside.

"You don't want to hear any more?" Maria asked as she sat back in her chair.

"Maria, this here is political talk," Jorge shook his head. "It means nothing."

She nodded.

"When anyone says something is for your 'own good', Maria," Jorge continued. "It is them saying they want to push their ideas on you."

Maria's eyes widened.

"One of the teachers says that to us all the time in school…."

"And do you think this teacher is right?" Jorge asked.

Maria shook her head no.

"Always follow your instincts," Jorge instructed. "This here teacher does this to manipulate. No one knows what is for your own good except you and your family."

Maria looked troubled.

"What exactly is it that the teacher says?"

"She says it is for our own good that we work hard now to get into a good university," Maria said and thought for a moment. "She kind of makes it seems like if we don't get high grades, we are going to fail at life."

"This woman, her intentions might be good," Jorge said after some thought. "But she is going about it wrong. You may make mistakes, but this does not mean you fail at life. You can always turn everything around."

Maria nodded and was about to say something when a knock at the door interrupted her.

"That must be Marco," Jorge said as he rose from his chair and walked across the room. "He has some information to share with me."

Letting the Filipino in, he appeared cheery and calm until he saw Maria sitting in the room, as she turned to look at him.

"Oh, I am sorry, sir," Marco quickly replied. "If you are busy with Maria, I can wait."

"No, that is fine, Marco," Jorge insisted as he closed the door behind him. "Maria is sitting in a lot of my meetings now. I am spending the summer teaching her about my business."

"Oh, is this so?" Marco smiled but showed signs that he was ill at ease. "Well, this is good, no?"

"I am learning a lot," Maria smiled as she pointed at her red book as Marco sat beside her.

"Maria, she is a good student," Jorge said as he smiled at his daughter while returning to his chair. "It is a pleasure to teach her."

His daughter gushed while Marco held his phone up to show it was off.

"Maria, as we have talked about before," Jorge reminded her. "We always turn our phones off or leave them out of the room."

"Yes, we do have extra protection on them," Marco added. "But I would rather be safe than sorry."

"Marco, he has created something to make sure that we are safe from outside hacking," Jorge insisted.

"It is not just hackers," Marco reminded him. "It is Big Tech in general, sir. They steal information from us on apps."

"If you aren't buying a product," Jorge nodded. "You *are* the product."

Maria's eyes widened, and she looked away.

"So, Marco, what do you have for me today?" Jorge asked. "Please, feel free to speak in front of Maria. Do not feel you have to hold back."

"Well, sir, I was able to find some information regarding your concern that someone in Athas party was trying to undermine him."

"It almost seems," Maria spoke up with confidence. "That he does that himself."

With that, Jorge's head fell back in laughter.

"Well, Maria, this is true," Marco grinned at her observation.

"Marco, we have been reviewing the interview with Makerson," Jorge informed his IT specialist. "And I pointed a few things out."

"Oh, sir," Marco shook his head. "He did not come out strong in that interview."

"That is because he is not," Jorge said and shared a look with Marco, then his daughter. "I assume that is what you are going to report to me today as well?"

"Sir, in my research, I see that it is someone working on behalf of Big Pharma is lobbying various members of Athas' party to push laws that suit them. For example, this censorship bill was to stop indie media such as your own company from reporting unfavorable information. You have leaked about the pill that causes cancer, so they do not want more trouble. That company took a hit from your story, shares sunk."

"That is all these companies care about, Maria," Jorge pointed out. "It is all about money."

"They have heard that Athas is talking about making it harder to pass their new products," Marco continued. "So they have a propaganda campaign that suggests that by doing so, that he is holding back life-saving drugs because he does not care for the people. Also, they have certain members of parliament picked to argue for this bill to make Athas look bad to the public."

"Is that so?" Jorge calmly asked. "And do you have the name of this here lobbyist?"

"I do, but sir," Marco paused for a moment. "It does not matter because if this person were to no longer be in the picture, they would get another. You must prove that money is exchanging hands, that promises are being made for big jobs in their companies and expose them."

"Do you have this proof, Marco?" Jorge asked.

"I do, sir," Marco grinned. "I certainly do."

CHAPTER 39

"...the law would create stricter rules around pharmaceutical companies. This comes after a well-known medication originally deemed safe was proven to cause cancer..."

"I cannot believe that the mainstream media," Jorge leaned forward and closed the laptop before looking across the bar at Chase. "They covered something relevant for a change."

"It's because our story picked up steam," Chase reminded him as he leaned against the bar. "Otherwise, they'd bury it. But notice their wording. They highlighted how some people in the industry fear that this will hold up medications that might save lives."

"Well, the corporate media," Jorge reminded him. "Are bought and paid for. They say what they are told."

Chase opened his mouth to say something but was interrupted when his phone buzzed.

"Marco's here," Chase said as he started across the empty bar to unlock the door for the Filipino.

Jorge glanced at his phone before turning it off.

"Good morning, Chase," Marco's voice echoed through the room as he walked through the doorway, carefully placing his bicycle beside the main door. Glancing across the room, he spotted Jorge at the bar. "Good morning, sir."

"Marco!" Jorge replied. "Let us hope you have some good news for us today?"

"Well," Marco breathlessly spoke as he crossed the room, with Chase in tow. "I…sir, are you alone? Is Maria here as well?"

"No, I told her to take the day off," Jorge replied as he turned around on the barstool and noted that Marco was turning his phone off. "I had a feeling maybe this would be a dicey one."

"You are right, sir," Marco nodded. "Should we go into the VIP room?"

Jorge nodded, and the three men headed that way.

"When we spoke yesterday," Marco started as soon as they reached the room. "I did not have all the information. If I had, I do not know how much I should say in front of Maria."

"You can say some," Jorge replied as he closed the door behind them. "But if you think there is something she cannot hear, then you say that something is still under investigation. That will be a way to let me know that we will discuss more after I send her off on a mission of some kind."

"I do understand what you are doing," Marco said as he grabbed his usual seat as they sat down. "But I would warn you…"

"This here is fine," Jorge put his hand up as he cut off Marco. "I assure you, I am cautious how much my daughter knows. So what do you have for me today, Marco?"

"Well, sir," Marco took a deep breath. "Yesterday, I talk to you about the lobbyist that is pushing the government to remove the bill that would force more testing before new medications are available to the public?"

Jorge nodded as he listened.

"Well, late last night, I couldn't sleep, so I did more work," Marco said as he leaned forward on the desk. "Sir, they know that an election is likely this fall and are already planning to make Mr. Athas look as bad as possible, so he does not get re-elected."

"This I knew," Jorge said as he leaned back in his chair. "Who is doing this?"

"Sir, it is the company that sold the stomach pills that caused cancer," Marco said as he closed his eyes and waved his hand around. "I forget what they are called…"

"This is fine, Marco," Jorge cut him off. "So they have some concerns?"

"Probably not the only pills they got that will kill people," Chase muttered while Jorge nodded in response.

"It is bad, sir," Marco continued. "They already have plans in place to smear Athas the rest of the summer. They have even reached out to their *competitor* in hopes they can join together to make sure that Athas doesn't get in and that the bill disappears."

"So, we are gonna take care of the messages or the messenger?" Chase asked Jorge, who was in thought.

"There is one man," Marco leaned ahead. "His name is Rubin Murray and, he's the PR person in charge of making sure this happens. He is the one who plans to bring Athas down, and sir, he has even talked of bringing you down too."

"Oh, is this so?" Jorge asked with interest. "Do tell, Marco."

"I can show you the conversations he has had online," Marco said as he took a deep breath. "He wants to help push the censorship bill through. He is creating a serious online hate campaign against an immigrant family in the Toronto area. This is to bring attention to the fact that we need to control social media. Of course, he has one of the major networks prepared to cover the story when this happens, to highlight why this bill needs to go through. He will not mention the fact that it will cripple independent media."

Jorge exchanged looks with Chase.

"As for you," Marco continued with some hesitation. "Sir, they plan to attack Maria on social media as a way of getting to you. What he plans, it is *really* bad. That way, they can point out that you are against the bill even though your daughter...."

"Who the fuck is this again?" Jorge shot back as he leaned ahead on the table. "What is this motherfuckers name that plans to attack my Maria?"

"Rubin Murray," Marco replied as his face flushed. "Sir, he is a very bad man. That is why this company hired him. He has a reputation for taking some extreme measures to get what his clients want. Sir, you should see the terrible things he has done in the past...I need you to read what he wants to do with Maria."

"You do not have to convince me," Jorge said as he shared a look with Chase, who was equally angry, while Marco slid some papers across the table. "This man, he will be in the oven before today is over."

"Sir, I have already looked at his schedule," Marco jumped in excitedly as Jorge glanced over the sheet, his face growing hotter as he read the words. "I know where and when you can find him."

"Let's keep this simple," Chase suggested. "We'll get him and bring him right to the crematorium."

"He goes for a massage at 11," Marco jumped in. "I looked into the place he goes. I'm pretty sure he's getting more than a massage. And the women there, they want to keep under the radar."

"So they will keep their mouth's shut if we need to remove him?" Chase asked.

"Oh yes, sir, I am sure of it," Marco nodded his head.

Jorge and Chase exchanged looks.

"Are you coming to get him?" Chase asked.

"No, get Diego," Jorge replied after some consideration. "I think I prefer he be surprised."

The men went their separate ways while Jorge dropped by the production company to inform Tony of what was going on. He didn't get into the details. He didn't give names. The less they knew, the better it would be. They knew what they had to know.

"Is there anything we should do?" Tony asked as Jorge stood up to leave.

"I got this under control," Jorge grinned as he stood in the doorway. "Tell Makerson about it and also tell him that we will do everything to build up Athas this summer."

"As long as we know what kind of fight we might be in for," Tony said as he stood up. "It might be less intimidating to get in the ring."

"This fight," Jorge said as he turned on his phone. "It will be fast and...

His phone beeped, and Jorge glanced at it.

"Sorry, Tony," Jorge said as he headed out the door. "I gotta make a call."

"I will let Makerson know...

Jorge was already halfway down the hallway as he returned the call.

"You got something for me?" Jorge answered as soon as Andrew answered the phone.

"You know it."

"I will be right there," Jorge said as he headed out the door and into the parking lot. Jumping in his SUV, he couldn't get to the crematorium fast enough. The closer he got, the more Jorge felt his anger rise to the top. No one hurt his family. No one was going to target Maria as a way of getting even with him. That was a line you did not cross.

Arriving at the crematorium, Jorge flew into a parking spot and jumped out of the SUV. His anger continued to grow as he flung open the door of one of his less-known businesses and immediately made his way to the basement. He knew where they'd be waiting.

Andrew met him at the door. He glanced over his shoulder next to the crematorium oven.

"We got him," He calmly replied. "If you don't kill him, I will. The motherfucker spat on me."

Jorge nodded as he took in the older, white man who lay on the plastic-covered floor, wearing only a towel around his waist. His hands tied behind his back, he was attempting to sit up, but his girth held him back. Across the room stood Chase and Diego, both exchanging looks with Jorge.

"So, tell me, friend," Jorge said as he walked into Rubin Murray's view, noting the look of fear on his face. "Did we interrupt your rub and tug this morning?"

"They finished the rub," Chase commented. "Just starting the tug...."

"Oh, so we interrupted your hot date with a professional woman," Jorge said with a grin on his face. "This here is a good way to break up a morning."

"Please let me go," Rubin started to speak. "I have a family at home. They'll notice I'm missing and...."

"And probably be glad," Andrew jumped in as he casually strolled across the room toward the oven. "I'm guessing."

"They told me why I'm here," Rubin spoke abruptly. "I was just doing my job..."

"So am I," Jorge replied. "We all are just doing our job here. Chase brings you here, and Andrew, he stokes the fire before we put you in it. We all have jobs, Mr. Murray, and now it's time we do ours."

"Please," Rubin Murray started to beg. "I will do anything...we can work together..."

"You know that there might have been possible," Jorge replied as he looked across the room at an ax leaned against the wall. "But that is before I learn that you were going to target my daughter to make a point. And what you plan to do to her....there is no way you could expect to continue to live once I found out. Where I come from, family, it is everything. And you do *not* mess with a man's family."

"I...it was only an idea," Rubin breathlessly rushed to explain. "Just something I was rolling around...."

Jorge ignored his words as he crossed the floor and reached for the ax.

"Please," Murray began to cry. "Please, I....

"Mr. Murray," Jorge said as he walked closer. "You picked the wrong team to play for."

"Please, I'm sorry," Rubin began to beg as tears ran down his face. "I can help *you...*"

Jorge ignored the man's pleas. Lifting the ax above his head, he brought it down hard into the soft flesh of the man's neck. In a blinding rage, Jorge continued to pummel the man's body with the ax as blood splattered all around. Andrew stood aside with disinterest while Chase looked away. Diego watched with no expression.

CHAPTER 40

"Did I miss anything yesterday?" Maria's brown eyes expanded in size as she innocently tilted her head to the side.

Jorge didn't even flinch as he leaned back in his chair and looked across the desk at his daughter.

"Maria, I just, you know, went to the bar to see Chase," Jorge replied as he looked away, unable to lie to his daughter. "I drop by the production house to check in on things, the crematorium, and then I come home."

"That's it?" Maria asked as she opened her red book and looked down.

"That is about all," Jorge replied and cleared his throat. "But you must not worry, Maria. Yesterday was your day off. You must enjoy your summer too."

"It was ok," She shrugged. "I had to go to the mall and stuff. You know..."

"Well, I hope you had fun."

"So, *Papá,"* Maria thought for a moment. "Remember the other day when we were talking to Marco, and he said someone was lobbying for Big Pharma to cause trouble for Athas?"

"Yes, Maria, we think we found and resolved that issue," Jorge hurriedly spoke, hoping to change the subject. "But we continue to monitor the situation."

"How did you resolve it?"

Jorge was frozen for a moment, unsure of what to say.

"Well, we find the man that was going to smear Athas," Jorge thought for a moment. "And we explained to him why he should stop."

"What did you say?"

"Oh, Maria, I do not remember," Jorge replied and shrugged, glancing around his office. "It does not matter. Sometimes, you only need to have a conversation with people to make them see reason."

"That sounds simple," Maria suggested as she carefully watched Jorge.

"Well, Maria, you must choose your words carefully," Jorge replied with a smile. "But that lesson will be another day."

She seemed to accept this, nodding.

"Now, we continue to monitor the situation," Jorge said as he leaned back in his chair. "Marco, he will watch things and, we will take care of any issues as they arise."

"So, that guy," Maria continued to stay on topic. "He wanted to make Athas look bad?"

"*Si.*"

"By saying that he was holding up the good drugs," Maria continued. "So people wouldn't get better because of him."

"Yes, something like this," Jorge nodded. "You see, Maria, they must get these drugs out fast and make all the money they can before people see the negative side effects or before their competitors make something better. It is business."

"And the problem is that Alec cares more for people's health?"

Jorge cringed a little bit. Why did everyone think Athas was a saint?

"Yes, well, something like that, Maria," Jorge replied. "The point is that Big Pharma is the biggest drug cartel in the world. Athas, he chooses not to be part of it."

These words seemed to trigger Maria, and her eyes widened.

"You see, Maria," Jorge began to lecture. "The only difference between the pharmaceutical companies and the cartels in Mexico is that they are legal. Many of their drugs are also highly addictive. They will *also* go to extremes to protect their interests. They *also* bribe governments to sell their products. There is no difference, Maria. They have found a way to make it legal."

"Really?" Maria's eyes widened.

"Maria, some of the drugs these companies sell," Jorge shook his head. "They are bigger on the street than, you know, cocaine or any illegal drug."

"But it's legal?" Maria appeared stunned.

"*Si,*" Jorge nodded. "They do need a reasonable excuse to give the prescriptions, but who is going to question a doctor?"

Maria mouthed 'wow' and looked down at her book.

"At any rate," Jorge attempted to switch gears. "This is what Athas is dealing with now. In turn, this is what we are trying to help him with."

"Ok, I get it now."

"Good, Maria, we must move on from this," Jorge said, happy to get away from the topic. "As I said, the situation is being monitored. But, we always have many irons in the fire, so we must leave this one alone for today."

Jorge kept the lesson short for the day, his mind wandering to things he preferred to take care of after his daughter was out of earshot. Giving her a research project to work on, he hoped to keep her upstairs for a while. Jorge sent a text to Alec Athas to let him know that they needed to talk. His secure line rang shortly afterward.

"So, we had a problem, and it is taken care of," Jorge lowered his voice and glanced at the door. "But we must continue to monitor the situation."

"Is this about them smearing me before the campaign?"

"Yes," Jorge turned his chair around so that he faced the opposite wall. "Yesterday, it come to my attention that a man, Rubin Murray, he might be a problem."

"Oh, him," Athas sniffed. "Big Pharma hired that vulture a few years ago. He isn't exactly known to be ethical."

"Well, he will no longer be known for anything," Jorge muttered and looked over his shoulder in case Maria had returned. "This man will not be a problem anymore."

"I understand."

"He was planning to attack an immigrant family online," Jorge started to explain. "Trust me. I see the information. It was going to be bad. The media planned to pick up where he left off, make a case for the censorship law that they wanted to pass…"

"That doesn't surprise me," Athas replied. "But he's no longer…."

"You do not have to worry about him," Jorge cut him off. "He was planning to smear you all summer. This here, I also see. He had some very detailed plans to bring you down before you even call an election."

"Ok, I understand," Athas replied in a tense voice.

"But just because he is no longer a concern," Jorge continued. "This here does not mean that no one else will be a problem. We must be diligent."

"Yes, well, I don't think they quite make 'em like that guy anymore," Athas replied. "He had no scruples. Last year, a journalist dug into a Big Pharma story, and he ruined her reputation. She was fired from her job and wasn't able to get back into it after that."

"Some people, they have no scruples," Jorge said with a grin on his face. "You are lucky that the other person like this, he works for you."

By the time Maria returned, Jorge was off the phone and checking his email messages.

"*Papá,* I did some research, but I can't find any bad stories about Athas in the news today," She returned to her seat, red book in hand. "Just the usual, boring political stuff."

"It is boring, isn't it?" Jorge shared a smile with his daughter. "This here is a lot more of my job than you think. It is not always exciting, Maria."

"I guess that's any job," Maria shrugged. "When I work with Chase at the bar, it's kinda the same. I do boring little jobs."

"They are boring, Maria," Jorge pointed out. "But they are also necessary. Most jobs, even though they seem irrelevant, they must be done. This here is a part of life."

"I know," Maria shrugged. "I mean, they're easy."

"You know, Maria, you have worked hard today," Jorge pointed toward the window. "It is a nice day. Maybe you should go outside, enjoy the sunshine. Take Miguel out."

"Tala already has him outside by the pool," Maria replied. "But it is a nice day. I mean unless you have anything else for me to do?"

"Maria, things, they are quiet today," Jorge said with a shrug. "I do not mean to take up all your time this summer. It is still your vacation. You should enjoy it. Go spend time with friends, sit in the sun, practice your dancing, whatever it is you would like to do…"

"I would like to go to shooting practice again."

"Talk to Paige," Jorge nodded. "I am sure she would be happy to take you."

"She said she would," Maria replied. "But she's been busy with Miguel a lot. Tala has been taking her English course, so she hasn't been around as much. But you know, I'm sure she will take me when she can….or you could?"

"I could, Maria," Jorge nodded. "But Paige, she is a much better shot than me. I think she is a better teacher too."

"Oh, I don't know," Maria slowly rose from her chair. "I'm learning a lot from you."

"Well, this is good," Jorge replied as he filled with pride. "Maria, I only want to make you prepared for whatever the future holds."

"But, you know," Maria shrugged. "You have to show me the bad stuff too, right? Like not just that easy stuff."

"In time," Jorge replied. "It is like a hill that you must climb to the top. You cannot expect to arrive on the first day."

"I know," Maria hesitated. "But even if you don't teach me everything right away, you can tell me stuff. You know I can handle it.

"I know," Jorge nodded as the smile slid from his face. "But I also know that you are sensitive, Maria. So, I do not wish to overwhelm you."

"I'm fine."

Jorge watched her as she looked down at her hand, then slowly looked up.

"*Papá,* can I ask you something?"

"Of course, *Princesa,* you can ask me anything."

"Why did Paige leave here yesterday with a duffle bag?"

Jorge hesitated.

"Well, Maria, I do not know," Jorge felt flustered. "You will have to ask her."

"I will," She started toward the door, and Jorge felt his heart racing.

"But," She turned around. "Why did you come home with a different suit from the morning?"

Jorge froze on the spot.

CHAPTER 41

"Maria, I…." Jorge attempted to explain, but already his heart was pounding erratically in his chest. This was the moment he dreaded. He watched her return to her seat.

"*Papá,*" Maria cut him off before he could try to sidetrack her. "Please. Please tell me the truth. I don't want to hear a story about how you spilled something on your suit. I know it is more than that."

Jorge felt a cold sweat underneath his shirt.

"I know because how many times has Miguel spit up on you?" Maria confidently pointed out. "And you barely change your shirt. I know it has to be something major if Paige brought you another suit. And that's what was in the duffel bag, right?"

Jorge looked away and considered his options.

"If you *really* mean it when you say you want me to learn," Maria continued as she sat up straighter with a strength he had never heard in her voice before, it was almost as if his little girl had suddenly transformed into an adult in front of his eyes. "You have to tell me the truth. I can handle it."

"Maria, I…" Jorge shook his head. His eyes pleaded with hers from across the desk. He suddenly felt small. "I do not think that we…"

"Yes, we *do,*" Maria corrected him. "We *need* to talk about this."

"But *Princesa,* I…"

"I'm not a little girl anymore," Maria cut him off and shook her head. "I'm almost 15. Everyone wanted me to have a *quinceañera* this year. That is a celebration to welcome me into womanhood, but *Papá,* you don't want me to go, do you?"

"Maria, it is not that," Jorge finally managed to get a word in. "It is not that I do not wish you to grow up. If that were the case, I would not even be doing what I have been all summer. The first sign of concern, I would have sent you off to boarding school. Somewhere safe, far away, but I did not. However, what you do not understand is that some things, they are difficult for me to say."

"It's because it's really bad, isn't it?" Maria asked in a softer voice, causing his defenses to fall. "It's because you killed someone yesterday, didn't you?"

Jorge stared into his daughter's eyes for the longest moment of his life before he finally could answer.

"*Si,* Maria," He said in a stronger voice than he thought he could muster as a cool breeze enveloped his body. "I killed a man yesterday."

"It was someone lobbying for Big Pharma, right?"

"It was a man," Jorge started to speak and stopped. "Maria, I do not think you should know..."

"Please," She asked in a softer voice. "Please be honest with me. I don't want any more secrets between us. You talk about loyalty above all, but if that's the case, then you have to trust me with everything."

"I know," Jorge hesitantly agreed, briefly looking away before he continued. "Maria, the man was a great concern. He had a lot of plans to smear Athas all summer, leading up to the election. Athas, he is weak, so he could never withstand this here plan."

Maria nodded.

"Also, he had created fake Twitter and Facebook accounts," Jorge continued as he looked past his daughter. "Because he wanted to attack an immigrant family, very aggressively, including their children, then have the media make a huge story out of it. This was to justify having a censorship bill created limiting what Canadians could say on social media, saying it was to eliminate hate speech. This would make it illegal to attack anyone online, but more importantly, people who might deserve to be publicly attacked."

"Like Big Pharma?" Maria asked as she watched him closely. "Politicians? Companies who do bad things?"

"Yes, Maria," Jorge continued to explain, "It is censorship. It is about control."

"But how would that get past Athas?" Maria wondered. "He's the prime minister."

"The prime minister, he does not have the power you would think," Jorge insisted. "Plus, he would have to cave under public pressure."

"After this person created a fake scenario to justify it," Maria nodded her head.

"But Maria," Jorge leaned forward in his seat. "There is more."

She didn't reply but nodded.

"Not only was this man planning to push for censorship," Jorge continued. "He was going to attack someone else, and this here, it crossed the line."

"Who?" Maria asked with such innocence that he briefly wondered if he should tell her at all.

"You," Jorge finally answered. "Maria, he was going to attack you as a way to get to me. He knew that to attack me would be useless because I would humiliate him in the media. But he knew that hurting you would, in turn, hurt me."

"Oh," Maria looked deflated and sat back in her chair. "What was he going to say about me?"

"Maria, it does not matter," Jorge shook his head. "He would make things up, you know, stories..."

"I want to know," Maria insisted. "Does he know I shot that man and..."

"No no," Jorge shook his head. "He knows nothing of you. That is why I say he was going to make things up."

"Like what?"

"He was going to suggest that you were with the Mexican cartels," Jorge started to reply and hesitated for a moment before going on. "That you were dangerous, just like me. He was going to say that you were violent."

"How could he do that?" Maria seemed puzzled. "I hardly even talk to anyone in Mexico anymore....like, would he just make up stuff?"

"Yes, Maria," Jorge nodded. "A man like this, he would go to great lengths to damage your reputation. I could not have this."

"But, how?" Maria shook her head. "I don't understand."

"Do you remember when you had that fight in the bathrooms at the mall?" Jorge reminded her. "The two girls?"

"He found out about that?" Maria's eyes widened. "Do people know?"

"No," Jorge shook his head. "What I mean is that he would put you in a similar position where you would have to defend yourself, but he would make sure it was recorded but only at the point where you looked bad. He had plans to do something like this. He knows you know self-defense because of that tour to the various reserves with Chase. That last year you two did teach women to look after themselves. He knows this, so he decided to put you in a position where you had to fight back but suggest you were trying to collect money."

"But I never even had drugs on me in my life," Maria pointed out.

"Maria, these people, they are not beyond planting something like this," Jorge reminded her, and her face fell. "I am sorry, but this is true."

"That's scary," Maria's face turned pink, and she looked ill. "That they can do something like that."

"I know this, Maria," Jorge nodded. "That is why you must send a powerful message to those who think that they can get away with it. If they fear you, they will never do such things."

"He didn't fear me because he thought I was weak," Maria shamefully replied. "That's why he chose me to attack."

"Maria, this here is not right," Jorge shook his head. "This here, you should never have to deal with such things. It is not because you are weak, Maria. It is because you are young. But I have…I feel, eliminated this problem."

"By killing him?"

Jorge looked into her eyes and nodded.

"You did it for me?" Maria asked with tears in her eyes.

"I would do anything to protect you," Jorge replied in a soft voice. "You know this already. I will stop at nothing."

Maria didn't reply but started to cry. Jorge felt his heart drop as he rose from his chair and slowly walked to the other side of the desk.

"Do not cry," Jorge sat beside her and gently pulled her into a hug. "I was not trying to upset you, Maria. This is not why I tell you such things."

"I know," She continued to sob. "I can't believe someone would want to hurt me because they hate you."

"Maria, this here is business," Jorge attempted to comfort her. "It was not personal against you. You must not let it upset you."

"I know," Maria sniffed. "Now I'm crying, like a baby. No wonder he decided to go after me. I'm *your* weak point."

"This here is not true," Jorge said as he moved away from her. "You are *not* weak. When a man come to kill our family, it was *you* who saved Paige and Miguel. That is not a weak person, Maria. And when those girls at the mall tried to hurt you, you stop them. To me, this is not a powerless, weak woman."

"But I'm crying," Maria sobbed. "Over this!"

"I do not want you to turn into a machine like me," Jorge curtly replied, causing her to laugh. "You are safe with me. I do…I understand."

"I guess I'm just very emotional," Maria sniffed. "Because I can't believe you would do so much to protect me. I mean, I know you would, but…I guess…."

"Maria, I would do anything to protect you, and I *have,"* Jorge reached out and touched her hair. "That is what you do for family. You protect them. You have done the same for us. I want you to know that I will always protect you. I love you very much. I love my family. You are all that keeps me sane."

"But to kill him…"

"Maria, there were many reasons why I chose to do this," Jorge replied. "It was not based on one thing, but I will admit when I hear what he had planned to do to you…"

Even though he did not finish his sentence, he didn't have to. Maria knew.

CHAPTER 42

"Is your boy toy here?" Jorge bluntly asked as soon as Diego opened his door. As a response, his friend's face puckered up as if he tasted something sour. "Because if he is…"

"I'm alone," Diego answered as his defenses started to fall, his eyes carefully taking in Jorge as he moved aside to let him in. "What's going on with you? You never come to see me anymore."

"Diego, you are never home!" Jorge reminded him as he stepped in and glanced toward the sunroom, where a row of miniature lime trees stood side by side. However, today he wasn't in the mood to comment on Diego's strange obsession with growing limes. "How can I visit if you're off with your boy toy all the time?"

"I'm at work most of the time," Diego corrected him as he gestured toward the bar. "I'll have you know! I'm working hard to keep *Our House of Pot* a success. It's a lot of work."

"See, me, I never went to the office," Jorge started to lighten up as he climbed on the bar stool.

"That's because you were everywhere else, and the rest of us took care of things," Diego bluntly pointed out.

"I was more of a…how you say? A visionary than a CEO," Jorge spoke bashfully. "I will admit it."

"I can't argue with that," Diego said as he walked behind the bar and grabbed a bottle of tequila. "Want a real drink, or do you want a beer?"

"I want a beer *and* probably the rest of that bottle there," Jorge gestured toward the tequila. "It has been a long day."

"Oh yeah," Diego asked. "Sitting by the pool all day can be tough on a man."

Jorge shot him an amused look as Diego slid a shot glass of tequila toward him and poured one for himself. Holding it up in the air, Jorge did the same.

"To world peace," Diego said flatly, causing Jorge to laugh as they tapped their glasses together.

"Yes, Diego, this here is our whole motivation," Jorge sarcastically commented before downing the liquid, briefly making a face before sitting the glass back on the bar and loudly sighing.

"So, what's going on with you?" Diego suddenly appeared concerned. "You never get like this."

"Well, Diego, it is not every day I have a conversation like I just did with my daughter," Jorge admitted. "It was…difficult."

"What's going on?" Diego's face softened. "Is she ok? Did something happen?"

"She is fine," Jorge gestured toward the bottle of tequila to indicate he wanted another shot. "It is her *Papá* that is not so good right now."

Diego didn't reply but poured them another shot. Both downed the liquor and fell silent.

"She knows," Jorge finally said as he looked away, as if too ashamed to look into Diego's eyes, "about me. Fuck, I could use a cigarette right now."

"I thought she already did," Diego leaned closer as if confiding a secret. "About when you were in the cartel…."

"No, I mean, she *knows,"* Jorge looked back into his face. "About what I do when people don't play nice."

"Oh," Diego said and puckered his lips together as he nodded.

"I tell her the truth," Jorge shook his head. "Because she figured it out. She saw Paige bring me a new suit yesterday, and she put it together. Diego, I could not lie. Maria would never trust me again if I did."

"How did she react?"

"She was upset, but this is because I told her why I kill him."

"Everything?" Diego's eyes widened. "Because I read what Marco found and..."

"No," Jorge admitted. "I could not tell her *everything*. I tell her that they were going to have someone attack her, maybe record it, post it on social media. Say she was in the cartel, but that was all."

"You weren't lying," Diego said as sadness washed over his face. "But what he had planned..."

"Diego, that would kill me," Jorge shook his head. "I would rather die than have anyone hurt my Maria in that way."

Diego nodded and looked away.

"I am glad I kill him so brutally," Jorge continued. "That man, he deserved it."

"If you hadn't," Diego confirmed. "The rest of us would have. Anyone who would do that to a teenaged girl is a fucking piece of shit."

"It was meant to humiliate her," Jorge confirmed. "To violate her in the worst way. You know, Diego, I have done some terrible things over the years, but we had our limits. We did not hurt children. We may threaten to scare the parent, but we never hurt the kids. That is why I often say it is the white man in a suit, who has a prestigious title, that is more the devil than I have ever been. But the world, they have certain ideas about who is the good guy and who is bad."

"Yeah, well, most people see things in black and white," Diego reminded him as he reached under the bar and pulled out two Coronas. "And their brains can't see any other colors."

"That is most people, Diego," Jorge replied. "It is easier to process and people, they like easy."

"So, Maria knows they were threatening to attack her," Diego nodded. "You tell her about the immigrant family? The other stuff?"

"Yes, I tell her the rest," Jorge nodded. "She thought it meant they saw her as weak."

"Oh no," Diego shook his head. "That's not true."

"I try to tell her that was not the case," Jorge insisted. "But she was very emotional about the fact that I kill for her. I say, Maria, this is for everyone I love, but especially my children. This is what it means to be family. Loyalty above all."

"Loyalty above all," Diego repeated before taking a drink of his beer. "There are no exceptions."

"That there is the biggest lesson I tell my Maria," Jorge said as he reached for his beer, but he paused before taking a drink. The powerful shot from earlier was traveling through his chest, warming his body, causing him to relax. "I think this here, it will be the most important summer of her life. It will make her more of a woman than a *quinceañera* ever would."

"She could still have one," Diego suggested. "I can plan it."

"This here, it is not for my Maria," Jorge shook his head as pride filled his face. "She is her own person. She does not follow along with the tribe or feel the need to fit into what society says, and you know, I am proud of this fact. If she wants one, I will give her one. But if it is not for her, then I am proud to respect her wishes. She will learn much this summer."

"Sounds like she already has," Diego replied with a raised eyebrow.

"I still have some reservations," Jorge admitted. "But at the same time, I would like her to be prepared for anything. Because it is often *anything* that comes knocking at my door."

"I think she can handle herself," Diego pointed out. "She's already proven it."

"Did I tell you that some kids," Jorge said as a grin appeared on his face. "Try to attack her in the mall bathroom recently? She fought back, and she won. I do not like her getting in a fight. I would like her to be under the radar, but if she must, I am glad she could take care of things on her own."

"Wow," Diego puckered his lips together and nodded. "That deserves a shot in itself."

Jorge laughed as his friend poured him another tequila shot, and they both knocked them back.

"So now what?" Diego finally asked. "What you got planned for the rest of the summer?"

"Well, Big Pharma, they are mad because Athas wants to put stricter regulations on new medications," Jorge said as he reached for his beer. "And that is why we had the issue with that man yesterday. I suspect others will come along too. He was planning to attack Athas, which, let's face it, is an easy target."

"He's weak."

"He's a fucking pussy," Jorge corrected Diego. "And always has been."

"You got no love for him."

"I got no love, but I gotta keep him as prime minister," Jorge insisted. "I got plans."

"Oh yeah?" Diego tilted his head. "Like what?"

"It is not important now," Jorge said with a grin. "But we must keep his head above water, and more importantly, keep him away from the sharks. Once they smell blood, he's fucked."

"So we gotta babysit him all summer?"

"Yes, while he prances around on his unicorn," Jorge nodded. "Even though he does not seem to be able to control the people around him. They are creating censorship bills behind his back, and Athas cannot admit he didn't know anything because it makes him look like a fucking moron."

"Which he *is,"* Diego complained. "He's too much of a hippie to be a prime minister. That don't work."

"Tell me about it."

"It should be *you* running the country," Diego pointed out. "I don't know why you didn't the time Athas got in. No one could've beat you. You're direct, strong, and no one would pull this shit behind your back."

"Diego, there is no question that I would win," Jorge boldly replied. "But I do not like politics enough to live it every day. Paige would not wish me to be in the spotlight, and she is right. But do not think it does not cross my mind, especially when I'm dealing with the *Greek God* all the time. The man has no backbone."

"I think that's why *they* were happy to get him in," Diego reminded him. "He's easy to control. They'd never control you."

"This here is true," Jorge replied. "That man, he gives me more headaches than he's worth."

"I think a lot of people feel that way," Diego suggested. "But just for different reasons."

"This here is true," Jorge replied as he lifted the beer to his mouth. "But Diego, you must remember, a man's worst trait is sometimes also his best trait. You just need to know how to play the game."

CHAPTER 43

Jorge sat his phone aside and reached for his coffee. Moving his sunglasses closer to his face only caused his discomfort to worsen. The headache was so severe that he wasn't sure where it started or ended. It was as if a freight train was running through his brain, and the coffee gave him no comfort.

Glancing at his croissant, he pushed it aside as his stomach flip-flopped. The last thing he wanted was food. He briefly considered going back to bed, but that would be weak. He refused to admit defeat to a hangover. Nothing else had taken him down over the years, and liquor certainly wouldn't be where it started; it was a slippery slope once a man allowed anything to get the better of him.

Sensing a set of eyes on him, Jorge turned his head to see a large crow sitting on the fence that divided his property from Diego's. They exchanged looks, and the bird immediately turned away. Jorge glanced toward his coffee, and the bird swooped down, boldly joining him at the table. Ignoring Jorge, he began to rip pieces off the croissant, his claw holding down the remainder of the fresh-baked delicacy that Jorge usually enjoyed.

The crow suddenly stopped and looked toward the door before grabbing the remainder of the croissant and flying away. This caused Jorge to laugh, even though it caused a shot of pain to drill through his head.

"Papá," Maria was sliding the patio door open while holding Miguel in her opposite arm. "Did that crow take your croissant? Like, the *whole* thing?"

"Bird!" Miguel pointed toward the sky before giggling and placing his tiny hand on his lips.

"That is a crow, Miguel," Jorge replied to his son, who continued to giggle. "And yes, Maria, you saw right. The crows are bold and take what they want. I admire this trait."

"Weird," Maria said as she put Miguel down and closed the patio door.

"Maria, make sure you keep an eye on Miguel," Jorge instructed. "Do not allow him near the pool. Your *Papá,* he has a bad headache this morning, so he cannot move very fast today."

"Paige said you were hungover from tequila with Diego," Maria replied as she reached for Miguel's hand, and they walked toward the table. Jorge reached down for his son. "I can't believe the crow took the *entire* croissant. That's crazy!"

"Maria, we have a lot to learn from crows," Jorge said as he pulled his son up, and the child attempted to reach for his coffee, which Jorge quickly moved away. "They are smart and fiercely loyal to their *familias."*

"Familia," Miguel repeated the word and pointed toward Jorge.

"Si, Miguel, familia," Jorge kissed him on the top of his head. "And crows, Maria, they recognize your face. They remember you. If you are good to them, they remember. If you are bad to them, they never forget."

"I like that," Maria replied as she sat down. "Kind of like you."

"Maria, there is a lot of similarities between me and the crows," Jorge nodded, then quickly stopped as pain shot through his head, his stomach turned. "*Princesa*, can you take Miguel, *Papá* is not feeling so good."

"Are you going to be sick?"

"I do not think so," Jorge replied. "But my old man body, it does not enjoy tequila as much as it once did."

Maria laughed as she reached for Miguel, who tried to slap her.

"Miguel, do not hit your sister," Jorge instructed. "She might beat you up. She's quite ferocious, you should know."

His daughter giggled and pulled Miguel onto her lap. He quickly settled in and watched Jorge with wide eyes.

"You know, Miguel, he reminds me so much of my brother," Jorge referred to the child's namesake. "It is how he looks at me sometimes, I see my brother again for a second. It is wonderful."

"I wish I had known him," Maria sadly replied.

"You would have liked him," Jorge nodded. "He was a beautiful soul."

The patio door slid open, and Paige walked out, a coffee in hand.

"How's the headache?" She called out as she closed the door behind her.

"It is not good," Jorge replied. "Everything hurts."

"Bird!" Miguel pointed toward the sky as a crow flew over and landed on the fence.

"I got no more food for you," Jorge spoke toward the crow. "You got a French bakery croissant as it is. I think you did pretty good for the day."

The crow continued to watch him.

"That's creepy," Maria made a face. "Isn't a crow about death? He keeps hanging around you, *Papá.*"

"Ah, Maria, do not be silly," Jorge grinned. "This here is fine. He just wants food."

"He looks like he wants to hang out," Maria observed.

"Bird!" Miguel pointed toward the crow, who shuffled as if he was about to fly away. "I want!"

"No, Miguel," Maria held back the squirming child. "You can't have the crow. He's just visiting."

"Visiting," Miguel appeared amused.

"We better get going, Maria," Paige gestured toward the door. "Your dentist appointment is coming up. Traffic is probably terrible."

"Do you wish me to take her?" Jorge offered but felt his head pounding even as he moved as if to stand.

"No, that's fine," Paige shook her head. "Besides, you get road rage when you're *not* hungover, let's not tempt fate."

Maria giggled at this, and Miguel quickly joined in, even though he was still staring at the crow.

"Can you take him downstairs to Tala's apartment?" Paige asked Maria. "She's expecting him."

"Sure," Maria stood, and the little boy struggled to get out of her arms. "Come on, Miguel. Let's go see Tala."

"Tal!" Miguel excitedly rushed ahead to the door.

"She is good with him," Jorge commented as his children headed back inside the house.

"Do you need anything?" Paige asked.

"I would fucking love a cigarette right now."

"Don't start that again," Paige shook her head. "I heard that repeatedly last night."

"But hey, it was a good night," He winked at her as she started to move away.

"I can't argue with that," She said as she headed toward the door.

Jorge briefly felt his libido stir, but his pain quickly took over and removed his desires. His body could no longer handle liquor as it did in his youth.

Glancing toward the fence, he noted the crow was gone.

Closing his eyes, the warmth of the sun gave him comfort. He felt his body relax. Maybe he would take a short nap on the couch.

His phone beeped, causing him to jump. Glancing at it, he grew angry.

"What the fuck!" Jorge complained as he stood up, his headache almost knocking him back down. He slowly made his way toward the door.

Once inside the house, he locked the patio just as the doorbell rang. He headed toward the main door. Looking out, he saw the last face he wanted at his door that morning.

"Athas!" Jorge complained as he tore the door open, another shot of pain running behind his eyes. "What the fuck are you doing here?"

"We have to talk," Athas replied with concern in his eyes. "It's kind of important."

"It better be important," Jorge shot back. "I am not in the mood for your nonsense today."

"Can we go to your office?"

"Nobody is home," Jorge shook his head. "What you want?"

"I'm getting a lot of pushback about the Big Pharma bill," Athas replied as he closed the door behind him. "They're threatening to close down and move to another country which would take hundreds of jobs away from the Toronto area."

"Would that not cost more?" Jorge wondered as he glanced at his empty cup in hand and decided he needed more coffee if he wanted to get through this conversation. "I do not know what you want me to tell you? Expose them."

"I can't do that."

"Why the fuck not?" Jorge asked as he reached for the coffee pot and poured another cup but leaving it on the counter. The smell turned him off, so he instead returned to where Athas stood. "You got a mouth."

"It was a private conversation and a subtle threat," Athas attempted to explain. "So I can't really…"

"Do it anyway," Jorge insisted. "Athas, this here is your problem. You are too fucking soft, and people, they do not like soft. They like tough. They like powerful. Pretend you are me for a change and stop being such a pussy."

"Just because I don't kill anyone who pisses me off doesn't make me a pussy," Athas countered. "We don't all play by your rules."

"Yeah, well, if I did not take care of the man I did this week," Jorge quickly pointed out. "You'd be *slaughtered* in the media. An innocent family would be ripped apart and probably deported when he finished. And my family, it would have also suffered. So maybe you do not *approve* of my methods, but at least I get the job done. What do you do? Push paper around your desk? Have a few photo ops? Like seriously, Athas, what do you do all day?"

"I work!" Athas shot back. "I know you don't like to think I do anything, but that's the truth. I work. I know you don't like me, but I'm getting a little sick of these snide remarks all the time. You have no idea what my life is like."

"I do," Jorge insisted. "You go to work, let everyone else tell you what to do all day, then you go home to an empty house and jerk off to pictures of the redhead with the big tits."

"You should like the fact that I let everyone else run the show since you're one of the top people who does," Athas countered as his face turned red. "And your problem with me isn't that I don't do enough. Your problem with me is you're afraid I go home and jerk off to pictures of your wife!"

A shot of fury overpowered the discomfort his body felt as Jorge swung around, and his fist shot forward to punch Athas in the face.

CHAPTER 44

"Can you at least tell me what he said that made you react that way?" Paige followed Jorge into their bedroom. Since punching the Canadian prime minister in the face, his hangover only got worse. This was even though it was something he had wanted to do for a long time. "What did he say?"

"Paige, please, I do not want to get into this," Jorge replied as he slowly turned around and touched her arm. "It does not matter. It was inappropriate what he said."

"Jorge," Paige moved closer to him. "I know you. You *also* say inappropriate things. Can you at least tell me *something?* I know there's tension between you and Alec, but I never thought you'd punch him."

"Well, *mi amor,* I do not know why you think this is not in the range of possibilities," Jorge shook his head as he walked over to the bed and sat down. "He come to my house to complain because of this and that, I mean, how is that appropriate? I cannot hold his hand every day."

"So you punched him instead?" Paige asked as she shook her head. "I don't understand."

"I want to tell you because I am sure he will come crying to you soon," Jorge insisted as his weary body fell back on the bed, his head continued to pound. "But I do not feel well, and I cannot deal with this now."

There was a silent pause before Paige spoke again.

"We'll talk about this later," She calmly replied, and then he heard the door close.

Unable to move, Jorge lay in an uncomfortable position because the idea of moving sounded too painful. Death was starting to look good. Closing his eyes, he began to relax. The sound of shuffling outside his door caused him to open his eyes in time to see Maria walk into the room with a plate of crackers and a banana in the other hand.

"*Papá,* I looked online, and it says that bananas are good for hangovers," Maria started toward the bed. "But I know when my stomach is upset, I eat crackers. So I brought them too."

"Thank you, Maria, but the last thing I want is food," Jorge replied and slowly sat up.

"*Papá,* sometimes what you want and what you need are two different things," Maria sternly replied. "And that's *my* lesson to *you* today."

Jorge grinned and reached for a cracker.

"Thank you, Maria, I do appreciate this," He reluctantly bit into the oddly shaped cracker. "You are probably right about this one."

"I've never been drunk before," Maria admitted. "But hangovers sound terrible."

"Well, Maria, do not drink like I did last night," Jorge advised. "It is not worth it. I feel like death today."

"Is that why you punched Alec in the face?" Maria calmly asked as she sat beside him. "Or because he's so whiny?"

"A little of both," Jorge replied, and they exchanged smiles.

"He must've said something really bad for you to do that," Maria observed.

"He was out of line," Jorge insisted. "But then again, maybe I was too."

"Why was he even here?"

"Good question," Jorge replied.

"Were you expecting him?"

"No, I was not," Jorge shook his head as he finished the first cracker. "So, a banana, this here will take away my hangover?"

"Yeah, it said online that it was one of the foods," She replied and turned toward him. "It said greasy foods sound like a good idea, but they aren't."

"That usually works for me," Jorge replied. "But I do not know if I want to put my body to more abuse today."

Maria giggled, and Jorge felt his spirits lift.

"I think Alec maybe called Paige," She leaned in and whispered. "I'm not sure. I heard her talking to someone when I was in the kitchen."

"Oh, is this so?"

"Yeah, she left before I could hear anything," Maria replied. "Is his eye black?"

"Maria, I did not look," Jorge admitted. "He left right after, but my guess is it will not be pretty."

"I'm sure he has makeup home to hide it," Maria spoke in a matter-of-fact tone, causing Jorge to laugh.

"Oh Maria, that is good," Jorge laughed as he removed the peelings from the banana and sat them on the plate. "I like that. I am sure his people will find a way to explain it away."

His prediction was correct. Prime Minister Athas' black eye was minor compared to the stories of how large pharmaceutical companies were threatening to leave the country over a proposed bill that would hold them to a higher standard. Within hours, propaganda was all over social media, indicating that Athas was cruelly attempting to hold back lifesaving drugs from Canadians. A woman in a TikTok video cried that her disabled son would have to wait even longer for a medication that would take away his unmeasurable discomforts. By mid-afternoon, Athas was shamed throughout social media as well as the news.

"You piss taxpayer money on these news channels," Jorge shouted into the phone while Maria quietly sat across the desk from him. "And they cannot even support you at this time. How is *that?* Why is *that?* You must explain this to me."

"Because I don't give them as much money as Big Pharma," Athas spoke innocently, and Jorge exchanged looks with his daughter, who sat up a bit straighter and shook her head. "If I did, then they'd flip flop. That's how it works. I thought media wasn't biased until I got this close to it."

"Go talk to Makerson," Jorge insisted as he took a deep breath before things got too heated again. "Tell him the truth."

"Which part?" Athas pushed. "I can't tell him what I just said about the media."

"You can tell him that they pay off the media with advertising money for their non-pharmaceutical products since the law prohibits them from advertising their pills," Jorge insisted. "Get Makerson to get the actual numbers."

"Then Big Pharma will drop them, and they'll be coming to me for more money," Athas complained.

"Too fucking bad," Jorge retorted. "If they want eyes on the screen, they gotta do better work. I got no sympathy for a sinking ship when no one bothers to seal the leak."

"Ok," Athas replied with a loud sigh. "I'll call Makerson."

"He is already researching the woman with the disabled kid," Jorge said as he leaned back in his chair. "So, we will see what the real story is there."

"The real story is that the medication she wants for her kid," Athas calmly replied. "Could do him a lot more harm if not sufficiently tested. But they got to her first and insisted that I was the devil and wanted her kid to continue suffering."

"There's only one devil in this conversation, and it's not you," Jorge shot back. "Go talk to Makerson. He will blow this out of the water."

"I will, thank you," Athas replied with sincerity in his voice. "Thank you for everything."

Jorge exchanged looks with Maria. Surprise filled her face.

"And regarding yesterday," Athas went on. "I did explain to Paige that I was out of line with you. I barged into your house, demanded something of you, and said something very inappropriate. I do appreciate everything you do for me, and I hope we can get past this."

"That's a very politician answer," Jorge replied as he glanced toward his bulletproof window. "Should I expect the RCMP to break down my door and put a bullet in my head after we end this call or what?"

"I think we both know that you have more power with the RCMP than me," Athas reminded Jorge, causing his ego to soar. "And I'm being sincere here. I was out of line, and I admit it."

"Well, if that is the case," Jorge said as he leaned ahead in his chair. "I accept your apology. I noticed your black eye didn't look very harsh when you were in the news earlier today."

"They said it was a tennis ball that hit me in the face," Athas said with a sigh. "No one cared anyway, especially with everything else going on."

"Those tennis balls," Jorge replied. "They can be quite ferocious."

Maria covered her mouth, and she squeezed her eyes shut as if to hold back a laugh.

"If that is all," Jorge continued. "Then we must end this call so you can phone Makerson."

"Thank you again."

Jorge ended the call.

"Wow," Maria appeared impressed. "He wasn't even mad."

"He knows better than to bite the hand that feeds him," Jorge insisted. "I helped him get this job, and I help him keep it. Athas would be nothing and nobody without me."

"So, what happens now?" Maria appeared intrigued.

"Makerson will do his research and spin things in the opposite direction from the other news," Jorge predicted. "Maria, it is often easier to respond to the monster in the closet than to prove that he's there in the first place."

"What do you mean?"

"If Athas exposed what Big Pharma does in the first place," Jorge attempted to explain. "People would not listen. They would suggest he only brought it up to get political points, but when Big Pharma attacks him first, he can now respond and knock down their claims and show proof of what they are really up to."

"So, they kind of screwed themselves over?" Maria bluntly asked.

To this, Jorge threw his head back in laughter before finally replying. "Maria, the toilet just blew up, and there's about to be shit everywhere."

CHAPTER 45

"*So, what you're saying*," Makerson calmly spoke as he sat across from Alec Athas. *"Is we need to be testing new pharmaceuticals more carefully before releasing them to the public?"*

"It is perhaps more than necessary," Athas nodded in agreement, his overall demeanor was relaxed as if he had no worries in the world. *"But, I would rather take an abundance of caution rather than take the risk of a Canadian being exposed to a medication that isn't yet ready to be approved."*

"Is this decision concerning the medication taken off the market earlier this summer because it caused stomach cancer?" Makerson asked him the question but then continued to speak. *"My understanding is that there's currently a class action lawsuit underway. I would think that it would be to a company's benefit to be certain that their medications are tested thoroughly before releasing them to the public?"*

"Yes, but then they couldn't make a shit load of money before they get sued," Jorge said to Chase as the two men watched the interview at the bar as it live-streamed from HPC news. "They make more money from the medication than they stand to lose in the lawsuit."

"That's all they care about," Chase muttered. "The people who die are collateral damage."

"Interesting enough, Chase," Jorge said as he looked around Chase's office. "They say the same about cartels when innocent civilians get shot.

But apparently, an accidental shooting is much worse than purposely poisoning people."

Chase said nothing but nodded and raised an eyebrow as the two men continued to watch.

"*....complex situation and I would guess that sometimes we can't see the potential dangers until time has passed,*" Athas was saying as he grew slightly agitated. "*I'm sure they hope that the drugs they sell help people, not hurt them.*"

Jorge rolled his eyes.

"*Unfortunately, they have a pretty long track record of these medical snafus,*" Makerson commented as he reached for a stack of papers beside him. "*In fact, in the short time I had to research the topic, I already found several incidences where pharmaceutical companies had to remove products from the market because they were proven to help one thing while creating another illness. Some of these illnesses were minor, such as stomach upset, but others were far more serious. What do you have to say about this?*"

"*Obviously,*" Athas started to reply as he gestured toward the documents. "*This is very concerning, and it's the reason why I'm creating new laws that will make this as infrequent as possible. We can't have our citizens entrusting their doctors and the pharmaceutical industry, only to later learn that the pills they were taking created new problems or worsened the issue they already had. There has to be checks and balances when it comes to something as concerning as our health, and I'm taking a serious approach to resolving this issue.*"

"*What about the threats that these companies will leave Canada and in turn, take jobs with them if you continue to pursue this path?*" Makerson's voice grew stronger. "*Would this make the government back off on any plans to enforce stronger regulations?*"

"*Clearly,*" Athas appeared more stressed. "*This is something we will have to look at more closely if the situation does arise. As of now, it's merely rumors and no official announcement from any of the companies that they might take this action. I hope that they won't, that they will be able to meet the government halfway in this concern because I would assume it's also a concern of theirs that the public suffers no ill effects after taking their medications.*"

"*But your hands will be tied?*" Makerson pushed.

"*Well, no, not really,*" Athas showed unexpected strength. "*I won't back down on this issue. My job is to protect the Canadian public, not to satisfy a company. My hope, as I said, is to meet them halfway, but I certainly won't bend when it comes to the health and safety of our citizens. That's my primary concern and the reason why my staff has been working on this bill. We need to make sure that these companies are accountable."*

"This here is getting boring," Jorge commented. "However, he is not as much of a pussy today, so that is good."

"You can barely see his black eye," Chase muttered.

"Good makeup and lighting, I'm guessing," Jorge grinned.

"Oh, they're talking about that woman from TikTok," Chase nodded toward the laptop. "The one who went viral."

"*....says that your rules might prohibit or delay the release of a new medication that will greatly help her son's discomfort,"* Makerson was glancing at an iPad. "*Let's play the short video."*

"You know, these here people," Jorge was pointing at the laptop. "It is always hard to say if they are sincere, or if they are propaganda from somewhere like Big Pharma, to pull on heartstrings."

"It's hard to tell what's real on the internet anymore," Chase agreed. "It's a marketing machine for everybody."

"That it is."

"They're talking again," Chase said as he watched the screen.

"*....goes out to her and her son,"* Athas solemnly replied. "*Of course, I want him to be in as little discomfort as possible, but at the same time, I want to make sure that the medication won't harm him in any way. We can't be too careful."*

"*We reached out to..."*

"Chase, now you gonna want to see this," Jorge grinned. "This is where the shit hits the fan."

"*....sources revealed that a large deposit was transferred to her account on the same day that the video was released on TikTok,"* Makerson calmly delivered the news as images appeared on the screen, showing the proof of what he was reporting. "*If you look here...."*

"I kind of thought that," Chase nodded. "The timing was too coincidental."

"Oh, but it gets better..."

"Does Athas know this going into the interview?"

"Some," Jorge shook his head. "but not all."

"*...was also planning similar attacks against your government in response to the news that tougher laws were about to come in place,*" Makerson continued as more documents appeared on the screen. "*You can see here a message where they contacted other people they knew were also speaking out on social media about their fears. However, these people backed out at the last minute, worrying about the legalities of making such claims online.*"

"He found four other people," Jorge spoke gleefully. "This here, it is not a good look for Big Pharma. They have to worry about public image and this shows their true colors."

"Aren't there laws for this kind of thing?"

"Anything with the internet is iffy," Jorge shook his head. "It's a clusterfuck at the best of times."

"Look at Athas' face," Chase laughed as the two men moved closer to the screen. "It looks like his head is about to explode."

"He should be happy because it proves his point," Jorge commented. "The man does not see a winning hand when it is in front of him."

"That's because he is a puppet, and no one told him what to say."

"*...this is concerning,*" Athas was commenting. "*Deeply concerning and the government will be looking into this further.*"

"They won't do a fucking thing," Jorge assured Chase. "It is just another card to play, a power card, even though this dumb fuck don't see it."

"Big Pharma is gonna be out for blood," Chase predicted. "Can't wait to see the spin the big media guys will have on it."

"Big Pharma and Big Media are in bed together," Jorge replied. "And they fuck like rabbits then cum on the public. And the public, they ask for more."

"That's a very disturbing image," Chase laughed.

"It's a very disturbing situation," Jorge countered.

The unsettling interview ended shortly after the big reveal, leaving an aghast audience to comment on social media, causing #BigPharmaBigScam to trend on Twitter. People were outraged by the information revealed. Few were willing to stand up for the companies that deceived the Canadian public. Even mainstream media had to cover the topic, with some attempts to play down the situation, but in fact, only making it worse by enraging the public.

"The fact people are so surprised by this," Jorge informed both his daughter and wife over their dinner that evening. "Is perhaps the most disturbing thing of all. Do people blindly believe everything big companies and the media tell them? It is quite unsettling."

"People will eat whatever you feed them," Paige commented. "We're trained to be that way, so you can't be angry when they do."

"Right now, a lot of people," Jorge commented as he glanced at Miguel in his high chair as the child concentrated on his food. "They feel stupid for believing that woman. But they should feel stupid because the next time someone else comes along, they will not question if it is real, but blindly following along again. That is the problem. People are sheep."

"Always be a wolf," Maria quipped. "That's what Diego always says."

"And Diego, he is right," Jorge assured her. "But you must never tell him I said that."

Maria laughed.

"It will be interesting to see how things look when the dust settles," Paige commented.

Jorge said nothing but looked down at his food. He knew it would get messy, but he had no idea how bad it would get.

CHAPTER 46

"They can issue all the apologies they want," Paige commented as she glanced toward the laptop on the kitchen table, as the couple finished their breakfast. "It's not going to make people have faith in them again, at least, not anytime soon."

"This here is something they feel they need to do," Jorge reminded her. "It is not sincere, however, many will believe whatever they say."

"Do you think?" Paige appeared skeptical. "With the negative media attention they had in the last week? I can't see it."

"Paige, the people," Jorge shook his head as he pointed toward the laptop. "They want the Hollywood, happily ever after ending. So, if someone tells them everything is all right, they believe it. Trust me on this. I have seen it many times."

Paige made a face but said nothing.

"It will blow over as they wish," Jorge insisted. "But Athas has to bring it up again before the election this fall. Remind people. It is more ammunition when he needs it. If he can do that and avoid any scandals this summer like fucking a married woman, then it should be smooth sailing to the election."

"I'm not sure," Paige made a face. "I don't have a great feeling about this."

"Paige, there is not much else we can do until closer to the election anyway," Jorge reminded her. "People are on vacation. They do not care what politicians are doing."

"The problem is that I don't think they care even when they should," Paige suggested.

"Well, in fairness, Paige," Jorge pointed out. "There isn't much reason to believe in politicians in the first place. They lie all the time. They make speeches not based on facts but on what sounds nice. It is a game, not real life."

"It feels like real life when their politics affect people," Paige replied. "Like that censorship bill."

"That bill, it has quietly been removed," Jorge reminded her. "It will not return. Athas finally did something powerful and had it quashed. That is out of the way."

"For now," Paige reminded him.

"For now is all we have," Jorge grinned as he leaned ahead and kissed her cheek. "Do not worry. We can take on anything that comes our way. We have so far."

She said nothing but looked down at her food while he turned on his phone.

The morning was a peaceful one. After breakfast, Jorge flipped through his usual sites to see what was going on in the world. It was while doing this that he sensed a darkness overhead for a brief moment. He looked up to see a crow sitting on the back of the opposite chair.

"You come at the wrong time," Jorge commented as the bird watched him. "I already had my breakfast this morning."

The crow continued to watch him, tilting his head slowly. He cawed then flew away.

The patio door slid open, and Maria started out, coffee in hand.

"Ah, Maria, can you get a slice of bread from the kitchen?"

"Ok," She appeared puzzled. "What did you want on it?"

"Nothing," Jorge shook his head. "It is not for me. It is for the crow."

"You're *feeding* him now?" Maria grinned.

"Maria, I was feeding him all along," Jorge reminded her. "It just was not always on purpose."

"Ok," She agreed as she came over and sat her coffee on the table. "I will be right back."

The crow reappeared and landed on the fence.

"I will take care of you," Jorge commented to the bird, "in a moment."

Maria returned with a slice of bread.

"Just sit the whole thing at the end of the table," Jorge instructed. "He will come get it."

"You don't want me to rip it up?"

"No, Maria, these here birds," Jorge pointed toward the crow. "They do not need to be babied. They can take the whole slice."

She gave a sheepish grin and followed his instructions, gently placing the bread at the end of the table before sitting down beside her father.

"So, Maria, you sleep in today?" Jorge asked as he glanced at his phone.

"It's like 8 o'clock!" She reminded him. "This isn't sleeping in for me."

"I guess it would be sleeping in for me," Jorge replied.

Maria giggled as she reached for her coffee and took a sip.

Just then, the crow flew down and landed at the end of the table. Looking at Jorge, he stabbed at the bread, the fluffy white piece disappearing in his beak. He continued to do this before finally greedily grabbing the remainder of the slice and flew to the other side of the patio, where he savagely tore it apart.

"How come he's not scared of us?" Maria wondered. "Usually birds are scared of people, aren't they?"

"Maria, these here birds," Jorge pointed toward the crow. "They have sharp senses. They know who they can trust and who they cannot trust. This here is a good lesson for you."

"I left my book upstairs."

"You can add it later," Jorge reminded her. "Today, *Princesa,* we are going for a drive out of town."

"Where are we going to?"

"We are heading to a rural community where Paige and I decided to build a safe house."

"Oh, yeah, I forgot about that."

"They have been working on it for some time," Jorge continued. "It was on some property we discovered last year. I will not get into how, but as soon as it was for sale, we buy it, and now we have a house being built."

"What does a safe house mean, exactly?" Maria appeared curious. "Like bulletproof windows, like our house?"

"Yes, of course, one can never be too careful," Jorge nodded. "But it is not only the structure and safety of the house but the fact that the house is kind of, as they say, off the grid. The neighbors, they can barely see it because it is away from the road. You see, there is an abandoned house closer to the road, and most people do not look beyond that. They do not realize that there is a road behind the home, and it takes you to our safe house."

"So you can't see it from the road."

"No."

"But the people in that town must know it's there?"

"They think it is a warehouse for a farmer," Jorge insisted. "We make it seem like it is not a real house. It is a bit deceiving, but this is what makes it safe. You do not suspect that it is a house at all, let alone one for people to live in."

"Is it nice?"

"I have seen the pictures and have had Chase go to check it out," Jorge nodded. "It is nice. Modest, but that is fine."

"So no pool?" Maria pointed toward their pool just as the crow flew away with the last scrap of bread.

"No pool," Jorge shook his head. "But enough rooms so that our family, Diego, Chase, anyone that must, can hide out there if needed."

"Is it almost done?"

"Yes, Maria, they are putting on the finishing touches now," Jorge replied. "That is why we must go see it today. I want to have a look, you and me."

"That sounds fun," Maria took another drink of her coffee. "Is Paige and Miguel coming too?"

"No, Paige she must go to the office today," Jorge replied. "And Miguel, he is going with Tala for an event at the library. He must socialize with other children."

"That never goes well," Maria reminded him. "I mean, he got kicked out of his daycare."

"Maria, that there was an overreaction," Jorge shook his head. "He was playing, but people today, they bring their kids up to be so sensitive that they cannot handle anything. Miguel, he is not that kind of child. Paige has his enrolled in Pre-K, whatever the fuck that is, for the fall. So this here is good."

Maria giggled at his comment.

"So, we can leave after you have finished your coffee," Jorge said. "If you wish?"

"I wanna go!"

"*Perfecto.*"

Maria went upstairs to finish getting ready, and Jorge made his way to the office. He wanted to check a few things before heading out for the rest of the day. It was while on the phone with Diego that his secure line rang.

"Diego, I must go," Jorge complained. "Athas, he is calling. He probably has a hangnail or something stupid."

"Yeah, well, that's usually the case," Diego replied. "Take some pictures of that house when you're there today."

"I plan to do so," Jorge replied. "Talk to you soon."

Ending the call, he picked up his secure line and made a face.

"What's up, Athas?" Jorge gruffly spoke into the phone. "I thought you were flying high in the polls this week."

"I am," Athas nervously replied. "But I think that's the problem."

"What do you mean by this?" Jorge asked. "Must I remind you it is a good thing to do well in polls?"

"That's not the problem," Athas replied. "I think…I'm in danger."

"Why do you say this?"

"I had the head of CSIS here today…."

"Oh, *now* you can talk to the head of CSIS," Jorge cut him off. "But last year when we were trying to find out who was writing a book about me, this here was a problem?"

"It wasn't by invite," Athas calmly replied. "He showed up for an emergency meeting."

"Oh?" Jorge was intrigued.

"He has reason to believe," Athas hesitated before continuing. "That someone wants to kill me."

CHAPTER 47

"Wow, this is *really* like a million miles away from *anything,*" Maria remarked as they drove through rural Ontario. "Like there's like, nothing here."

"Maria, you exaggerate," Jorge shook his head. "There was a grocery store and pharmacy back there and a gas station up ahead."

"Yeah, but like, you know, that's it," Maria stumbled on as she continued to look around.

"What did you expect, *Princesa?"* Jorge teased. "To find an H&M or Guess store out here?"

"Well, it would be nice!" Maria mockingly replied. "A girl's gotta have nice clothes."

"But Maria, the beauty of this here area," Jorge pointed out. "Is that it is quiet, peaceful. You don't sit in traffic for an hour trying to get home."

"Well, unless you're driving from Toronto to here," Maria reminded him. "And when did you ever sit an hour in traffic, *Papá?"*

"Maria, you know what I mean," Jorge grinned. "The point is that it is a more peaceful life, and there are days that I think it would be better."

"It would be so boring out here," Maria observed.

"That is because you are young," Jorge pointed out. "When you are young, you crave the excitement. When you are old like me, not so much."

"There always seems to be some excitement in your life."

"A little too much," Jorge said as he continued to drive. "We are almost there."

"It seems like it's getting more...*rural,"* Maria said as she looked down at her phone. "I barely have one bar on my phone."

"But Maria, isn't that kind of nice?" Jorge asked as he exchanged looks with his daughter. "To sometimes be away from it all."

"But what if there's an emergency?" Maria wondered. "Back in Toronto?"

"Maria, we still have some reception, so we will get the message."

"Maybe."

"Maybe I will look into improving the reception in this area," Jorge commented.

"What if Alec has an emergency and needs to reach you?" Maria asked in a serious tone, causing Jorge to cringe. However, a glance in her direction and he realized she was purposely taunting him.

"Let the fucker figure it out for himself," Jorge sharply remarked, causing his daughter to laugh.

"But you had that call..." Maria started to remind him.

"Maria, part of being a politician," Jorge pointed out. "Is to accept that you will get death threats. This here is reality. You cannot run a country and not expect that some people want you dead. I am not sure why Athas thinks he is the exception or that they are even real."

"You don't think they're real?"

"I do not know," Jorge shook his head. "All I know is that he has armed people around him at all times. I am pretty sure at least one of them cares if he is alive, so this here is not my problem."

"Then why did he call you?"

"Maria, Alec Athas is a scared little boy," Jorge pointed out. "And I somehow became his mommy."

His daughter laughed, causing him to grin.

"Me? I do not think this threat was very serious," Jorge bluntly replied.

"But you said CSIS was talking to him?" Maria said. "Wouldn't that mean it was more serious?"

"No, I think these people here have to err on the side of caution," Jorge replied. "Someone probably sent a message to a friend on Facebook saying they wish Athas were dead, and they all overreacted."

"They read our messages?" Maria appeared surprised.

"Maria, do not trust social media," Jorge warned. "Never have any secrets on there. They spy on you. That I promise you."

They drove a few minutes longer before Jorge slowed down on a quiet road. He turned into the driveway and past a small house, following a path that led into the trees. Maria remained silent on the passenger side but observed her surroundings. They quickly lost sight of the main road as they approached a large, warehouse-type building. Jorge stopped the SUV and grabbed his phone. He tapped on the screen, and a large garage door opened, and he drove inside.

"Wow," Maria said as she looked around. "It doesn't look like a house."

"That is the idea," Jorge said as he stopped the SUV then tapped on his phone again. The door behind them closed. "It is important that no one knows the difference."

"So, they think..."

"It is a warehouse," Jorge replied. "Those who even know it's here at all. We are quite far from most people, and Maria, that is what I like."

Glancing down at her phone, she appeared surprised.

"I have better reception now than on our way here."

Jorge didn't reply but winked at his daughter.

"Let's take a look," Jorge said as he reached for the door handle.

"This is awesome," Maria jumped out of the vehicle, and Jorge did the same. "Is anyone here?"

"Some men, they are working," Jorge replied as he opened the door to enter the house. "Normally, there will be an alarm, of course, but the security system is hooked up. I can check to make sure they are always working, and no one else is here."

Maria nodded as they walked through the door.

They entered a room that was a reasonable size.

"This here will be the living room," Jorge commented as he walked ahead, and Maria followed. "And this here, the next room, the kitchen."

The carpenters, all Mexican, looked up, surprised to see Jorge Hernandez walking through the house.

"*Senor* Hernandez!" An older man said. *"No te estábamos esperando."*

"Finge que no estamos aquí. Solo estamos mirando a nuestro alrededor," Jorge replied and turned to his daughter. "Do you know what I said?"

"My Spanish isn't that bad!" Maria complained. "You said we are just looking around and pretend we aren't here."

"Good, I worry that you forget," Jorge commented as he continued to walk-through, passing the carpenters, who nodded in respect. "We do not want to get in their way, Maria, so we will do a quick walk-through."

"Is that stairs safe to go up yet?" Maria pointed toward the stairway that didn't have a banister.

"Yes, Maria, but be cautious," Jorge warned as he forged ahead.

Rushing up the stairs, it took a minute for him to realize that his daughter had barely made it past the first step.

"Maria, do you not want to come with me?" Jorge asked.

"I'm scared of falling," She spoke nervously, appearing self-conscious.

Jorge didn't reply but walked back down and reached for her hand. She bashfully took it, and together, they walked upstairs. There was hammering on both levels.

"Now, this here," Jorge said as they reached the hallway, and he let go of her hand. "Is all the bedrooms. We have enough for our family, including Chase, and Diego, and maybe a couple more if necessary."

She nodded as she glanced around. "It seems bigger up here than down there."

"Not really, we did not see all the downstairs," Jorge commented. "There is also an office and another bedroom there as well."

"Wow," Maria started to walk to her left. "It looks almost done."

"They can put these places together fast," Jorge replied as he tapped on his phone. "Come here. I will show you where the cameras are."

"I don't see cameras in the house," Maria commented as she returned to his side.

"That is the point," Jorge said as he raised an eyebrow and showed her the phone. "They will be in all rooms except bathrooms and only at the entrance of bedrooms. But most will be outside the house, as you can see."

Her eyes scanned the phone.

"Yeah, and that one is at the house we passed when we came in," Maria observed.

"And there's another between there and here," Jorge commented as he pointed toward his screen. "I have a lot of cameras outside. I want to make sure everything is secure."

"Wow," Maria replied. "Do you think we will need this house anytime soon?"

"It is always a possibility," Jorge shrugged as he put his phone away. "But the most important thing is that we are always prepared."

Maria nodded as she glanced around again.

"Let us finish looking around," Jorge said.

Twenty minutes later, they were back in the SUV and on their way home. Maria appeared subdued, which made Jorge unsure if he should bring up something on his mind.

"Maria, I have something important that I wish to discuss with you," Jorge said, catching her attention. "It is about Miguel."

"Ok," Maria turned to him. "What is it?"

"Maria, if anything were to happen to me," Jorge slowly continued. "I want you to make a promise to me that you will teach him everything I have taught you."

Appearing startled, Maria froze.

"I am not saying anything will," Jorge continued. "But we never know what will happen to any of us. I want to be prepared."

"Of course," She finally replied. "Is there something you aren't telling me?"

"No, Maria, I promise," Jorge reached over and squeezed her arm as he continued to watch the road. "I am just saying this in case something *did* happen. You must always protect him, and you must teach him everything that I teach you. It is important that you do."

"Of course, *Papá.*"

"I know that Paige, Diego, Chase, they all would do the same," Jorge continued. "But there is a difference. What I tell you, they are special lessons. And you would need to teach the same ones to Miguel."

"But you're going to be fine, right?" Maria continued to look worried.

"Maria, none of us know how long we will be on this earth," Jorge reminded her. "So, that is why I say this to you. There are never guarantees. But I certainly do not plan to leave without one hell of a motherfucking fight."

Maria giggled, appearing to relax.

The two continued to drive along, slowly making their way back to Toronto. And that's where he got the news.

CHAPTER 48

The atmosphere in the VIP room was somber when he entered it. A glance at the faces around the table, his eyes quickly landed on his wife's face in an attempt to read her reaction. Her expression was blank, showing no emotion, while Chase, Marco, and Diego appeared equally morose. He quickly sat down and took a deep breath, but before he could speak, Paige asked a question.

"You took Maria home?" She glanced past him toward the door. "I figured she'd want to be here."

"I told her I would feel better if she was at home," Jorge gently spoke. "Since Miguel is there. To watch over him."

"This might be a bit much for her," Chase quietly added.

"I think it's a bit too much for us all," Diego cut in. "I can't believe this fucking happened."

"He's fine," Jorge put his hand up in the air as if to calm the room. "Athas isn't dead. He's not even in the hospital. So let us take it easy."

"But it was close," Paige reminded Jorge. "The shooter was bold."

"They shot the guy before he could get near," Chase replied. "I think they killed him."

"Sir, he is dead," Marco jumped in, his comments directed at Jorge. "They are not releasing it to the public yet, but I did see it before I turned my laptop off."

Jorge nodded his head and didn't say anything.

"The thing is that if they did it once," Paige added. "They might do it again. And next time, they might be successful."

Jorge again attempted to read her expression when he looked into her eyes, but nothing alerted him.

"Well, ok, so we must look at exactly what happened here," Jorge said as he took a deep breath. "What was it? He was walking toward parliament, and what?"

"He was going in, and some lunatic came out of nowhere and was about to shoot him," Diego spoke excitedly. "Like, holy fuck! How does someone like that get past security?"

Jorge raised an eyebrow but didn't comment.

"You'd be surprised," Paige answered. "When I was an assassin, I found some clever ways to get the job done. These things are well planned. The subject is watched carefully. They follow their routine, monitor their general behavior, and work around it."

"But with all that security?" Chase asked.

"Everyone has a vulnerable spot," Paige shook her head. "Even the security that watches him. They're watched too."

"So, Athas, he is fine?" Jorge asked, unsure why they were meeting. "They give him more security, do whatever, and he will be fine. I cannot see anyone trying this soon after the first attempt."

"Sir, this may mean nothing," Marco jumped in. "But I have read that sometimes parties will do this on purpose to create compassion for the leader. When presidents and prime ministers escape these situations, they are viewed as brave and often win another election. Of course, they have a fall guy who takes the blame."

"You don't think the party was doing this on purpose?" Paige wrinkled her forehead. "And if they did, Alec would know."

"Not necessarily," Jorge shook his head. "And I doubt that they would kill the assassin."

"They would if they thought the assassin would talk," Paige reminded him.

Jorge didn't say anything, but his thoughts were springing into action.

"But that may not be it," Marco shook his head. "I just thought of it."

"Come on," Diego jumped in. "It was obviously Big Pharma. They got a lot to lose if he fucks around with the standards to pass their shitty pills. They lose money. It's easier to lose *him.*"

"Or scare him into submission," Paige quietly added.

"See this here," Jorge shook his head. "Are all guesses. We do not know for sure."

"Sir, I am trying to hack CSIS and the RCMP to see what they say," Marco said as he looked around the table. "But there is concern that there will be more attempts."

"They must be basing that theory on something," Chase commented. "So they must know something."

"Not necessarily," Paige shook her head. "Probably erring on the side of caution."

"I assume later today I will be getting a call from Athas," Jorge sighed and leaned back in his chair. "Probably ready to retire his position because he's scared."

"Probably a legit response to almost being shot," Diego nodded his head. "I mean, come on….he ain't us."

"This isn't his world," Paige added.

"Well, he is running a fucking country," Jorge argued. "So it is reasonable to expect such things. This is not the first time a country's leader has been shot at, even though, I know in Canada, it may not be so common."

"So, what we gonna do?" Diego asked. "Do we gotta babysit him, or what?"

Chase grinned and looked away.

"Diego, we have been babysitting him for the last few years," Jorge reminded him. "Why would this be new?"

"He has security," Paige shook her head. "They aren't going to let in any of us to watch him."

"And if they did," Diego leaned ahead on the table. "Paige, you would be the perfect person with your background."

Jorge glared at Diego, who shrank back.

"I'm pretty sure they aren't aware of my past," Paige grinned as she waved her hand in the air. "To them, I'm just a stay-at-home mom."

Laughter sprang up around the table, and even Jorge managed a grin.

"Anyway," Diego continued. "Yeah, there ain't much we can do."

"Well, we might have to do something," Paige reminded them. "We don't know for sure that his security *or* these agencies aren't in on it."

Jorge glanced at his wife and thought for a moment.

"I am looking into everything," Marco said. "But it is hard to say. I did not even see this coming."

"Nothing with Big Pharma?" Jorge asked.

"If it was them," Marco shook his head. "They left no trace."

"Maybe it's someone for them," Paige reminded the group. "As I said, maybe if we find out who the assassin was, that might help us find out more. If I can get a name, I can do my own research."

"Do you still have connections to that world?" Chase asked.

"I do," Paige nodded, without getting into the details. "And I probably have access to information that the RCMP and CSIS won't. If I can find that out, I can trace back to who hired him."

"They'll just say it's a terrorist attack," Diego sniffed. "I can see that a mile away."

As it turned out, Diego was right. The news speculated that it was a terrorist attack, causing the entire country to live in fear of what could happen next. Who was doing this? What country? Why? The news channels misled Canadians down a rabbit hole that didn't make sense, but fear led them.

It was when Jorge was back in his office alone that his secure line rang.

"Hello," Jorge answered. "I hear you had an exciting day."

"Maybe in your world," Athas complained. "But it scared the fuck out of me."

"So, let me guess," Jorge leaned back in his chair. "You want to quit politics now."

"No!" Athas was quick to reply, causing Jorge to lean ahead. "If they think they'll scare me away, they can think again. I won't be bullied."

"Well, I must say," Jorge commented. "This here is refreshing. I did not expect it from you."

"I know it was Big Pharma," Athas continued. "They're trying to scare me into backing down, but now, I'm going to make these laws even tougher."

"You might want to wear a bulletproof vest to the grocery store," Jorge replied. "Because these here people aren't going to back down easily."

"I know," Athas had a hint of concern in his voice. "But neither am I."

"So, tell me," Jorge was intrigued by this change in character. "What information do you have so far? I have my people working on it, but I need to know if you have anything that might help."

"I wasn't told much," Athas confessed. "They keep me on a need-to-know basis."

"Yes, well, that is nothing new," Jorge replied. "But they must have told you something."

"They were too busy assuring me of my safety," Athas replied. "I tried to ask, but no one was telling me much. They just said it was 'still under investigation'. That's another reason why I'm pissed off."

"I think that's fair," Jorge nodded. "If someone tried to kill me, I would also want to know who and why."

"Yeah, well, if I find out who and why," Athas snapped. "You should get your crematorium ready because I'm not fucking around with these people. If it's Big Pharma, like I think, this is fucking war."

Impressed, Jorge couldn't help but grin.

"I must say, Athas," he finally replied. "I did not expect this here from you. Who knew it would take almost being shot to bring out the fight in you."

"Like I said," Athas sharply replied. "Enough is enough. This means war."

"And luckily for you," Jorge replied. "You have a whole army behind you. And we fight to win."

CHAPTER 49

"But of course, it's a terrorist attack," Jorge shook his head as he glanced at his laptop and back at his daughter. "This here is what the media fall back on in this situation. Nothing gives them higher ratings than fear."

"But *was* it a terrorist attack?" Maria wrinkled her nose and leaned forward on the table. "I mean, wouldn't someone say they're attacking our country if that were the case?"

"But now it's *domestic* terrorism if they can't do that," Paige chimed in as she walked toward the table, coffee in hand. "If they can't link it to a group outside of the country, they still make sure they get that terrorism word in there. It's a great way to keep people frightened."

"And the more frightened," Jorge continued. "The more people turn to the news to see what the latest developments are…"

"And there's usually nothing," Paige shook her head as she sat down. "They want more people watching, more advertising money, it's completely disgusting what they do."

"We live in a world that thrives on fear," Jorge reminded his wife, who nodded her head. "I mean, useless products would never sell if people weren't scared."

"What do you mean by *that?*" Maria asked with a grin on her face. "Like what?"

"Like that expensive lipgloss you wear," Jorge pointed at his daughter's face. "Why do you buy it?"

Flustered, his daughter stuttered over her words.

"It's...like, better for the environment, and it helps so your lips don't get dry from the sun and heat...."

"Ok, so a cheap one, it is not the same?" Jorge countered.

"I...I guess not."

"Exactly," Jorge pointed out. "That there lipgloss is the same as a cheaper brand. They make you feel guilty by saying it's better for the environment..."

"Giving the impression," Paige jumped in, "that the other one is not."

"And fear," Jorge continued. "They make you feel scared your lips are going to turn to sandpaper if you don't use their product year around. Do you think the cheap one does not do the same?"

"I don't know," Maria blushed. "I can buy the cheaper one from now on..."

"Maria, this here is not the point," Jorge shook his head. "I am not saying that. What I am saying is that advertising creates a problem you never thought you had. I have seen the ads for this here brand, and that's what they do. But it's twice as much as..."

"Try three times as much," Paige cut him off.

"Exactly!" Jorge nodded. "The news, it does the same. They play up everything to scare people. People react to fear. If people turned their backs on television when they do this, they would stop. It is like when Miguel has a temper tantrum. If we run to him each time, he will continue doing it. This here is no different."

"So, you don't think it's a terrorist attack," Maria pointed to the laptop on the table.

"Maria, there is no proof," Jorge shook his head. "They jumped on this idea and ran with it."

"Wow," Maria looked ill. "That's terrible because now everyone is scared all the time."

"They got extra security at baseball games and concerts over this," Paige added. "And airports, all these places."

"Welcome to the modern world," Jorge shook his head. "People are scared and people are dumb."

Maria looked discouraged.

"I have a meeting with Marco," Jorge said as he glanced at his phone. "I must leave now."

"Can I come too?" Maria asked.

"I would rather you stay here," Jorge shook his head. "Maria, you have learned much from me this summer, but there are still some things that I would rather wait for now. We will discuss whatever happens later. For now, stay with Paige. I think she needs you here today."

"I do," Paige nodded. "We're going to discuss what we want to teach you for the remainder of the summer. I have some ideas."

Jorge said nothing but exchanged looks with his wife.

It was better his daughter not get both feet in yet.

Heading out, he noted there was less traffic as he made his way to the club. Many people were working from home out of fear of another attack. Jorge had no idea why since the attack was directed at the Canadian prime minister. The fact that the public believed otherwise was ludicrous.

Only Chase's car was outside when he arrived at the bar, but he walked in to see Marco's bicycle beside the door. Locking up behind him, Jorge made his way to the VIP room, where Chase was hovering over Marco's shoulder, looking at the laptop on the table.

"Good morning," Jorge said as he walked through the door, noting that neither man took their eyes off the screen. "Did we find something here?"

"We did," Chase commented as he moved away. Glancing at Jorge, he sat in the chair beside Marco.

"Sir, it is *not* a terrorist attack," Marco confirmed as Jorge sat across from him.

"Did we not already know this?" Jorge asked as he fixed his tie. "Let me hear what you got."

"Well, sir, it wasn't Big Pharma," Marco continued. "At least not directly, but they aren't clean either."

"There's definitely blood on their hands," Chase assured Jorge.

"But the masterminds behind all this were people in Alec Athas own party," Marco continued as he pointed toward the laptop. "It was *them* that *encouraged* this attack."

"I am not surprised," Jorge leaned back in his chair. "Paige, she has been looking into it and was speculating the same thing."

"The name she gave me last night," Marco continued as he scratched his head, causing his hat to be crocked. "Billy Marshalton? This man, he works behind the scenes in Athas' party."

"He does PR or marketing or something," Chase shook his head. "He's being told by the party that Alec's the problem and has got to go…"

"So, this Marshalton guy did what?" Jorge asked.

"He joined an online anti-government group," Chase began to explain as Marco tapped on his keyboard, his face very pensive as he worked. "And he found this guy, who, let's say, clearly had mental health issues. This was the same guy who ended up shooting at Athas."

"I see," Jorge nodded. "So they got him to do the dirty work?"

"Yes, sir, Marshalton encouraged him," Marco stopped typing and looked across the table at Jorge. "He said things like, 'You know Athas is the reason why this country is such a mess' and that kind of thing."

"Yeah, Marshalton wanted to make him angrier," Chase explained. "He told him that they were cutting funds for the program that this guy relied on to keep his sanity. Marshalton even went so far as to make up a fake article headline that said Athas thought it was a waste of money because 'those people' never got better. Of course, this wasn't true, but the shooter guy didn't look into it at all. He believed it."

"So that was what pushed him?" Jorge asked.

"It was a lot of things," Chase pointed toward the screen while Marco nodded. "We are talking months and months of conversations that built up to the point where the shooter was ready to go. Marshalton was pushing his buttons."

"But technically," Marco jumped in. "He did not do anything illegal."

"So, this here sounds like he slipped under the radar," Jorge replied. "Unless he is doing the same with someone else."

Chase and Marco exchanged looks.

"What?" Jorge asked. "What is that about?"

"He's got some kid persuaded to do something at an event Athas is attending this weekend," Chase spoke in a quiet voice. "He's 14."

"Maria's age," Jorge said as he raised an eyebrow. "That is...that is young."

"Sir, this man, he does not care," Marco spoke solemnly. "His only goal is to get Athas out of the party at any cost."

"And this here is coming from..." Jorge asked.

"You name it," Chase shook his head. "Big Pharma, the members of the party, the overlords who control politics behind the scenes, they want him out because he's not toeing the line. He was supposed to be *their* puppet and not yours."

"And sir," Marco continued. "They know that they cannot do anything about you, so it's him they have to take care of."

Jorge said nothing but nodded.

"So, now, they have this kid that's going to shoot him instead," Chase reminded Jorge. "What the fuck kind of savages are these people?"

"And they say the cartel is bad," Jorge complained. "At least, back in Mexico, we never pretended to be saints. Here, there is always a more sinister monster hiding in the corners. I might be a monster too, but I do not hide it."

"So, what are we gonna do?" Chase shook his head.

"We need someone to hack this man's account and talk the kid down," Jorge instructed Marco, who nodded in agreement. "Say whatever you have to, and this Marshalton guy, just tell me what I gotta know."

"It seems like he's been working behind the scenes for some time," Marco commented. "He is one of the key people who help find ways to get Athas out of the party."

"But none worked, so they want to get him out *permanently*," Chase added. "Before he can win another election."

Jorge fell silent. A million thoughts flooded his head, memories, conversations with Athas.

"Sir, I am tracking this man to see his usual behaviors," Marco attempted to explain. "I see a few opportunities where you could...find him alone."

"We can take him out tonight," Chase pointed toward the laptop. "I was thinking..."

"No," Jorge cut him off, causing both men to fall silent and look at him. "First, I must decide if I want to stop him."

"What are you saying, sir?" Marco appeared confused. "The 14-year-old..."

"No, you gotta stop the kid from whatever he was going to do," Jorge confirmed, causing Marco to appear relieved. "But the other guy? I don't know if I disagree with him. Maybe I want Athas dead too."

The room fell silent as the three men exchanged looks.

CHAPTER 50

When you watch the news, do you ever wonder why it's so dramatic? Rather than focusing on the facts, we're instead caught up in the emotional aspect, much like we would for a soap opera or a nighttime drama. Shouldn't we instead be concerned with details, policies, and actual facts? The proof might be in the pudding, but who's making the pudding? And what did they put in it? You might want to consider that before you dip your spoon in.

Jorge Hernandez spent a great deal of time alone in his office that day. He considered everything, and just when he thought he had made up his mind on whether or not Athas should live or die, a knock at the door grabbed his attention.

"*Si,*" he called out, expecting Maria to be on the other side.

It was Paige.

"Ah, *mi amor!*" Jorge forced a smile on his lips, attempting to hide the fact that he was distracted. "Come in."

"I know you said you wanted some time alone," Paige seemed hesitant as she closed the door behind her. "But I thought I should check in. You tend to get in your own head."

"Don't we all, *mi amor?*" He attempted to brush it off as she sat across from him.

"So, I don't know the details," Paige reminded him. "But I know enough to be concerned about Alec's life. They want him out, one way or another."

"And you are worried they will kill him?"

"And I'm worried they will kill *you,"* Paige corrected him. "After all, you're the person who *really* has control here. We know that. They know it too."

"Paige, come on…"

"If they don't get him," She continued. "They will want to get you."

"Paige, I…"

"Enough is enough, Jorge," Paige cut him off. "We have to be careful here. I don't want either of you dead, but more specifically, I don't want *you* dead."

There was a silence as the two shared a look, with Jorge finally looking away.

"How many times have we had this discussion?" She continued. "That you can't be in the limelight. That you need to keep out of their crosshairs."

"I am keeping a low profile," Jorge argued. "I stayed home all summer with…"

"I know," She spoke in a more soothing tone and leaned forward in her chair. "But I'm starting to fear that is not enough."

"They are focused on him," Jorge finally confirmed. "Not me. I know this because Marco did some research."

Paige didn't say anything. Jorge felt his heart begin to race.

"Paige, it isn't what you think…."

She didn't reply but gave him a cold stare.

"I did not know how to go about it," Jorge stuttered through, attempting to sound confident, but knew it was lacking.

"Really?" Paige quietly asked. "You weren't sitting here trying to decide whether or not you wanted Alec to die?"

"Paige, I…"

"Jorge, I know you," She continued to speak in a calm voice, even though her eyes were showing emotions that put him ill at ease. "You were considering whether or not you wanted them to kill Alec. You hate him. And you hate him because of me."

“Paige, it’s not that,” Jorge attempted to reassure her but looked away. “The man, he infuriates me. He is so weak.”

“I know,” Paige surprised him in her answer. “But that’s not the real issue you have with him, and we both know it.”

Jorge didn’t reply, and the two exchanged looks. He felt his stomach turn as she stood up and walked out the door. His body felt weak. A cold sweat took over as a pain shot through his chest. He closed his eyes and turned his chair around for fear that Maria would walk into the office and see him that way. His breath was short, erratic until he finally felt light, calm, relaxed. Opening his eyes, he looked around.

Athas had always been loyal to Jorge. And despite any animosity, Jorge had to be loyal to him.

This wasn’t about him or Athas. It was about Paige.

Jorge slowly turned his chair around and called Athas on his secure line.

“Hello,” Athas answered with some hesitancy in his voice.

“You got a rat.”

“I do?”

“In your office,” Jorge continued. “A big rat.”

“Why do I feel like we went through this and…”

“This one here has been working against you from day one,” Jorge cut him off. “He’s in talks with the big shots that want you out.”

“They said,” Athas slowly began to speak. “That someone was encouraging the guy who tried to shoot me on some anti-government…”

“It was someone from your office,” Jorge cut him off again, and the two fell silent.

“But I thought…”

“You thought wrong,” Jorge sharply replied. “It’s your own party that wants you out. Have we not seen this again and again? They started small, but they keep upping the ante.”

“I see,” Athas suddenly had anger creeping into his voice. “But what about Big Pharma and…”

“They are involved,” Jorge confirmed. “There’s a lot of powerful people who want you out. They thought you’d be compliant for them, and you aren’t. They want you gone.”

“I’m not leaving!” Athas’ voice grew angrier. “I try to reason with…”

"They don't want to hear reason," Jorge reminded him. "They want it their way, but you ain't playing ball."

"Who?"

"Do you know a guy named Billy Marshalton?"

"Him?" Athas sounded surprised. "But he's been so supportive and..."

"Yeah, well, think again," Jorge cut him off. "He's waiting for you to turn around to stick the knife in your back. *Literally,* stick the knife in your back."

"But you must be mistaken," Athas sounded alarmed. "He's been so helpful to me. I thought he was in my corner."

"Look, I don't know what he says to you," Jorge insisted. "But I got a whole lot of evidence that says otherwise. He wants you the fuck out and sooner rather than later."

"He's meeting with me later today," Athas continued. "He said..."

"You're meeting him today?" Jorge cut him off. "Where? When?"

"Well, I'm in Toronto today," Athas stuttered along. "He's from here...I mean, that's one of the reasons why we connected. He always talked about how much I did for the community when I was a social worker."

"And nothing set off a bell?" Jorge asked. "Nothing seemed odd?"

"No, I....oh fuck!"

"What?"

"He knew about Sheila Proctor-Wade," Athas sounded infuriated. "I confided in him because I thought I could trust..."

"Think again," Jorge reminded him. "I bet if you look back, you will see a pattern here. Now, when and where are you meeting him?"

"Here, at my home office, in Toronto," Athas sounded confused. "Then that means, he also..."

"*When* will he be there?" Jorge cut him off, annoyed with the naive prime minister.

"In about a half-hour," Athas replied, his voice full of anxiety.

"I'm on my way!" Jorge said as he jumped up from his chair. "Do not do anything."

Hanging up the phone, Jorge grabbed his gun and headed for the door, almost running into Paige.

"Where are you..."

"I gotta go, Paige," Jorge gave her a quick kiss as he passed. "I gotta go to see Athas. Call Andrew. Have him on standby."

"Wait! What?" Paige followed him.

"Paige, do not worry," Jorge halted for a moment. "He got a meeting with a rat."

She didn't reply, her eyes full of emotion.

"I promise, Paige," He quietly continued as he leaned in to kiss her forehead. "This here is fine. Athas will be fine."

Before she could say anything, he rushed out the door and jumped in his SUV. Flying down the road, he felt his heart race as he hit a button on his phone. Chase answered.

"I'm taking care of the rat problem we talked about this morning," Jorge abruptly spoke.

"Need any help?" Chase asked. "Just tell me what to do."

"Hang on for now," Jorge replied. "Tell Marco no cameras at the house of the pussy boy. He'll know what I mean."

"Gottcha."

He ended the call and focused on his driving. Glancing at the time, he realized it was rush hour. His head began to throb. What if Marshalton was going to kill Athas himself? What if he was too late? Would Paige ever forgive him? Would she believe he had tried his best?

Arriving at Alec's house, he noted that the usual security wasn't around. Expecting to see a sniper or RCMP officer jump in front of him as he approached the door, he thought it was concerning that neither was in sight. No cars were in the driveway, which he assumed was a good sign. Perhaps Marshalton was stuck in traffic too, but Jorge had a bad feeling. There was an eerie vibe as he approached the door.

He was about to ring the doorbell when he heard a gunshot inside.

Glancing around, he knew Marco had nearby security cameras turned off by now, but were eyes watching him. What if he was being set up? Wouldn't it be convenient to kill Athas and have him arrested for murder? That would take care of two problems at once. He sheepishly glanced around again before using his sleeve to try the doorknob. To his surprise, it opened.

Reaching for his gun with the other hand, he walked through the doorway and looked around. Quietly closing the door behind him, he locked it and moved forward, listening for any sound that might indicate the location of the gunshot. He walked through the entryway and headed toward the room where Athas had his office. Although he had only visited it once, Jorge recalled the location as he quietly moved ahead. Jorge listened for any sound but continued to hear nothing. If Marshalton killed Athas, he'd be rushing toward a door. That was unless he was expecting Jorge to arrive.

Creeping ahead, he found the office. The door was open ajar, and blood was seeping into the hallway. Carefully, he pushed the door open and prepared to shoot when he discovered a dumbfounded Alec Athas standing with a gun in hand. There was blood everywhere, including on his face and suit. On the floor lay a man. He was indistinguishable because he no longer had a face.

Stunned, Jorge exchanged looks with the Canadian prime minister, who finally spoke.

"I...I think I might need some help."

Jorge took a deep breath and nodded.

"You got it."

Loyalty above all.

There are no exceptions.

If you enjoyed this book, please give a review on Goodreads or your favorite online retailer. Learn more about the series at www.mimaonfire.com. Check out Mima on Twitter, Instagram, Facebook and TikTok @mimaonfire

Printed in the United States
by Baker & Taylor Publisher Services